# Twenty-six Nil

Published by Honeybee Books

www.honeybeebooks.co.uk

Printed in the UK using paper from sustainable sources

ISBN: 978-1-913675-22-6

Cover image: a formal grouping of Preston North End footballers, 1887 (origin unknown)

# Twenty-six Nil

*A Novel*

Brent Shore

*To the memory of Fred Shore,*
*Hyde United footballer 1924 – 26*
*(78 appearances, 9 goals)*

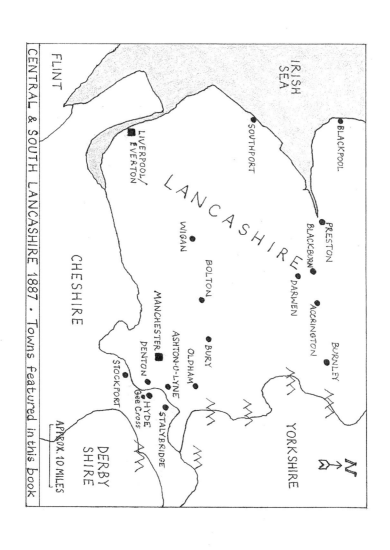

CENTRAL & SOUTH LANCASHIRE 1887 · Towns featured in this book

# Contents

# Prologue

## Saturday, 15th October, 1887

Thirty miles or so north out of Manchester, thirty miles or so of clickety-clack, of whistles hooting, of coal smoke billowing past the window, and we are rolling onward through the sharp air, chugging ever closer to our destination. Ten minutes ago our locomotive heaved itself out of the grimy railway station serving the town of Chorley and the damp grey-green hills of Lancashire envelop us once more. Every man is fidgety, shuffling a little, nervously, on the hard parallel benches. Each one faces another, knees touching, noses barely a yard apart. Some exchange a glance, a shallow smile, then run a palm over their whiskers and look away. Conversation dried up some time ago and a sense of anticipation, so palpable we can almost taste it, has filled the space.

"Ay up, Wally!" Bowers had shouted back on the platform at Victoria. "Come on, step up, old man! Mind your feet! I've saved you a spot. I said I would."

We had cut it fine, Berry and I and a score of fellow supporters, since the first stopping train from Hyde was unexpectedly full. We were obliged to wait for the next one, hearts in mouths: would the special wait for us?

"Is there room enough for two of us?" I enquired, climbing into the carriage with my knapsack, looking around for a space between the crowded ranks of footballers – familiar men, yet curious to the eye in their woollen suits and high collars, each with a cloth cap folded in his lap or balanced on a knee. They had been ordered to dress this way, for show, to represent the club in the most appropriate manner, but rather than heading for a prestigious sporting occasion they did look, to my mind at least, as though they were on their way to a wedding. Or even a funeral. Harry Bowers' shaggy blond mop had been combed through with a palmful of hair oil but it was already springing back here and there to its unruly ways. I had kept my thoughts to myself.

"Two o' you?"

"Yes, I told you Edward was coming."

"Edward?"

"Yes, Edward Berry. You weren't listening, Harry."

He wasn't listening now. The engine fitter's eyes were aimed at the rows of bare heads, above which a faint tropical tang of Macassar was hovering, judging where a gap might be found. Obligingly, one or two of the young men were already squeezing up together.

"'Ere, sit theeself down, lad," said one, touching the soft knot of his necktie self-consciously. It was Robinson, the boilerman. I recognised him even though I had never seen the fellow so tidy, his auburn hair so neatly brushed and parted.

"Thanks, Robbie," I said. "You all know Edward Berry, I think."

There followed a few nods, murmurs, pats on the arm. Berry was already on board, forcing himself between Bowers and the tangle of knees, aiming for the narrowest of spaces for his bony backside.

"Eddie, how do, lad?" asked one of the players. "Squeeze in 'ere. You've not got so much fat on you, 'ave you? Right skinny arse."

A long, deep-throated whistle had suddenly pierced the steamy air. Carriage doors up and down the platform had been slammed shut, and within moments the engine had groaned, valves had hissed and puffed, great wheels had started to turn and the train had slowly lurched out of the shelter of the station like a lazy Goliath might stagger out of a warm bed.

The conversations we had interrupted quickly picked up again: details of the journey, the weather, comical insults, bits and pieces of nonsense, unanswered remarks here and there, a serious dialogue up and running over in the corner. The compartment was alive with guttural, untutored voices as we were pulled along the tracks, through the tight, smoky Mancunian streets, past the flanks of a mill, a gas works, across wide bridges, here running by the side of a dark canal, there so close to the wall of a great brick warehouse you felt you could lean out of the window and trace your fingers along the lines of mortar.

There were eleven of us in the space. Somebody opened a window to let in a draught, welcome in spite of the autumn chill, exaggerated by our velocity.

"How are you all feeling?" I enquired.

Bowers was the first to speak, answering for everyone:

"Feelin'? I feel perfectly alright. Like I allers do of a Sat'day afternoon. It's no diff'rent today, really, is it now?"

"Well, it is," said Robinson. "Course it is. It *is* diff'rent. Today's the biggest game we've ever 'ad. Ever."

"No mistakin' that," added another.

"Aye, but it's still a game of football," insisted Bowers. "Nowt else. We're doin' what we do every week. No-one's askin' us to do owt scary, are they? No-one's askin' us to sail a boat across th' Irish Sea, are they? Or climb a mountain, or fight a bloody tiger…"

"That's true."

"Might stand more chance if we were," said Pressdee, the grocer's assistant.

"If we were what?"

"Fightin' a tiger."

Pressdee was a newcomer to the town and to the team. Bowers laughed. I knew that he had already taken him under his wing; Harry had recognised a handy footballer, quick-witted and robust, as well as a friend, a man he could trust.

"Any road, it's only Preston," said Robinson, full of mischief.

"Only?" echoed another. "Only North End. Only the best bloody side in the country!"

"There'll just be eleven of 'em," said Bowers. "No more than eleven. And there's eleven of us."

"You all know how to play," added Berry, if only to encourage. "I've watched you often enough. You're a good side yourselves. You'd give anyone a fair match, I'd say."

"Let's just ger up there," said Robinson, stretching his arms. "I can't wait to ger out of this bloody suit an' tie. Get kickin' a ball about."

To which comment, general agreement.

I looked up to the wire racks above our heads. There was no less of an encumbrance up there: stuffed together and overhanging the shelves were bags and bundles of all shapes and sizes, containing the players' jerseys and trousers, stockings and boots, and a knobbly sack which self-evidently held at least half a dozen footballs.

The train was picking up speed, rattling through a landscape that had turned distinctly rural. We saw fields and farms, sloping woodland, low lumpy walls of stone dividing up the grazing land, crags of white and grey on the horizon, set beneath a sky of soft clouds and patches of mournful, steely blue.

A lull in the conversation had not signalled a period of quiet, for over the rattle of the train could be heard voices from either or both of the compartments adjacent to ours. They too, indeed the whole carriage, had been commandeered by Hyde's footballers and their supporters – those who could afford the ticket – for this special occasion. I asked if anyone knew if Joseph Maloney, the club secretary and a fellow I had come to know quite well during the past twelve months, was amongst the occupants of the neighbouring compartments. An innocent question, I had believed, but it raised a guffaw of sarcasm.

"What? Maloney in this carriage?" Bowers laughed. "In third class? You'll not see any of t' committee on greasy wooden benches, Wally."

"'Appen if you 'ad a look in first class, lad," offered Robinson. "Mr 'Ibbert told me it were t' most illusprous day in t' club's 'istory."

"Illusprous?"

"Aye."

"You mean *illustrous*," suggested Pressdee.

"You mean *illustrious*," I interjected, in spite of myself.

6

"That's what I said," insisted Robinson. "Special. Like why we're 'avin' to wear suits. Any road, they're all in first class. Livin' it up in t' posh seats. There an' back, as far as I know."

"As long as they're payin' for 'em from their own purses," said Pressdee, "I dunna care. It does seem a bit much payin' double just to sit on a cloth cushion."

"An' 'ave a lot more elbow room, mind," added Hopkinson, the foundry labourer, expressing himself with an exaggerated wriggle which upset his neighbour. Hopkinson was a skinny fellow, a player who was new to the team, almost hidden amongst the limbs of his mates, covered in their folds of worsted. I had barely noticed him until this moment; he must have been quietly lost in his own thoughts, in his own insecurities.

"They'd better not be usin' club funds to pamper 'emselves with," Robinson was rambling on.

"You're alright, Robbo," said Bowers. "You'll not be needin' any pamperin'. No cushioned seat for you, pal. You've got all the paddin' you need on your own backside!"

"Bugger off!"

"Fat arse Robbo!" somebody said, to loud amusement.

"It's all muscle," claimed the boiler man, stifling a smile of his own. "It's why I'm so bloody good at stoppin' a full back gettin' t' ball off me."

"I'd not noticed," said Bowers.

"No, there's not much you *do* notice," retorted Robinson, with a wink in my direction.


A moment of calm had been filled by raucous laughter from the compartment up ahead.

"I dunno why I bother," came a strident voice through the wooden panel. "I put a couple o' beauties in t' goal, give us a flyin' start, an' you donkeys still end up costin' us t' match. Tackles like a bloody nursemaid might make! I've seen more fight in a new born lamb."

"Jimmy's off on a rant," said Bowers, laughing to himself.

"If only we 'ad eleven Jimmy Woods," mused Pressdee.

I smiled to myself and saw that Berry was grinning too. We had stood together as usual a fortnight earlier when Hyde had suffered a reverse by three goals to two at the hands of Halliwell F.C., a very capable team from Bolton. Somebody had mentioned that they had reached the third round of the F.A. Cup the previous winter. We had enthused, along with many of the spectators around us, about the first-half performance of our new outside forward James Wood, a manager's assistant at Longfellow Mill.

"He's a lad with a high opinion of himself," Berry had claimed, "but he's a handy addition to the team, and no mistake."

Like the majority of the first-team players, Wood was signed as a professional. There was a range of individual terms for these footballers, and in the case of the ones brought in on contracts from outside the town, part-time employment had to be found to supplement wages and fill the days of these young men who had moved far from home and family to pursue a career kicking a leather ball up and down a field. Wood was an exception, being a Hydonian, a worker in the town's cotton mills since the age of fourteen.

"Slow? Tommy's as slow as a lame dog wading through treacle."

We could hear him in full flow, giving his mates a taste of his repertoire, each barb more extravagant than the last, all for show, all greeted with laughter, all part of the release of tension amongst the players.

"Sprint? You wouldn't sprint even if you were bein' chased through a field by a ragin' bull!"

"Pass the ball to a teammate? Ashworth couldn't even pass wind after a cabbage stew an' a skinful of ale…"

Eventually his voice had been drowned out by muffled boos and cackles from behind the dividing board.

By the time our locomotive had pulled us clear of Bolton, offering fleeting views of forest and farmstead and with each hillside blessed by the watery sunlight of early afternoon, a fug of tobacco smoke had filled our tight space. I am not averse to the habit of smoking in others but I do not share in the enthusiasm. Thankfully a pair of open windows allowed a fresh breeze to prevent asphyxiation in every last man of us. One or two of the players produced tobacco for their pipes while at the same time, and a little self-consciously, here and there a fellow, Hopkinson and Pressdee amongst them, set about rolling flakes of what I believe is called shag into flimsy smoking paper. Once lit, they held the fragile cigarettes between their forefingers, bringing them to their lips to suck on the unfired end like a babe on a mother's teat.

I have spoken to physicians about the benefits of tobacco and am not surprised at its popularity amongst sportsmen: it is said that it refreshes a weary man, can calm the nervous system and yet awaken the brain and quicken a fellow's understanding. I must say, however, that in the religious circles that I frequent, the smoking of tobacco and its effects have few supporters.

I was expecting a comment from somebody when I found an apple in my knapsack and noisily took a tidy bite, but nothing came. Men were momentarily deep in their own thoughts, staring out of the window or at their knees, imagining in their own minds what the afternoon might hold. Pressdee started bickering with Robinson about where the larger man insisted on putting his feet. I chewed the fruit heartily, not as a wordless reproach to the smokers, but simply because, several hours since breakfast time, I was pricked by hunger.

Thirty miles or so north out of Manchester, thirty miles or so of clickety-clack, of doors rattling on their catches, of lifting and shifting on our unforgiving seats, and we are rolling onward, chugging ever closer to our destiny. Hopkinson and the lad by his side are dozing, conserving nervous energy. Pressdee has been telling a joke or two but nobody is in the mood to give him a fair hearing. Berry and I listen in as Bowers and a couple of the others discuss plans for the routines they have been drilling in practice for today's momentous match. The players have had a brief insight into their opponents: Frank Hibbert, the club chairman, visited North End's ground at Deepdale a few weeks ago to watch them perform. "They play imperially," he reported – not a description that was welcomed in the Hyde camp. F.A. Cup semi-finalists last season, Preston are a fully professional club, well stocked with lithe and skilful Scottish players whose game, it is said, is well advanced in technique and formation. It was indeed a misfortune for Hyde to have been drawn to face them, and up in north Lancashire on an unfamiliar pitch besides, in their first ever F.A. Cup tie.

Only football clubs which hold themselves in high esteem would wish to enter the famous competition, now in its sixteenth year, with a final at London's Kennington Oval: clubs which expect not necessarily to lift the trophy (that is indeed the preserve of the exceptional), but to win a match or two along the way and take more than an ounce of prestige from the results. It is a competition, as I understand it, for clubs with ambition, for teams that want to announce themselves, so that the rest of the English game will sit up and take notice. This season one hundred and forty-nine have entered. The number represents a very small proportion of the footballers who play a sport which is growing ever more popular in all corners of the nation. Just one hundred and forty-nine teams and one of those is Hyde F.C., a club that was born barely more than two years ago.

As merely an adopted Hydonian, I have detected a feeling of envy that has propelled the club so rapidly to its estimable position. Other folk may prefer to call it local rivalry, an urge to match and then surpass the achievements of Hurst F.C., the principal club in the neighbouring borough of Ashton-under-Lyne. That town, similar in character but larger than Hyde, developed some years earlier, growing in size and influence with the expansion of the cotton industry: spinning, weaving and the mining of coal flourishes there just as it does in Hyde, only three miles distant. Ashton achieved the status of municipal borough in 1847, a good thirty years before Hyde did the same – by which time its town hall had been constructed, to be followed in quick fashion by a stately public baths and a free library. Divided by the dark waters of the river Tame, Ashton is a Lancastrian town whereas Hyde sits to the south, at the north-eastern tip of the county of Cheshire. I have met many Hydonians who, perhaps resentful and a little jealous, mischievously regard Ashton-under-Lyne as a younger child might consider an older, haughtier and uglier sister.

I have been busy perusing the records: Hurst made their bow in the F.A. Cup in 1883 and in the meantime they have enjoyed some minor successes. Two years ago they beat Newton Heath Lancashire and Yorkshire Railway F.C., one of the strongest teams in east Manchester, in the inaugural Manchester Senior Cup final. Conscious of the shadow the Ashton club casts, Hyde F.C. have a deal of catching up to do, but I can guarantee that all those involved are determined to do so.

The jolting carriage shakes me from my reverie and I glance up at the red faces of the men that surround me. The fortunes of the club are in their hands – and their feet – today. Harry Bowers sees me looking down the row and pats me on the knee.

"Cheer up, Wally!" he says. "Win, lose or draw we'll give 'em a game."

"Of course you will, Harry," I reply, forcing a smile.

Before long I notice that the train is decelerating. Below us courses the grey curve of the river Ribble. Beyond the track there are buildings now, casting shadows: factories, rows of houses, a municipal park, the backs of more houses, street after street. There is a sudden squeal of brakes, metal on screechy metal, and the harshest of whistles rips into the air. The men around me are stirring, stretching their legs, starting to button up their jackets. One by one they try to remember exactly where in the racks they had lifted their luggage, one by one they reposition their caps on overheated heads.

Moments later we are being shunted to a crawl, edged by a wide concrete platform dotted with folk who walk this way and that. Some stand waiting, eyes eagerly following the carriage doors that pass slowly before them. And large black signs with bold white lettering display the information that nobody needs telling: we have arrived in Preston.

# Book The First
# Summer 1885

The arrangement was for all groups to gather punctually in Crook's Square by the town's Wesleyan Chapel but the space was already overflowing. Excited children were comparing new clothes and polished shoes, uniformed members of several marching bands were unpacking shiny musical instruments, knots of solemnly dressed gentlemen in pristine neckties were in deep discussion. There flitted amongst them teachers and preachers, parents and grandparents, constables and firemen, not to mention the Hyde Company of the 4th Cheshire Rifle Volunteers, their scarlet tunics criss-crossed with dazzling white straps. Already groups had noisily spilled out into Crook Street by the time we arrived: some were unfurling colourful banners which here announced the Union Street Congregational Sunday School and there the Independent Order of Oddfellows, elsewhere the National and United Free Gardeners and others of that ilk. Disobedient children were being shepherded into uncertain lines by shrill-voiced ladies in fussy hats. Trumpeters and trombonists were beginning to tune up their horns, creating a random cacophony of something a far cry from music. I remember consulting my pocket watch: our contingent, still incomplete I am embarrassed to admit, was by no means late, but it appeared that the organizers of the procession had, at least when the idea was originally discussed, considerably underestimated the number of participants. There were hundreds of people milling around in anticipation.

I left our children – scholars past and present, well over a hundred of them – under the supervision of Frederick, the youthful Reverend Ashton, and the many parents who had wished to support us. I wriggled through the throng towards the centre of the square where a pair of young constables were cheerfully attempting to clear a central path; the crowd was good-natured and folk were generally doing what they could to conform. It being a bright sunny morning, the committee had set up a table outside the entrance to the chapel. I recognised a grey-whiskered gentleman – a clerk to the new grouping of councillors – and tried to catch his eye but his attention was for the moment diverted towards a stout woman ahead of me, who announced more than once that she represented the Methodist Free Church Sunday School in Newton and was wondering aloud where in the procession her charges should expect to be. The clerk adjusted his spectacles and consulted the details written in a large ledger open in front of him. *Position number eight,* she was told after a moment's hesitation. *Directly behind St Thomas' Church School.* Position number eight seemed to suit her for she took the man's ticket with a gracious smile. Eventually when it was my turn to speak I had a very similar enquiry relating to Hyde Chapel Sunday School, a group of children and adults from Gee Cross.

"Mr Rowbotham, is it?"

"Yes, it is."

"Hyde Chapel?"

"Hyde Chapel."

The man raised a pencil over his ledger and looked me in the eye.

"How many in your contingent?"

"At least one hundred and fifty, I would say. More will join us in the Market Place at the finish."

"You'll be lucky to find them."

"Really?"

"Can't you see how busy it is? It'll be chock-a-block down there at noon."

"You're probably right."

"One hundred and fifty on the march, you say?"

"Thereabouts."

I watched him carefully scribe the number in a column of others.

"You have musicians?"

"No. No musicians."

"A choir?"

"No, we have no choir."

"A banner?"

"Yes, we have a banner."

"Large or small?"

"Small, I would say."

I opened my arms to give the man a clue as to what I would estimate the width of a small banner to be.

He scratched something quickly on the page in front of him: I assumed the word *small*.

Yes, we had a banner, yet to arrive, I failed to add. I was praying that Mr and Mrs Booth from the bakery would be waiting in the street when I returned. Not only had they volunteered to bring the banner but they had offered their cart to transport their two young sons and eight others of our scholars.

"Mr Rowbotham?"

"Yes?"

"You'll take your place in position number fifteen," said the clerk, keeping the tip of a bony index finger at a strategic place on a wide page of lists. "In front of the St Paul's Catholics and at the back of the Fire Brigade Band. You'll find them gathering in the square. Look yonder, the navy blue uniforms."

He handed me a slip of paper printed with the number fifteen and told me I'd need to show it to the sergeant.

I squeezed out of the square and searched for the imposing, bewhiskered figure of Frederick Ashton, who had added a jaunty red cap to his clerical cravat for the occasion. It appeared that ever greater numbers had swollen the crowds. I quickly spotted that he had directed our group halfway up Crook Street. When I rejoined them they were still depleted; several families were missing and there was no sign of the Booths or their wagon. I was fearing the worst, for such was the congestion in the traffic, both human and horse-drawn, that I could see little chance of the bakers meeting us before the procession set off on its way. Already constables' whistles were piercing the hubbub and I could see the sergeant gingerly climbing a large set of step-ladders with a megaphone in his hand.

There was at the least a veneer of organization to the chaotic scene of assembling and reassembling, instructions given then overridden only to be redelivered more loudly moments later. People had formed their groups and waited patiently in the sun to be barked at by the ever more flustered sergeant. We were no exception. I was too distant to see the head of the parade move away from the square but we heard rousing music and I later discovered that it was led by the splendid Rifle Volunteers and their regimental band. Deliberately held back in the square, in the shade of an awning, was the pack of dignitaries in their Sunday best: the town's first mayor, Mr Thomas Ashton, and various officers of the town council and gentlemen of the borough. Apparently the plan was for these most important members of the community to bring up the rear of the procession, their eventual arrival thus providing a spectacle for the assembled crowd waiting to greet them.

And so, at five and twenty minutes before ten on the sparkling morning of Saturday, 27th June 1885, the majority of members of Hyde Chapel Sunday School, lacking our banner, were signalled forward to take our place behind the stiff backs of the Fire Brigade Band – their drums and brass at the ready – to step out and join the march edging towards Market Street.

The streets were lined with hundreds of clapping supporters, some of whom were enthused to join the procession in random gaps and so swell our ranks with conversation and song. And gaps there were for this was far from a march of military precision, yet all the more convivial for that fact. One minute our group would be lagging – a girl had a stone in her shoe, a little boy was complaining of thirst – the next minute the fireman's bass drum was inches from our ears, the parade having compacted together for an unknown reason like a concertina. There was singing up ahead: one of the larger Sunday schools had formed a choir. Their hymn was largely lost on us, however, drowned by the lively brass of one of several bands behind us. There was a collective joy in the chaos and I saw very few people in poor humour; it was a morning full of smiles and pride. Smiles of good fellowship, pride in our splendid new Town Hall.

We followed the procession up Newton Road and presently

into Floweryfield, stopping and starting as needs be: a short halt for a stationary performance of a band ahead of us, I was assuming, or perhaps a delay caused by an unexpected bottleneck of some kind. Any pause was welcome, as a matter of fact. A number of our children were already complaining of sore feet, and here and there we were able to avail ourselves of the refreshments offered by the townsfolk whose open front doors we happened to be passing. Onward we marched, returning to the town by way of Ashton Road and Commercial Brow.

The mood of our group was raised yet a level for up ahead, at the very top of Cheapside I caught sight of a familiar horse and cart. At the reins was Mr Booth and close by, already disembarked and jumping with excitement were the children we had left behind. On the footpath his wife was unfurling the banner emblazoned with our name.

"I couldn't get down as far as Crook Street," Booth was shouting as we approached. "Not for love nor money. Too many wagons and folk in t' road."

As I reached him I shook him by the hand.

"Not to worry," I said.

"Sorry I missed you," he ploughed on, "but here we all are. We turned around and took Back Lane, came out at that corner over yonder."

"The children have all had a drink while we waited," added his wife, handing me one of the banner's poles. Frederick took the other as the scholars joined their friends with talk of blocked streets and frustration, of their anxiety and their relief to catch up with us. I was pleased to see Daniel Harrop amongst them, at twelve years one of the more responsible boys, and at the same time surprised to find his mother clambering down off the cart at the rear of the group. She must have decided to come along late in the day.

"Now folk can see who we are," said the Reverend, raising his end of the banner. "We're no longer nameless interlopers."

"Sorry, Mr Rowbotham," said Mrs Booth sheepishly, tidying her boys' hair before stepping out of the road to climb back on to the cart to sit beside her husband.

Though the centre of Hyde was less than half a mile away, the ambitious organisers of the march wished for every parish in the entire borough to be visited. The final leg would take us halfway to Gee Cross and we followed the increasingly raggedy procession up Lumn Street towards Back Lane. Once the towering chimneys of Slack Mills were behind us – starkly inactive, I noticed, as redundant on that day as a line of cannon during an armistice – the Fire Brigade Band were greeted with a lively reception from many of the drinkers gathered outside the Ring O' Bells alehouse. A trumpeter later told me that the men had extinguished a blaze in an outbuilding there the previous week, saving hundreds of bottles of spirits from detonation.

In spite of a few fair weather clouds the sun was still doing its best to smile on us all, and was now approaching its zenith. We were finally heading down Market Street in fits and starts. We must have tramped for four miles from start to finish and the children in our midst were not the only ones to complain of fatigue, but gradually the encouraging sound of applause grew louder in our ears. Ahead of us the firemen struck up another marching tune. Our spirits were lifted by the sight and sounds of a long avenue of well-wishers lining the approach to the Market Square; we passed public houses, shops and private dwellings all decorated with flowers and flags, with bunting and bannerettes.

"Well done, Hyde Chapel!" came a voice I recognised.

Standing outside the Royal Hotel with a circle of friends was Charlie Knott, flaxen hair catching the sunlight, a glass of ale in his raised hand. He was a young man from Gee Cross, a former scholar of mine, someone I had watched grow up.

"How d'you do, Charlie?" I called back with a little salute.

"Well done, Walter!" he shouted. "Good for you!"

The cheering and clapping continued as we were funnelled into the main area, now with a view of the new Municipal Offices. For these were, strictly speaking, what were housed in this impressive brick edifice with its stone dressings, large mullioned windows and domed bell tower. Displayed at the oriel windows and on the balcony above the central doors were groupings of flags of the Union, imperial red, white and blue, which hung lazily in the warm air. Over the past two years, with both astonishment and pride, Hydonians had witnessed the demolition of Greenfield House and the construction of this brand new building; although a large public hall, not to mention courtrooms and a police station, was to be added in the future, most locals had already chosen to call it the Town Hall. In spite of the adjacent dusky bulk of Greenfield Mill, reverentially silenced, the new façade caught the late morning sun and its fresh brickwork glowed orange, bathed in a heavenly light.

Taking, by my estimate, a middle position in the snaking procession, I had seen neither its head depart nor its tail arrive but before too long the signal was made for the ceremonials to begin and the boisterous crowd gradually composed themselves one and all. The band of the Rifle Volunteers, now stationed directly in front of a temporary stage bedecked with a banner proclaiming the words "Floreat Hyde" and upon which sat lines of eminent gentlemen, briskly played the opening bars of the national anthem. The lines of eminent gentlemen rose as one, straightening their jackets and dutifully removing their hats from their heads simultaneously like rows of clockwork figurines. Every single one was an elegant top hat, grey or black, the type worn in my memory by Lewis Carroll's Mad Hatter; I wondered if, in their haste to impress, any of our worthies had distractedly left the price ticket (ten shillings and sixpence?) tucked into the black ribbon. We all sang heartily, beseeching the Lord to save our noble Queen and send her victorious. On that sunny Saturday morning, filled with thousands of smiling faces (*The North Cheshire Herald & Hyde & Glossop General Advertiser* later reported that the procession itself could not have been composed of less than nine thousand people), the centre of Hyde could indeed have been described as most happy and glorious.

Somebody tugged at my sleeve. I turned to find young Harrop with a question:

"What does that big banner say, Mr Rowbotham?"

"Floreat Hyde?"

"Aye. What's a *florry-at*?"

I have never been one to pass up the chance to educate and inform.

"It's Latin, Danny," I said. "It means 'May Hyde flourish', I suppose. 'May Hyde prosper'. 'May Hyde do well', perhaps more colloquially."

"I were askin' for me mother," said the child. "She were bustin' to know."

I caught sight of the woman, partly hidden behind her son: short, pale of complexion, she smiled shyly before looking away.

Thankfully the speeches of the principal dignitaries were brief. With so many children and elderly folk standing cheek by jowl under the midday sun, I was grateful to whoever it was who had offered an advisory word to our mayors. For it was the pair of them who were to address us: our town's first mayor, Mr Thomas Ashton, spoke to the gathering before handing over an outsized ceremonial key to our second, our new mayor, Mr Edward Hibbert. He too was keen to let us hear a dash of his skill in oratory. He accepted the trophy and made a theatrical performance of entering the building and reappearing on the balcony above us all, loudly declaring the Town Hall open.

Even from a distance it was clear to me that unalloyed pride displayed itself in both men's faces, certainly in the tremor in their voices and indeed in the hearts of the congregated townsfolk upon hearing their words. Ashton spoke of the rapid growth of the town in just eighty years: at the start of the century the semi-rural settlement was populated by a thousand souls. Thanks to industrialization, the locality's geographical advantages in the mass production of cotton cloth, not to mention the enterprise, hard work and good sense of its people, Hyde (and at this point he was eager to include the parishes of Gee Cross, Godley, Newton and Floweryfield) now had a thriving population of nearly thirty thousand. He reminded us that its status as a municipal borough had been granted four years ago and was well earned. The Town Hall was the natural next step in its development. He felt obliged to remind us also that it was he who had laid the foundation stone only two years past. Before resuming his seat he drew most applause by insisting that it was a town hall to compare most favourably with any other in the orbit of Manchester.

To raucous cheers (at this point it crossed my mind that the alehouses had been serving for longer than was customary on a Saturday morning) Mr Hibbert, still clasping the ceremonial key like a weapon, made reference to the future. Repeating the town's significant motto "Onward", he spoke with unashamed optimism of projects on the near horizon: a free library, public baths and the establishment of new schools. Wiping sweat from his brow with a white silk handkerchief, he talked of the expansion of Corporation Street where there were plans for a post office, and a fire station, and before too long we would enjoy public gardens and even a new theatre. Surely I was not the only one who could sense that the gentleman's excitement was running away from reality at this point, but nobody was of a mind to care.

There followed a blessing by a vicar I did not recognise (I guessed he was the fellow from Hyde St George's) and finally the crowd slowly dispersed. We had come to mark a grand moment in the history of our town but beyond the parochial pride I wondered if we were there to celebrate the providence of the Lord or the benevolent majesty of our Queen. I supposed both, in an English sort of way.

Here and there musicians started up their singing and playing and the beer stalls were serving once more. Much chattering and laughter filled the air. As we edged out of the square on such a wave of good hope and aspiration, I noticed so many folk, parents and children alike, with their chins up high and their chests puffed out. In that moment we could be forgiven, each one of us, for thinking that we were indeed blessed, for believing that we really were the inhabitants of the Promised Land.

If I consider myself a Hydonian and write as such, it is only partly the performance of an imposter. The truth is that the town of my childhood was Oldham, somewhat earlier established as an industrial centre but for all that a place whose growth and prosperity through cotton production ran on a parallel path to that of Hyde. It lies less than ten miles north from here, on the edge of high moorland disputed for centuries by Lancastrian and Yorkist. It has become one of several boroughs which these days encircle the city of Manchester like the numerals on a clock face: if Oldham is five minutes after the hour, then Hyde is just gone quarter past.

My father was a Methodist minister in Lees. Unlike my younger sister I was sent away to school – a draughty and rather unforgiving establishment in the West Riding – and a future in the clergy was envisaged for me. Without abandoning the church entirely I decided to train as an educationalist and spent my days as a student in Manchester, supported by the Unitarians. Once qualified, I remained in the city for twenty years, employed as a teacher on the whim of the Ministry in a seemingly random succession of schools in the insalubrious central districts. I was a dedicated schoolmaster, willing to sacrifice my own social development to the calling and prepared to contribute further to the religious education of the local children by managing Sunday schools.

I cannot guess whether my posting to Hyde was some kind of reward for service or simply a matter of expedient reorganization on the part of my employers, but when I arrived here in 1870 at the age of forty I was pleasantly surprised by an escape of sorts from the smoke and deprivation of the city. I remain here a happy man, approaching retirement, nearly twenty years later. For at Hyde Chapel, my new place of work, I discovered a generous and inspiring man ministering the church and, in Gee Cross, a bustling village barely a mile south of the town yet already on the fringes of pale green hills. Two great rumbling mills sit deep in the valley bottom but I felt blessed to be in sight of sloping fields and to breathe fresh air. I lived in the schoolhouse on Knott Lane for over sixteen years and have never felt so settled, my spirits more at peace, than here. As a result I feel quite free from duplicity in calling myself a Hydonian. I was not born one but no man can tell me I have not become one.

It was as we were preparing to leave the Market Place, gathering our fragmented group together and looking for the least congested route through the throng, that Frederick pointed out the Reverend Henry Dowson standing on the raised platform, hat in hand, in friendly conversation with Thomas Ashton. I knew the men were well acquainted: indeed the former Mayor had been something of a mentor to the younger man, both having spent formative years in the German city of Heidelberg. They were fellow Nonconformists and sharers of radical opinions. Had Mr Dowson been amongst the selected dignitaries all the time? I must have missed him, perhaps seated to the rear and out of my eyeline. I had spoken to him only the previous evening: he had confirmed his attendance but made no mention to me that he would have a position of honour. I have no doubt his reticence was born out of modesty, one of his many qualities.

It is a question of mild curiosity as to which of us, Frederick or me, knows Mr Dowson the better. The Reverend Ashton (no relation, incidentally, of our former mayor's family, the property-owning Ashtons) has fewer years to his name but has worked as a close assistant in the affairs of the Chapel. No matter.

I have nothing but respect for the man and he deserved his place on the dais with the great and the good of our community. His reputation has long since spread beyond his ministry and his influence is felt in wider circles these days. His interests and his desire to make his mark in the town extend beyond religion to matters of education, health provision and the importance of organized leisure activities for working families: indeed, politics in its broadest sense. Like Mayor Ashton, he is a leading light amongst the local Liberals. He is a most inspirational man, possessed of a sharp mind, and a fine orator; it is a privilege to work in his service.

In the sporting realm, Mr Dowson's passion as a younger man, so he has told me on more than one occasion, was swimming. He grew up in Great Yarmouth, close to the beaches of the Norfolk coast. Sadly for him and his family there is no such provision in this corner of England. Lately he has turned his attention to cricket and he arranges matches in the summer months for the Chapel team against other church groups, notably the Methodists of both Hyde and Newton and the Unitarians of Floweryfield. Being a few years younger than me he is still an active participant in what is, after all, a most sedate sport. As for myself, although by no means yet decrepit, I prefer to abstain and seldom even spectate. Alert to a certain natural agility in my gait, the Reverend had of course invited me to join the players but I had so far respectfully declined. I am a brisk walker and carry little fat around my middle but give me a heavy bat to strike a ball and I become as inept and uncoordinated as a blind man on a frozen pond trying to catch snowflakes. I once accepted the invitation to make up a foursome at tennis. The parsonage has an enclosed court of neatly tended lawn and Mrs Dowson is a proficient player. Once was quite enough for me. After a game or two without accident, I swung at a ball with misplaced confidence only to mistime the stroke so dreadfully that it sailed far over the perimeter fence into a field of ponies where it was chewed into small pieces by the most curious of the beasts. I believe it must have mistaken it for a fallen apple.

# Book the Second
## Season 1885-86

# Chapter 1

Two months following the great opening of the Town Hall, on a Sunday afternoon in the middle of August, I was busying myself in the schoolroom when a timid knock at the open door disturbed me. I looked up from my labours – I was preparing arithmetical puzzles or some such – to see a red-faced boy standing on the threshold, panting from running from who knew where.

"Mr Rowbotham," he exhaled. "Mr Rowbotham, sir."

I recognised him at once as one of my scholars: it was Jack Hill, the youngest son of the shopkeepers at the dairy, a ten-year-old with a wild mop of hair but a tamed spirit.

"What's to do, Jack?" I enquired.

"Cricket, Mr Rowbotham," he replied almost inaudibly, embarrassed to find himself suddenly alone in the classroom with his teacher.

"Cricket? What do you mean, Jack? Who sent you here?"

"The Reverend sent me, sir."

"The Reverend? Which one? Mr Dowson or Mr Ashton?"

I allowed him a pause to catch his breath.

"Oh, Mr Dowson, sir," said the child after a moment as if my question had been fatuous at best. "Mr Ashton is busy in t' middle."

"In the middle?"

"In t' middle o' t' field." Another deep breath. "T' cricket field."

I remembered that a match had been arranged for the

afternoon. It had been the subject of intermittent conversation during the course of the week but it was one of which I had very much been at the fringes.

"Alright there, Jack," I said. "Thank you for coming."

"You're welcome, Mr Rowbotham."

He seemed to be about to turn heel and leave the room there and then.

"But no, tell me, pray, what is the message you bring? The message from the Reverend Dowson. The message about the cricket. Have you run up here to tell me the score?"

"No, sir, it's not that," he answered, sailing over my needless sarcasm. "The Reverend said you 'ad to come down to t' field."

"The cricket field?"

"Well, aye, sir. The Chapel are a man short. Mr Gee…" And here he paused to cogitate. "Mr Gee…"

"Mr Gee, the farmer's lad? William? William Gee?"

"I think so, Mr Rowbotham. He took a ball in t' face. Broke 'is nose, they said. Blood all down 'is shirt."

"Oh, my goodness. How terrible."

"They sent a lass over for Mrs Gee."

"I'm sure they did."

"An' they sent me up 'ere. For you, Mr Rowbotham."

"For me? You mean they want me to play?"

The boy was nodding.

"The Reverend said you could take Mr Gee's place. They can't play a man short, he said. He told me: *Go an' fetch Mr Rowbotham, Jack, lad. It'll do 'im no 'arm to run around a field on a summer's afternoon.* That's what he said, Mr Rowbotham."

"Oh, he said that, did he?"

"His very words, Mr Rowbotham."


A quarter of a mile down Knott Lane, where the track peters out to a rough path, is a flattish field over which, a year or two ago, the Reverend Dowson and the owner of the land had come to an agreement. If the farmer mowed it regularly throughout the summer months and allowed Mr Ives the Chapel groundsman to prepare a pitch, a nominal sum would be paid to rent the field as a space where cricket matches could be held. It was for the benefit of the community, Mr Dowson had insisted, nudging the fellow to lower his price.

Sure enough, as I approached the ground, even before I cast eyes on the cricketers, I heard raised voices which told me that a competitive match had resumed. Under blue skies dotted with wispy, benign cloud the scene was unarguably bucolic. Faith in Mr Ives had been well placed: the tidy field was edged on three sides by trees and the fourth offered a view of a flock of desultory sheep. Pegged down at various intervals, and delineating an approximate oval, were lengths of frayed old rope, suggesting the boundary of the playing area.

I recognised most of the men standing at strategic positions, waiting for the bowler: fielders is the term, I was told. Mr Dowson, of course, was prominent, prowling dangerously close, I thought, to one of the batters, or batsmen. He was crossing what I believed was called the square. Or was it the wicket? And there was Robert Howarth, the greengrocer's son, crouching behind the stumps. The stumps, or was *that* the wicket? A few players wore white shirts and a couple had even produced white caps, such as I had seen in illustrations of cricketers who were deemed good enough to represent the country.

About to bowl was Charles Knott, my friend and former pupil. I believe he was Mr Dowson's most important player; in any case he seemed to be invited to play in every match. I watched the delivery: a fiercely quick one which passed the flailing swing of the batsman and landed in Howarth's thick leather gloves with a loud smack. From both his stature and the scarlet cap on his head I recognised the umpire as Frederick Ashton. He appeared to be exchanging a joke with Charles. Then I noticed a second umpire. So there were two of them. I assumed each team provided one in the interests of fairness. Finally I was surprised to spot a young woman fielding for the Chapel team at the far boundary.

Small groups of spectators stood at various places at the pitch's perimeter. A few children were throwing balls between them and squealing as excited children sometimes do. Grouped together for the use of those who needed to rest their legs were chairs I recognised: hard-backed things, about two dozen of which had been carried down from the Chapel rooms. Several of them were occupied by members of the opposition who were wiping down their bats and lacing up their boots and talking quietly as if a conspiracy was being hatched.

"The Wesleyans of Hyde Central," said Ives in reply to my inquisitive look.

The groundsman was the first person I addressed, finding him seated at a small table with a battered sunhat shading his face and a pencil between his fingers, filling in a large scorecard, a kind of record of the play. Next to him was an unusual wooden frame, standing about six feet tall. On its crossbar were four hooks, spaced three and one, attached to which were tin squares the size of roofing slates, painted with numerals. At his feet was a box filled with dozens of such tin squares.

"They're a decent team, Walter," he went on in his raspy voice, talking through a mouth almost empty of teeth. "They beat us this time last year."

My arrival had not been noticed by any member of the Chapel team, not even the young man fielding just ten yards away: it was the butcher's apprentice whose name I had forgotten. I did remember, however, that he had only one good eye: every cutlet he chopped had one thick edge and the other a fair deal thinner.

Ives looked a little morose. He kept dropping his pencil. I could tell he was bored by recording the score. Perhaps in return he could sense that I was a most reluctant player.

Suddenly I heard my name being called. I looked across to see Charlie Knott waving to me to come on and join the match.

"It's th' end o' th' over," said Ives, marking the record.

"It's over? Already?"

"Th' end o' *the over*. A run o' six balls bowled."

He was adjusting the numbers on the frame.

"I see."

"Walter!" came the shout again. "Come on! You can take Margaret's place."

I realised the girl was Margaret Dowson, the eldest of the Reverend's daughters, who must have been covering for the injured William Gee.

"Give her one more over!" I cried, already absorbing the specialist vocabulary. "I'm not quite ready."

From the opposite side of the field a different bowler was preparing to play: I recognised Jesse Thornley, the ironmonger, whom I knew to be older than I was. I had to respect his willingness to put his creaking body through such an ordeal in the name of sport. For here he was, trotting in like an old dressage pony: his delivery was slow and gentle – it was an invitation to be hit hard and without mercy, I thought, but as the ball landed in front of the batsman's feet it appeared to spin off its course and sailed past him in perilous fashion, narrowly missing the target. The stumps. The wicket.

"Listen, Walter," Ives resumed. "I can see your 'eart's not in it. Why dunna you let me play? You take over t' scorecard."

"But I've no idea what to do with it."

"It's dead easy. Follow this next over and see 'ow it's done. You'll pick it up right away, Walter. Clever bloke like you."

As luck would have it I had my spectacles in a carrying case inside my jacket pocket. I put them on and leaned over to see what he was writing. As each ball was bowled I watched him filling in the squares on the page one by one, marking dots and singles and then a figure four when a batsman hit the ball to the boundary. He told me to keep an eye on the umpire's signals and explained what they meant. He showed me how to mark a wicket (that word again) and what the numbers on the frame signified. He referred to it as the scoreboard.

"They're fifty-two for three. See? Total score there, and then wickets down."

"Wickets down?"

"Wickets they've lost. Three. Three batsmen given out."

"Out. Right. I understand."

"Easy, see."

"Easy," I nodded, acknowledging all the while to myself that I had very little instinct for this game.

Ives explained that he had agreed to fill in the scorecard for Hyde Central's innings only. He had a pit to dig out for the morrow. It occurred to me that it was quite a novelty to be taught the finer points of the scoring etiquette of cricket by a gravedigger.

"But I'll get it done first thing in t' mornin'. If they bury 'er 'alf an 'our late she'll not be frettin', will she? She'll be in no 'urry."

"Someone I know?"

It was Sarah, the old charwoman at the Grapes Inn who had collapsed and died a week ago.

"Miss Margaret said she'd score our innin's," he added.

At the conclusion of Thornley's over Mr Ives stood up and started stretching his limbs. The man was about my age, I supposed, but he carried a good deal more bulk.

"What's going on?" shouted Frederick Ashton from the middle.

"I'm takin' 'is place," called the groundsman. "Walter'll do t' scorin'."

Nobody was in a position to argue and indeed Ives was already crossing the boundary at a jog. At the far side of the ground, watched by a few curious sheep and to an appreciative ripple of applause, the seventeen-year-old Margaret Dowson stepped away and gracefully took her leave from the game.

*

The Wesleyans completed their innings of twenty overs by the middle of the afternoon. Expertly tutored, I was untroubled in my role of recorder and my only moment of mild drama occurred when I noticed a ball flying high towards the boundary in the direction of two young ladies who were deep in conversation. My shouts alerted them just in time and, giggling in embarrassment, they narrowly avoided being struck. It was Louisa Thornley, Jesse's daughter, and a friend I failed to recognise.

According to my records, which I believed to be wholly accurate, the visitors had scored one hundred and twenty-two runs and had lost eight of their batsmen. Charlie Knott took five of their wickets and was the centre of attention in the Chapel rooms, for to my surprise (and delight, for the fresh air had given me an appetite) the entire body of players and spectators walked up the lane at this interval to enjoy a collation of sandwiches and cakes displayed on a pair of trestle tables.

Busily supervising the refreshments was Maria Thornley, the self-possessed wife of slow bowler Jesse and mother of the distracted Louisa. When I came into the room she was pouring hot tea into rows of cups.

"Oh, it's you, Mr Rowbotham!" she exclaimed upon noticing me in the queue. "I didn't expect to see you here today. You're not so much of a player, are you?"

"I suppose I'm not, Mrs Thornley," I replied, feeling slightly belittled, however much inadvertently. "I offered to keep the scorecard."

"Very noble," she smiled. "Milk? The sugar's in that bowl at the end."

"Thank you."

"I should be thanking you, by the way," she said as an afterthought. "Our Louisa tells me you all but saved her life."

"Saved her life?"

"From a flying cricket ball."

It was then that I noticed the younger woman, still with her friend, amongst the ladies in the background who were buttering bread and slicing cake. She wore her hair loose that afternoon and it fell to her neck in thick shiny locks, the rich deep brown I remember her mother's being before it began to fade to grey. Perhaps she had been listening to our conversation for she looked up at me and offered a friendly smile, not only with her rosy lips but also with her soft blue eyes.

"It was a near miss," I conceded, "but I doubt the lady's life was ever in any danger. At worst a bruised ankle was avoided."

The mother was smiling too: the same generous smile as her daughter, albeit perhaps a touch more theatrical.

Now in her sixtieth year, Maria Thornley had lived in Gee Cross almost all her life and in spite of being a married woman for half of those years, many local folk still referred to her, quite incorrectly, as Miss Gledhill. As a girl and indeed as a young woman (the most beautiful in the village, it was said) she was unflinchingly devoted to her mother, the widow Mrs Gledhill. Both women were equally devoted as a pair to Hyde Chapel and the word of the Lord. Maria was still a handsome woman and was fortunate never to have to worry about praying to Him for the means to maintain a polished appearance. In her late twenties she had briefly been employed in a lawyer's office in Hyde where she met Jesse Thornley, a blacksmith who had his works around the corner.

He was a skilled craftsman with a full book of commissions who already employed three young apprentices. Having given every man in Gee Cross the cold shoulder, Maria saw a future with the shy but entrepreneurial Hydonian and they married with very little delay.

Shortly before I arrived in the village Jesse bought the ironmongery (and shuttle and picker manufacturing business) on John Street previously owned for generations by the Oldham family. All the while he maintained the smithy in Hyde and employed a manager to run it for him. As a matter of interest, one of his smiths produced the ceremonial key used in the grand opening of the Town Hall. Meanwhile the Thornleys, by now parents of a pretty young daughter, purchased a substantial house on Joel Lane and Maria's happiness was complete.

I carried away my plate of food to sit at a table with Charlie Knott and two other players who had already eaten. I took in good part his jest that rather than working up a sweat out on the pitch I had landed the easier option of sitting at a table filling in numbers.

"Just like markin' school work," he added with a grin.

I congratulated him on his successful bowling. Modestly, he was concerned that he had not actually bowled well enough.

"One 'undred and twenty-two is a fair score," he said. "It's a total we'll be 'ard pressed to beat."

For a moment or two we were left alone. I asked after his mother, about his job and his new lodgings. As we often did, we touched on politics and the state of the country, for he was a serious-minded young man with an impatience for social justice. He attended the Mechanics Institute on Hyde Lane where he could avail himself of newspapers and history books and political pamphlets, and there discuss issues with like-minded men. He was reluctant to join the Liberal Party, he had told me more than once, believing that though they moved in the right direction, their journey to what he called "an enlightened future" was at a snail's pace.

"Mr Gladstone's too timid," he said with a sigh; it was something I had heard him say before. "Or else 'is cabinet is."

We were both excited that a general election was due to be called later in the year. It was the first one, since the previous year's act of parliament, in which men such as me would be allowed to vote; not yet a householder, my friend remained ineligible. People were stirring around us, however, and we had no time to delve further into the subject.

"We need to get back," said Charlie, standing up and taking a deep breath. "One of our lot's goin' to 'ave to knock some runs in t' next 'our or two."

"Well, good luck," I said.

"You're comin', aren't you? Scorin' our innin's?"

"I believe Margaret Dowson is taking over," I replied, "but I've not seen her. I suppose I'd better come down in a minute just in case I'm needed."


Shortly after I had resumed my seat at the table by the scoreboard Louisa Thornley and her friend sauntered past me by the boundary. No words were exchanged. Louisa's eyes were aimed towards her father who was one of the Chapel's opening batsmen and who had scored five quick runs in the very first over.

There was no sign of Margaret. No matter. It was a fine afternoon and I was getting the hang of recording the overs. I am loath to criticise any volunteer but it must be said that for all his expertise, Mr Ives' handiwork was shoddy by anybody's standards. I appreciate that rows of dots and figures, columns of names and numbers, they are all components of a code of which he was no doubt a master, but there was no excuse for illegibility to my mind. I say in all modesty that the contrast at the point on the page where I took over was marked.

One or two of our players, waiting their turn to face the bowling, wandered over for a word. The Reverend Dowson seemed to think that I was doing a tidy job.

"You're probably better at the desk than in the middle facing a fast one," he remarked, patting me on the shoulder.

The match proceeded steadily, punctuated by applause for each shot that beat the fielders or the fall of a wicket, and by the regular exhortations of the players to the umpires for what reason I am not quite sure.

During a break in the play I noticed at one side of the field a group of boys: some of the same children who had been throwing a cricket ball around earlier. Now they had reappeared with a larger ball, an old leather football, and were gleefully scurrying after it. I guessed they were boys I taught or at least had once taught. They were too distant for me to recognise and, truth be told, the light was beginning to fade. The brightest of the day was beyond us and as the sun dipped slowly towards the treetops the players cast ever longer shadows over the grass. A thin veil of cloud was advancing from the west and the sheep had long since wandered down the slope out of sight.

Shortly afterwards a child broke off from the pack and ambled over to talk to me. It was Danny Harrop, his face red and damp with perspiration. His fair hair was in a tangle and the knees of his breeches were stained with grass.

"I've come to keep you company, Mr Rowbotham," he said with a smile. "What you doin' exactly?"

In the course of the next two or three overs I regaled him with my knowledge of the recording system. He might have assumed that I had been familiar with its intricacies for years, such was the confidence in my voice. He offered to change the tin numerals at the end of each over, for which I was grateful; I was becoming fatigued by bending down and reaching up every five minutes.

Wickets began to tumble. Charlie Knott, the fifth batsman, managed only a dozen runs and he left the field cursing his luck and swinging his bat this way and that as if he were swatting at a fly. The Reverend Dowson, poor man, was flummoxed by the first ball he faced and was bowled clean out for nothing. The Chapel needed to score fifty more runs and had only six overs in which to compile them. Suddenly I found that I was appreciating the value of the game as a genuine competition.

It was at this moment that Margaret reappeared. She asked me how I was managing.

"Oh, I'm coping, Miss Margaret," I said.

"Perfectly well, I can see," she said, casting an eye over the record. "But here I am and I must release you from your task. I'm sorry I was elsewhere, Mr Rowbotham, but I thought I'd better show my face for the last bit. I don't want to let father down, especially now that he'll be in a foul mood. That was him, wasn't it," she asked with a mischievous grin on her face, "hitting out at thin air?"

"Don't worry," I insisted. "Danny and I will finish off now. We're a team."

Danny laughed. Some of his friends had joined us, dribbling the football around the boundary. He explained to them what he was up to, proud of his new responsibility.

It quickly became evident that the Hyde Chapel players were not going to pass the score of one hundred and twenty-two. In their desperation the batsmen were imprudent, risking their wickets for reckless shots, and they were all out with three overs remaining. The Wesleyans were jubilant but gracious in victory and there were warm handshakes all round.

As the sun finally set I handed over the scorecard and found myself strolling back up the lane with Danny at my side.

"I dunna mind cricket," he was saying, "but football's t' sport for me, Mr Rowbotham."

"Why is that?"

"Dunno. There's more runnin' about. It's faster. I like kickin' a ball, I like jugglin' it, just playin' with it, I like t' feel of it at me toes."

"I must say," I said, "I do prefer a sport that's over and done with in less than four hours. I'm sure it's been at least four hours since I started watching that cricket match. Mind you, it did have an interesting finish."

"Football's better."

"I think you might be right, Danny."

"'Ave you ever watched a match, Mr Rowbotham?"

"No. Not a proper match."

"I'd love to watch a proper match. Even better, play in one."

"When you're older, Danny, I'm sure you will. If you're good enough."

"Oh, I'll be good enough," he said, smiling to himself.

We had reached the school building. The boy was still talking. I sensed he was reluctant to leave me, to walk down the Gerrards to his home in the Hollow – one of a terraced row of cottages owned by the Apethorn Mill estate.

"There's a team in Hyde now, you know."

"Yes, I read about that."

"Hyde Football Club."

"Yes, exactly. Hyde Football Club."

"They'll 'ave proper matches, won't they?"

"I'm sure they will. When the cricket's over."

"Where'll they play, then?"

"I've no idea. There'll be a field they can use somewhere in Hyde, I suppose."

"Can you find out, Mr Rowbotham? Find out where they'll play?"

"I'll do my best, Danny. I'll keep my eyes on the newspaper."

"Thanks."

Just as he was heading away, I called out a question I had been remiss in not asking earlier.

"How is your father, Danny? Any better?"

"Not really."

"He's still off work?"

"Aye, he's still at 'ome. It's 'is lungs."

"Yes. I remember your mother telling me."

"We 'ad a doctor come. Listened to 'im breathin'. Said 'is lungs were a mess. Nowt we didn't already know."

"I'm sorry."

The child stepped away.

"Bye, Mr Rowbotham," he called. "An' thanks."

"Thanks?"

"Thanks for lettin' me put them numbers up on that cricket board."

And without further ado he turned away from me and tore off down the street.

# Chapter 2

With less than one week before the Chapel school was about to reopen after the long summer holidays, I was pleased with the improvements I had made to the classroom. While most of my pupils had been out and about at play and some intermittently cajoled into work – helping their older siblings with haymaking and the early harvests, for instance – I repainted the walls and polished the woodwork, washed the windows inside and out and replaced faded displays the best I could with brighter ones. I had removed piles of dog-eared papers, thrown away cracked writing slates and worn out samplers. I washed every dip pen I could find and had ink bottles filled to the brim ready to dribble an amount into the little porcelain wells (also rinsed clean) in the desks where the older scholars would sit come Monday morning. I had wiped down sticks of chalk that were worth saving and had disposed of broken stubs. An allowance I had been granted to purchase new boxes of coloured chalks had been promptly spent, and in addition I obtained a stock of fresh booklets from Mrs Beech's little business on Hyde Lane.

A former teacher herself, Mrs Beech was a most enterprising woman, short-sighted and well into her late sixties, who ran a small bookshop which specialised in secular teaching materials. As a subscriber, along with many other local schoolmasters, I was able to avail myself of a regular supply of her children's readers, pages of puzzles and a range of copybooks for a modest annual sum. She was able to provide new stock throughout the year from a supplier in Manchester, and was prepared to recollect second-hand materials which were still in good condition.

I was in the middle of unpacking a new batch – simple arithmetical problems in the main – when there was a tap on the door and the Reverend Dowson strode into the room.

"Well, I must say," he said, casting his eyes over the freshly painted space, "you've made a good job of it, Walter."

"Yes," I agreed, "I am pleased with it. I hope the children appreciate it. But you can imagine how tidy it'll look after a week's activity."

Mr Dowson nodded but was keen to curtail inconsequential chatter.

"I haven't seen you properly since that cricket match a fortnight ago, have I? I did thank you, Walter, didn't I? For the scorekeeping? It was negligent of me if I didn't."

"No, I believe you did, Henry."

"Well then. I'll say it again anyway: you did a wonderful job, you really did. For all his good intentions, Mr Ives is better with a shovel than a pencil, let us say. He's a broad stroke man, if you understand my meaning. Not one with an eye for detail."

"I did notice."

"I'm sure you did. Give him a patch of ground to turn over, a tree root to unearth, a pile of bricks to move: Ives is your man. He's perfect. And a lovely chap too, of course."

"Yes, he's a reliable worker."

I wondered where the conversation was heading and had to wait yet a moment or two to find out. Mr Dowson seemed to be examining the contents of a bookcase. Then he coughed to clear his throat and, eyes resting on the books, said:

"Would you care to do it again, Walter? We'd be so very grateful."

"The scoring?"

"Yes, the scoring. Unless you'd rather play?"

He turned to face me and saw my reaction.

"No, I thought not," he went on without hesitation. "Would you treat us one more time to your incomparably neat handiwork? Your effortless accuracy?"

I was on the point of opening my mouth to respond but he was running ahead of me.

"We have one match left to play before the summer ends. It's at Woodley on Sunday afternoon. Against the Primitive Methodist Chapel. Down the hill, by the canal, I'm sure you know it. They use a pitch over the Stockport road. A two o'clock start."

"It's kind of you to offer."

"And they provide a superb tea. At least they did last time. Better than the one we put on, I have to admit. But please don't let my words ever reach Mrs Thornley's ears!"

I realised I had no reason to refuse.

"So, you agree, Walter? Wonderful. I'm sure it'll be a fine afternoon. And you'll have a lovely time tallying the numbers. Well done. And thank you. I'll be able to tell Mr Ives he can have a well-deserved day off."

When Sunday came the Reverend Dowson was unavoidably caught up in matters ecclesiastic and his place amongst the cricketers was taken *in extremis* by Jack Hill's father, the stout dairyman, who looked less like a sportsman than Father Christmas. Nevertheless my responsibilities as a record-keeper were unchanged.

I was not unduly surprised to see, an hour or so after the match had begun, the boy Jack arrive at the ground with a large bottle of milk and, tucked under his arm, a partially deflated football. Walking a pace or two behind him with a grin on his face was Danny Harrop. The pair of them joined our group by a long stone wall at the edge of the pitch. Jack found his father nervously waiting his turn to bat. Danny gravitated towards me.

"You've no big number board today, Mr Rowbotham," he said.

"It's over there," I answered, pointing across the green where Woodley's scorer had established himself. "It's the home team's job. I've just got the scorecard to fill in."

"So, you'll not be wantin' any 'elp, then?"

"Not really, thanks. You're free to kick your ball about. As long as you keep off the pitch."

The boy said nothing but seemed disappointed. He had no brothers or sisters and I fancied he was bored at the tail-end of the summer. In spite of his father's recent illness, both his parents had been regularly employed and, as far as I was aware, they had never struggled to find the money to pay for their son's schooling. In the wake of recent education acts, the Reverend Dowson has been keen to take advantage of the grants available from the government via the new school boards, but monies are slow to trickle to established schools and even slower towards non-conformist bodies such as ours. So for all the talk from our enlightened politicians, for the time being schools are rarely free. Rudimentary infant classes have been available for some years at many large factories, allowing young parents to continue working, but mill owners are oftentimes torn between their philanthropic principles and the desire for cheap juvenile labour. In these more prosperous times the new Anglican church in Gee Cross, Holy Trinity, has opened a schoolhouse on Higham Lane which is popular. As for Hyde Chapel, the number of our scholars has increased too, adding, incidentally, to my workload.

I was worried about the prospect of John Harrop becoming a permanent invalid. He was one of several workers I have known who have suffered from years of exposure to the mites of dust in the carding room at Apethorn Mill, where raw cotton is teased and stretched and cleaned of its impurities on the drawing frames. It is the home to an invisible menace; Harrop was one of many afflicted in the end by chronic ailments of the throat and the chest.

I had spoken to his wife Martha a few days earlier, meeting her by chance outside Booth's bread shop. The woman was by nature a cheerful soul and was not for long without a bashful smile for her fellow man. However, I sensed the expression she wore before she saw me that morning was one of an anxious traveller along life's path with a heavier burden to bear than most. Her eyes flickered to life when she noticed me: watery blue eyes ringed with shadow. She thanked me for taking an interest in Daniel. She told me that the mill owners had sent a doctor to the Hollow this week to see her husband.

"He has no energy, Mr Rowbotham," she said in a thin voice. "He takes a swig o' gin in th' afternoon to 'elp 'im sleep. Doctor said there's nowt to be done beyond rest. An' keepin' 'im well-watered. He reckons I should put ginger in 'is tea. Failin' that, a spoonful of 'oney. He wrote it down for me, what he said t' matter was. What's t' matter with my John."

I did not need to ask, nor did I wish to. There was little doubt the word would be *bronchitis*. I wondered what the man was thinking. What comfort was there in such a stark medical term scribbled down for her on a scrap of paper?

Instead I asked her if she was still in work. Of course, it had become a necessity. Yes, she was working longer hours, cleaning up for Mr Quigley and lending a hand in his shop. Quigley was a shoe mender, a widower, a Catholic Irishman, one of many such folk from over the water who had found work in the town's mills in the past forty years. They say he had saved every penny of his weaver's wages once his wife died, so determined was he to buy a little cobbling business and resume the craft he had learned as a boy back in County Meath.

"I've got some 'ours cleanin' at t' Grapes an' all," she added, pulling from her face a strand of colourless hair that a gust of wind had caught.

I told her it was nice to talk to her, that I was looking forward to the new school term, to teaching her son again.

"Thank the Lord our Danny'll be leavin' this next year," the woman sighed. "Sooner he gets 'imself a job, better for us all."

I was sure she did not really mean those words. She knew the value of education. She was a reader herself, Danny had told me once: there was always a book or two in the house. As we parted I asked her to pass on my best regards to her poor husband John.

The Woodley umpire signalled a change of bowler and I returned to my scorecard. Danny and Jack drifted off with the football, to be quickly joined by a couple of local lads who wanted to demonstrate their juggling skills. I concentrated on the cricket, marking off the outcome of each delivery in my newly acquired code and offering words of encouragement to the Chapel batsmen – those disappointed to be out and those impatient to be in. There was no sign of Charles Knott today. Somebody said he was playing for a team in Hyde. Someone else said he'd injured his hand on a franking machine at work. Somebody else again had heard he'd found himself a lady friend.

Tea was served in a tiny side room of the chapel of the Primitive Methodists. We spilled out into the lane with our cups and saucers and matching plates. Danny and Jack were instinctively drawn to the refreshments to which, strictly speaking, they were not entitled. They smiled politely and blind eyes were turned. Danny joined me on a low wall in the shade of a sprawling oak whose leaves were starting to turn the colour of toast. He was carrying a glass of lemonade and a large slice of apple cake.

"You 'eard owt else about t' football club, Mr Rowbotham?" he asked.

"I know the names of a few fellows on the committee," I said.

"No, I mean, like when they'll play. When they'll practise."

"I've no news on that front, Danny."

"You think they'll be playin' next week? Will it be a Sunday?"

"As soon as I know I'll let you know."

He took a mouthful of cake.

"Will it be soon?" he asked, swallowing.

"It's likely to be in the autumn, I'd say. They need to organise a team, a pitch, not to mention fixtures."

"I 'ope it's soon."

"It'll not be long. I'm sure they'll arrange plenty of fixtures. They'll probably try and play matches all through the winter months."

"That's alright. I'll not mind t' cold. Even if it's just watchin'. I'll borrow me dad's work coat. He'll not be needin' it much longer."

I let him take a long drink before asking:

"How is he today?"

"Same. He don't speak so much. Not to me, any road. Just coughs. Even before he got poorly he never said owt much."

The child looked at me with a quiet appeal in his eyes.

"Mother says he's *wee-sy. Wee-sy.* Is that a real word, Mr Rowbotham?"

"Wheezy?" I said, smiling. "Yes, it's a word. It means he's short of breath."

I spelt it out for him.

"W, H, like the question words you learned: *what, why* and *where.*"

"And *when.*"

"And *when.* Indeed."

"Come along, Walter!" a familiar voice suddenly shouted, jerking my attention from the boy. It was Frederick Ashton, again on umpiring duties:

"We're starting again in five minutes."

He was already ambling across the lane with some of the players.

"Are you coming back to kick your ball around?" I asked Danny.

"Suppose," he said, swallowing the last of the cake. "It's not

55

*my* ball. It's Jack's. But 'ave you seen 'im play? He's no good. He kicks like a lass. You watch 'im toe it!"

As I stood up we shared a moment of laughter.

Then the boy was staring down at his plate, picking up the last few crumbs, when he suddenly said:

"You know, Mr Rowbotham, I wish *you* were me father."

The words struck me like a jab in the ribs. I had no time to respond as he had dropped the plate on the grass and was already running off down the path to find his friend.

# Chapter 3

That same summer, while Martha Harrop was sweeping up dust and scrapings of leather from Mr Quigley's workshop floor, while her husband John lay wheezing in his chair clutching a bottle of gin, her son Daniel would have been excited to learn that grand plans were indeed being laid to establish an association football club in Hyde.

Ever since the labouring classes had been granted statutory paid leisure time, loose groupings of young men had formed themselves into informal sports teams. Whenever and wherever they were able to arrange to meet willing opponents they played matches, generally of cricket, rugby or football. Our town was not exceptional in this regard but until this summer informality was assuredly the byword.

On the evening of Monday 27th July a body of around forty like-minded gentlemen convened a meeting at the Royal Hotel in the Market Square to lay the foundations of a football club that might fly the flag for the town. Further meetings were held to put together a committee, to agree rules and objectives, and to consider all the practicalities of the endeavour. There was no denying that measures were being taken first and foremost to compete with other towns in the area. A good number of them were in their turn following in the footsteps of football clubs established to represent self-confident towns across Great Britain throughout the previous decade. Four years after Hyde became a municipal borough and four weeks after the official opening of its Town Hall, there were plenty of Hydonians who felt ambitious enough to promote their town through organised sport.

Many such men were casual players with their own aspirations, some were businessmen, even mill owners, who offered expertise in administration and financial affairs, others were simply interested parties from all walks of life who wanted to help the project in any way they could. I refrain from naming them all but I came to befriend a good number of such fellows in the course of the following years. Joshua Hall, one of the Halls from Kingston House, was instrumental from the outset, not only as a player but also as a leader; he was the club captain for several years. Along with members of the Hibbert and Horsfield families, Joseph Maloney, a print worker at Newtonbank, was another I came to know as a friend. He was no player but was elected as the club secretary in 1887 and as such had a role in selecting the team.

Forgive me, I am running ahead of myself.

By the early autumn of 1885 players had begun to assemble regularly to train as an embryonic team. Rudimentary pitches were marked and goalposts erected on sections of the large area of open grassland stretching south from the new Mottram road generally known as Walker Fold or Ewen Fields or many years before that simply as Owen Field. It was standing on the edge of one such pitch, along with my young companion Daniel Harrop, that for the very first time I watched a group of Hyde Football Club players stretching their limbs, running up and down the length of the field and purposefully kicking leather balls around.

It was a Saturday afternoon in September and when I mentioned to several of the older boys in my class that the session had been advertised in *The North Cheshire Herald*, inviting players to attend for trials, Danny was bursting with excitement. There was no question of him missing the occasion and of course I was prepared to take him down to watch. There was nobody else who could.

Happily it was a dry day but the weather had turned cold. Rusty leaves were shaken from the trees by a chill wind and I admit I was reluctant to stay outside for long. Nevertheless, once ensconced, I became curious to witness such a variety of activities on view, and fairly quickly my curiosity transformed itself into genuine interest.

As I have previously alluded to, I have never played much sport, and team sport hardly at all, but there were aspects of the training which I could understand, even relate to. In the first instance I was observing teaching. I saw groups of players being instructed by one of several trainers in a range of what I suppose must be considered skills: shooting at a goal, heading a ball (which looked particularly uncomfortable), running short distances with a ball at one's feet, and so on. In each case there was explanation, demonstration, individual tuition and group practice. I heard shouts of rebuke and correction, I heard words of encouragement and praise. It was not so very different from the teaching and learning that took place, at least theoretically, every day in my classroom.

Secondly I found myself wondering how a functioning team would be assembled from all these disparate parts. In many ways I could be considered a solitary man. With rare exceptions I have always had colleagues or acquaintances rather than friends. I enjoy my own company. I like solitary pursuits: walking, reading, playing music. Marriage was a mystery. Yet for all of that I do appreciate the particular richness of community, indeed of communion. The togetherness of a full chapel on a Sunday morning warms my heart, as does the energy of a group of pupils working as one. I love the collected majesty an orchestra can create, and the harmony of a choir. More functionally I understand committees, or at least committees of educationalists: I have sat on successful ones and on some others less so. I have even chaired a few. I know the value of a unity of purpose, of shared aims, of building a team spirit.

Wandering around the field I watched closely as players' strengths and weaknesses were assessed. Even from my perspective, inexperienced and simplistic as it was, I realised that I was actually assessing them myself: those men were better shooters at goal, these men had greater accuracy in their passing, and those others could dribble the ball better at speed. There were players who were predominantly right-footed and here their counterpart left-footers; it seemed so few were adept with both feet. And yonder was a separate species: the goalkeepers. One or two were more agile, braver, with stronger hands than the rest. Somehow from all these components a team would be built.

Presently I wandered away, found a fence to sit on and took the weight off my feet for five minutes. It was a paddock fence, enclosing half a dozen fine workhorses, a pair of which showed a silent interest in me. I was moved to pat the forehead of one, a handsome grey, and, lowering my hand to its muzzle, was alarmed when the animal snapped at my glove and ambled away from the barrier with the woolly object between its teeth.

A stable boy had appeared in the meantime bearing bales of hay.

"Hey, there!" I called across to him. "That horse of yours has stolen my glove!"

The breeze ambushed my voice and the lad looked puzzled at my agitation.

"He's got my glove in his mouth!" I shouted.

"It's a she," he corrected me. "That un's a mare, she is. What's to do?"

I was about to repeat my complaint but I saw that by this time the horse was standing in a corner of the enclosure by a large dung heap. She had dropped my glove and it was flattened under a heavy hoof in a brown puddle of septic juices.

"What's to do?"

"Never mind," I said, turning away. "It doesn't matter."

From some deep part of my memory came the rueful words of an old friend: *Me and horses*, he once said, *we haven't always been so friendly in the past.*

I smiled and wandered off absent-mindedly, away from the distant shouts of the footballers and the soft whinnies of the animals. I was in a part of Hyde I barely knew and found myself skirting a farmstead named Ewenfield and thence emerging into Fairbrother Street, which I did finally recognise: it led down the hill towards Godley but here I turned back.

I hoped Danny was not made anxious by my absence but I need not have worried: when I found him he had made friends with some boys from Mottram Road who had their own ball.

"Come and look at Toffee's skill, Mr Rowbotham," he said, pulling at my coat sleeve.

"Toffee?"

"That lad over there. I thought they were callin' 'im Tommy

61

but he says it's Toffee. Look at 'is face: he's got skin t' colour o' caramel."

I had seen a few children like him before: boys and girls in Manchester's central districts whose mothers were pasty-faced Englishwomen and whose fathers were Jamaicans who, by accident or by design, had found their way to Lancashire on the sugar ships.

I was made to stand and watch for more than a minute as a spindly lad with a shaven head and defiance in his deep brown eyes juggled with a football, keeping it off the ground with one foot, tap, tap, tap, then the other, then the knee, now the head, the shoulder, back to the feet: a study of soft control and deep concentration which brought to mind a musical étude. Finally, without loss of composure, he simply decided to stop, caught the ball between his grubby hands and looked up at me for approval.

"Very well done," I said. "You should be in a circus."

From the scornful look on his face I realised my remark was inappropriate and perhaps even insulting.

"Why you only wearin' one glove, mister?" he asked.

I looked at my hands. It was a fair question: they were decidedly odd.

"Oh, that!"

I was about to explain but he had already turned away. Even without sight of his face I could tell he was grinning. In his own knowing way the boy must have considered me ridiculous. He walked off without a further word.

"He should be in a football team, Mr Rowbotham," insisted Danny. "Not in a circus."

"How old are you, Toffee?" I called, but he had gone.

"He's fourteen," answered another lad. "He works at Slack Mills. Name's Mellor. He'll be captain o' this lot in a year or two."

By this time recognisable games had been set up on two adjacent pitches. Men with loud voices bellowed instructions from the sidelines. It was clear that there had been more triallists than the club needed and a cull of sorts had taken place. Disappointed young men who had been discarded had quickly swallowed their pride and were already organizing their own makeshift teams and more and more contests were kicking off at the fringes.

I was not disposed to staying for much longer. The damp cold earth was penetrating the soles of my boots and raw gusts of wind brought tears to my eyes.

Regretting leaving a scarf at home, I called Danny over and informed him that we would come again another day but for now it was time to be leaving.

# Chapter 4

A full week later and concerns aplenty relating to matters scholastic had taken my mind far from thoughts of footballers. There had been an incident of bullying amongst a few of the girls which I was obliged to deal with by speaking at length not only to the perpetrators but also their mothers. Another immediate matter to resolve was the discovery in a batch of handwriting samplers supplied by Mrs Beech that half of the contents had been printed incorrectly. I made a point of calling into her bookshop early on the Saturday afternoon to ask her to rectify the situation.

As I knew she would be, the old woman was a model of apologetic courtesy. She insisted it was not a fault of hers, which I dutifully accepted, as all the packets were collated and sealed at the printing stage.

"If I'd split a packet and given you half and half, then it could have been me to blame, Mr Rowbotham, I grant you. You know how my eyes are getting and it's so gloomy in that back space. I really should get myself some brighter lamps for in there. Or else employ a young girl who can see in the dark!"

The exchange was made with a minimum of fuss. I was lucky to catch her, she remarked as I was leaving: she had errands of her own to run and she rarely kept the shop open much beyond one o'clock of a Saturday.

I was halfway down Hyde Lane, a good quarter of a mile beyond the Big Tree which folk talk of as the northern limit of Gee Cross village, and had no urgent reason to retrace my steps. It was a fair afternoon, my bundle was not heavy and

I decided to stroll down the hill into town and see what the market might offer by way of diversion. The road was quiet and as it ran over the railway cutting I paused a moment to watch for goods trains but the line was empty, its steel tracks catching the light of the weak autumn sun.

I noticed no fellow travellers until I was approaching the looming chimneys and the huge flat-fronted brick edifice of the main carding and spinning rooms of Slack Mills. It was there, just as the road forked, that I heard a pair of men's voices behind me and the click-clack of their boots on the flagstones as they gained ground. The talk was of football, specifically a discussion of the merits of a goalkeeper whose name I had missed.

As they reached me one of the fellows bade me a good afternoon. He was the taller of the two, a distinguished, dark-haired young man with a full moustache and side-whiskers. His companion bore a resemblance to him facially but was clean-shaven and his hair was a shade lighter. Strange to say, but I did in fact recognise them both; I had seen them at the football trials a week earlier and I spoke up to tell them so. Now that he faced me the taller man said he believed he had noticed me on the fields too. *Was I on my way there again this afternoon?*

"Well, I was heading into Hyde," I told him, "on my way to the market, as a matter of fact."

"We're on our way to the fields. There's a session on again later. They're putting on a practice, then a match."

"Come down with us," said the shorter man, "If you've nowt else to do."

"I'm Edward Berry," said the other, offering a hand to shake.

"Walter Rowbotham," I confirmed.

"And this young reprobate is my brother Clarence."

A moment later we were walking in step down the street, in the shadow of the long eastern wall of Number Three Mill. Without realising it, I had fallen into their rhythm and had quite missed my turn down Hyde Lane. We were passing the squat, grimy rows of mill-workers' houses on Back Lane instead, heading directly towards Ewen Fields. No matter. They were genial fellows and I was happy to stay in their company a while longer.

I conceded to them that I was not by habit a follower of football and that my presence last week was first and foremost as a favour to a young man, a scholar in my class.

"Oh, you're a schoolteacher, then?" asked Clarence, raising an eyebrow. "Not my favourite sort of gentleman."

I was uncertain how to respond.

"Too many bad memories," he went on. "Too many canings."

His brother laughed.

"He's exaggerating," Edward insisted. "He was quite a scholar in his day. He's clever enough with numbers to keep himself out of the weaving shed, any road."

Clarence nodded, stuck his big hands into his coat pockets and said no more.

Both brothers had been educated well beyond the age of thirteen.

"It's something our parents believed in. We were lucky. They had a bit of money saved up."

Both now had jobs in offices where they could wear pressed shirts and keep their faces clean: Clarence was a clerk at the

66

gasworks by the canal and Edward's office was up there, he said, pointing to the left, *no, it's just out of sight.* He was a trader in cotton cloth, employed by the Slack Mills Company. He was clearly proud of his achievements and mentioned in passing that he was twenty-two years of age, which left an impression on me. What a future he might have!

"I'm still learning the job," he added, not wishing to appear boastful. "I've got plenty to learn. They send me into Manchester once a week to college. And sometimes with my manager to take notes at meetings at the warehouses."

I remembered seeing Clarence taking part in the goalkeeping drills the previous Saturday. Edward informed me that he himself was not much of a player but he loved the sport and he had been one of the fellows at the first meeting at the Royal Hotel where, as he put it, *our club was born.*

"Our Clarence had a go at the trials last weekend but he saw how high the standard is."

I could see the brother nodding again, this time in resignation.

"But they asked him back today, didn't they, brother? They want him to do some drills with T.H. I reckon he'll be the starting goalkeeper once we get some fixtures sorted."

"T.H.?"

"Tom Harry. Big bloke, fair hair, going a bit thin on top. You must have seen him. Tom Harry Drinkwater. A noisy cock, you'll have heard him yelling out his orders. He's the best goalkeeper we've got. Better than our Clarence, any road."

Clarence aimed a playful kick at his brother, who jumped out of the way laughing.

"I'll introduce you to him when we get down there," he went on. "And some of the others if you like."

Edward Berry was as good as his word. Together we spent at least two hours wandering around the fields, stopping here to watch a group of players drilling, there to have words with parties in dark woollen frock coats whose ambition it was to make something of this group of footballers and turn the club into a force to be reckoned with. I met one of the Hibberts, one of the Horsfields, both from mill-owning families, Joshua Hall and, of course, Tom Harry Drinkwater, who from beneath a floppy cap offered me a wide grin and a muddy gloved hand to shake.

There were just enough players on show on that afternoon to form two teams of eleven with a handful of eager replacements. We watched the majority of a practice match where I could see the beginnings of a first-choice team forming. After half an hour of the match a huddle of trainers decided to adjust the selections and the picture became even clearer. I was fascinated by how these decisions were made and discussed them with Berry. He brushed away some of my observations, ignored a few completely and, to my delight, complimented me on others.

"Very perceptive of you, Mr Rowbotham. I was just about to say the same thing: that lad is far more comfortable running in from the left-hand side of the pitch."

"Hey, mister."

I felt a tug on my sleeve and our discussion was interrupted. A youth was standing by my side with a supercilious smile on his face: it was Toffee Mellor.

"Is Danny comin' down?" he asked.

"Hello, Toffee," I said, surprised that the lad had wanted to re-engage with me. "No. No, he's not. Not today. I imagine he'll be at home helping his mother with things."

"Oh."

He looked disappointed. I had noticed that there were fewer boys of his age on the fields today.

"Are you his dad?" he asked.

"His dad? No, I'm not his dad," I laughed. "I'm his teacher. He's in my class at the Chapel school."

"I thought you was his dad," he muttered to himself, "but you're his teacher."

"I'll see him on Monday," I added. "I'll tell him you asked after him."

"Is he clever?"

"Danny? Yes, he's a clever lad."

Mellor nodded.

"Thought so."

He was already moving away when I called:

"I'm sorry about last week."

"Last week?"

"When you were juggling with the ball. It was very clever. I was honestly impressed. Quite dazzled by your repertoire."

"Dazzled by what?"

"By your repertoire. Your skill."

The lad smiled at me. I seemed to amuse him.

"Did you find your glove?" he asked.

I held out my bare hands to show him.

"No, I never did. Lucky it's a bit warmer today."

"Not much warmer," he said. "Ta-ra."

And with that he was gone.

I never ceased to be surprised by how adept children are at creeping up behind an adult without being noticed and then how they can disappear into thin air before you know it.

"Who was that child?" asked Berry.

"That was Toffee Mellor," I said. "He'll be captain of this lot in a year or two."

Eventually Edward Berry and I left Clarence behind and headed back towards Gee Cross. While watching the practice he had explained to me some of the rules of the game and how the umpires would enforce them. He also had a word or two on the shape of the teams and the tactics available according to the strengths of the players. Needless to say, his eye for a player's strengths – and weaknesses – was considerably sharper than mine. I realised how little I had ever known about the intricacies of the game. And yet I was gratified to see how easy it was to understand, with its confined spaces of two halves, a physical contest for a ball (no handling allowed) and a goal at either end. There was room for fluidity within its structure, a range of skills was encouraged and it had a beautiful simplicity compared with what had appeared, to me at least, to be the bewildering complications of cricket.

Now as we walked home he spoke in more general terms about the immediate plans for the club. He was by no means privy to committee decisions, he conceded, but he had his ear to the ground. I found the man's enthusiasm quite infectious and his optimism most endearing.

"If we're going to mix it with the best teams, we're going to have to spend some money," he said as we marched up Back Lane. "A lot of money."

The sun had long disappeared and the afternoon had drifted into gloom.

"That'll not be a problem, mind ," he went on. "The club's got funds. Or we can borrow. All the best clubs employ journeyman players. Semi-professionals from far and wide. There are a lot of good lads from Hyde – you've seen them with your own eyes, Walter. Look at T.H., for instance. And that lad Chatterton, the quick one from Floweryfield, scored a couple of lovely goals. But the team you've watched just now will need stiffening up. With experience, as much as anything else."

I nodded, accepting his wisdom without question.

"Are there any fixtures on the horizon?" I wondered aloud.

"I believe so. Happen a couple in October. Very local opposition, I'd fancy: sides from Stalybridge, Ashton. There's a cost to everything, of course. Travelling, for one thing. And more often than not, opponents will want paying to come to Hyde to play us."

"Well, it definitely sounds like there's a plan."

"Oh, there's a plan alright, Walter, believe you me. Hyde will have its team and it'll not be letting the town down."

As we rejoined Hyde Lane it started to rain: a soft light drizzle. Sweet rain, my mother had always called it. Not driving rain, not the wind-blown torrential stuff that caused streams to burst their banks. Sweet rain was gentle like a kiss. *It's what makes the hills so green and your complexion so fresh*, she would say to me as a child, hugging me to her bosom.

By the railway Berry stopped, indicating the road, Osborne Road, off to the right.

"That's where we live," he said. "You can come in if you like. Have a cup of tea or something? Meet my mother. Meet my sisters."

"That's very kind," I replied, "but I am rather tired. Regretfully, I'm not twenty-two like you. I think I'll get off home before the rain sets in."

"Our Blanche is a schoolteacher like yourself," he added. "You'd have plenty to talk about, I'd wager."

"Another time, I'm sure," I said, a little feebly. "I would love to meet your family another time."

I offered a cold damp hand for him to shake.

"Thank you for your company, Edward. I'm so pleased we bumped into each other. You've been an excellent teacher yourself this afternoon."

We separated and I trudged up the slope past Mrs Beech's darkened shop as the rain persisted. Sweet rain, soaking into my coat. I was comforted, however, by the faint echo of my mother's voice: I heard the words she would say to me half a century ago, tenderly stroking my cheek as I sat on her knee in the scullery of the parsonage in Lees. Surrounded by the smell of baking bread, warmed by a crackling fire, watching the mizzle outside wetting the windowpanes: *Thou's a bonny lad, our Walter.*

# Chapter 5

Edward Berry's predictions were largely accurate. In the months approaching Christmas, Hyde Football Club had fixtures arranged against several teams from the neighbouring towns. For the very first of these, a home match against Lower Hurst Seconds from Ashton-under-Lyne, the flattest pitch on Ewen Fields was neatly marked out with sawdust and flags were placed at the four corners. In accordance with the rules of the Football Association, a horizontal pole was attached to the top of the goalposts to mark the height below which a goal might be scored.

The match, played on the afternoon of 10th October, attracted the attention of over one hundred curious spectators, including myself and a few of the boys from my class, one of whom, of course, was Daniel Harrop. I remember standing with Berry and being the beneficiary of his lively and insightful remarks. Presumably in an imitation of cricket, I noticed that each team provided an umpire who patrolled the field between them, arresting play if improper roughness was deemed to have impeded an opponent. At a point approximately halfway along one side of the pitch was a seat for a third official (although he preferred to stand and move himself about a little to keep warm) who was referred to in the event of a disagreement and in regard to timekeeping.

Hyde, playing in their uniform shirts of pale blue and dark blue halves, and featuring Drinkwater, Hall and Chatterton, put up a spirited show but in the end were beaten by a score of four goals to two. Rather uncertain of what to expect, I have to say that I was royally entertained, not only by the vigour and skills of the players but also by the ribaldry of the crowd.

I pause here to admit that in recording snatches of conversation between footballers (and similarly amongst supporters), I refrain from including the more unpalatable vocabulary in my narrative. It is very true that in moments of extreme disappointment, anger, excitement and even joy, some men more than others are prone to stray beyond the boundaries of decency in their choice of expression. I hesitate to say that it is even a choice at all: I believe there is an element of engrained habit in their behaviour which precludes thought. I must say that obscenities and profanities do not shock me. I am not so sensitive as to be outraged. I worked for many years amongst the poorest families of central Manchester where a lack of schooling and exposure to life's hardships oftentimes conspired to produce a popular form of language that is heavy with vulgarity. I have visited factories where only the constant thunderous rattling of the machinery disguises the offensive vocabulary used between labourers, in some cases in the form of grotesque insults aimed directly at an unwitting overseer.

All that said, I do not believe that you, dear reader, need me, or would even wish me, to expose you gratuitously to explicit obscenities. As a Christian I have no truck with profanity. I can see my father spinning in his grave even as I write these sentences. On the other hand the sexual and the scatological I can find excuses for; after all, such allusions have been the stuff of comedy, insult and ridicule from poets Greek and Roman, through Geoffrey Chaucer, the foul-mouthed Frenchman Rabelais, even to Mr Shakespeare, our most feted bard. Nevertheless, you will find none such here. I leave it to your imagination to add, should you wish, a more earthy flavour to the dialogue, and to your own sensibilities as to where you might choose to draw the line.

Over the following weeks Berry was a regular attender of home fixtures and, with a small knot of fellow supporters, even joined the players on a few of their visits to opponents' grounds. I was somewhat less infatuated, oftentimes having Chapel responsibilities to fulfil or simply deterred by inclement weather. Standing on wet grass under threatening rain clouds has little appeal, no matter how enthralling the sporting spectacle might be. It did occur to me that some enterprising soul associated with the club ought to set up an umbrella stall on afternoons when the skies looked ominous. And moreover, if football were to become a truly popular sport for spectators during the months of winter, then surely, before too long, clubs would have to invest in building at least rudimentary shelters for folk to stand beneath and keep themselves dry. I could imagine the days when a supporter might even have to pay a nominal sum to stand and watch a match on Ewen Fields.

Hyde F.C.'s second game came a week later on a pitch provided by Stalybridge St George's. Sadly it was a second defeat, by one goal to nil. Revenge was gained on Boxing Day when, in a match I did attend in spite of the perishing cold, Hyde won five-nil. The team had a successful run up to Christmas, in fact, beating Oldham Olympic eight-two (I had no conflict of interests), Manchester South End seven-nil and Hooley Hill (a team from Audenshaw) three-one.

It was at the Hooley Hill encounter that Danny Harrop and I once again bumped into Toffee Mellor and some of his pals from up Godley. All of us were impressed by our team's performance, notably the commanding presence of Drinkwater in goal and the shooting skills of Will Chatterton, who scored twice and immediately became Danny's favourite footballer.

Six more matches were arranged for the New Year, which began with a deflating defeat at home, one-nil against Marple. Later in the month the result was more than reversed in fine style, according to reports, as Hyde won three-one in Marple, with another goal for Chatterton. This was the way of it: a defeat then a victory, ups and downs, no deadlocks (what is termed a tie or a draw) in sight. Indeed in all my time watching Hyde F.C. ties have been as rare as a winter swallow. At the end of the short season (the last match took place in March), the team had won nine times and lost six and it was clear to the cognoscenti that Hyde could hold their own against sides of a similar standard. The question on everyone's minds – and certainly on Edward Berry's – was whether the club would be able to compete against more established teams of a higher rank.

By springtime, after many hours in each other's company, my friendship with Edward Berry was well established. I had met his family on a few occasions, stopping briefly at the house on Osborne Road on my way up Gee Cross at the end of a football match. It was a large house set back from the road with a view of the railway cutting, woodland to the west and the mill chimneys and streets of the town to the north. Indeed it needed to be a house of many rooms, for Edward was the oldest of four brothers including Clarence and there were also three sisters.

I recall the first time I stepped across the threshold and met Mrs Berry. Edward had already mentioned to me that his father had died unexpectedly three years earlier: he had been a meat trader, principally in pork, supplying butchery businesses and pie makers across Hyde and Godley. His widow, bright of eye and plump of figure, pink-cheeked and very tidily dressed, stood on no ceremony: she introduced herself to me directly as Mary, Mother Mary in fact, with a self-deprecating smile. She had fine teeth and spoke with a slight nasal tone which I later discovered was an echo of her native Liverpool.

"So you must be Walter, the schoolmaster," she said, taking my hands in hers. "It is always a pleasure to meet an educated man."

With Edward melting into the background, she insisted I follow her into the drawing room.

"Here, take a seat, Walter – or do you prefer Mr Rowbotham? I'll not be offended if you do but we have a relaxed attitude to convention on Osborne Road, don't we, Edward?"

Her son was standing in the doorway smiling indulgently.

"I'll see if the girls want to take a look at you," she went on, backing into the hallway with a little squeeze of Edward's arm *en route*.

I must have produced a somewhat daunted expression.

"She's kidding you," he said, shaking his head. "But be prepared, she will fetch in the misses. The Three Graces, I call them. Don't look so worried, Walter. I can tell that she likes you already."

We were sitting in a cosily-lit room of simple but elegant decoration. Sisters Edith and Blanche appeared presently, each with a tray bearing a plate of buttered scones and a tea set. Sister Beatrice, a schoolgirl, followed with an embarrassed smile. Mother Mary brought in a very large china pot of freshly brewed tea. Heavy curtains were closed against the evening gloom and a coal fire was raging in the grate, adding a shimmering quality to the light.

"The scones are homemade," declared Mrs Berry. "Our Edith's the baker."

The older daughter raised an eyebrow and offered me a plate. It was a most genteel interlude after the earthy grunts, the deep-voiced bawdry and muscular competitiveness of the football match. The ladies were charming and I did my best to warrant their interest in me. With identical blue eyes, rosy cheeks and dark brown ringlets, the young women, sitting in a row along a wide cushioned settle, brought to mind a series of matching porcelain vases of diminishing sizes.

I found Blanche, the teaching assistant at Hyde St George's, to be especially personable. Thirteen-year-old Beatrice spoke eloquently of her interest in matters scientific. The two younger brothers, Charles and Henry, were allowed into the room to introduce themselves, were adamantly refused access to the remaining scones and, exchanging smirks, were encouraged to leave the party before they upset the guest. Edward observed the scene from his armchair, quietly amused. I had not seen him so short of words before but this was unmistakably his mother's domain; Mrs Berry was the conductor here, and the children danced to her lively tune.

Settling down beside me on the sofa, she was most desperate to know about my life, my career and my plans. Not given to talking about myself to women, I was succinct in my replies and was gratified that she continued to listen intently.

"And what on earth do you find to enjoy, Mr Rowbotham," she enquired, "in standing on a wet field watching unruly men kicking a football about?"

"Most probably I would have said not a thing if you'd asked me that very question only six months ago, Mrs Berry." I said. "But there is something noble in sporting competition, I have come to believe. As I am sure your sons will agree."

"Oh, they're quite besotted," said the woman, as if she was talking of a lost cause. "More tea?"

"Thank you, no. I really must be on my way. I'd like to be home before nightfall."

"Well, we shall all look forward to seeing you again, shan't we, girls?"

The three sisters nodded as one and in the corner of my eye I could see Edward trying hard not to laugh. Presently he showed me out.

"Mother is a little eccentric," he whispered, "but she has a heart of gold. Of course she misses Father. He was her anchor."

As I took my leave I crossed paths with Clarence, who had been delayed returning from the match by an impromptu visit to the Ring O' Bells alehouse with a group of friends. I bade him good evening as he walked up the steps to the house, but I believe my words were lost in the smoke and heavy rattle of a goods train lumbering its way towards the depot in Stockport, heaving its long, dark line of wagons filled with freshly mined coal from the pits of South Yorkshire.

# Chapter 6

The summer of 1886 arrived with unexpected haste. No sooner had the football season concluded than the young men in the village began to anticipate the return of cricket matches, hoping that more of them than before could be arranged for the long afternoons of June, July and August. Most of my time and energy was taken up, of course, by the demands of my profession and I do believe that the school year had been a most productive one, especially amongst the infants who were generally more receptive than ever. Nevertheless, it was the first year in my teaching career when the rhythms of organized sport affected the pattern of my own life. Saturdays had assumed a new significance for me with the anticipation before the event and then the joy of not only watching our developing team play a football match but also talking about it with new friends.

The prospect of a series of cricket matches held less appeal but even that gave a pleasing structure to my weeks, knowing that it was likely that I would be called upon to resume my well appreciated responsibilities with the scorecard. Edward Berry was interested in discovering this surprising string to my bow. Out of curiosity he did attend one of the Chapel's fixtures during those summer months but he had no inclination to offer himself as a player. By his own account his younger brother Clarence was an accomplished batsman and he was regularly invited to play for one of the millworkers' teams in Hyde.

So it was, at least temporarily, that I saw less of the Berrys and more of Charlie Knott, former pupil, fast bowler and politically conscious desk clerk at the post office. In the general election of November, with the disenfranchised young radical's approval, I had cast my vote for Thomas Gair Ashton, the son of the town's first mayor, the Liberal candidate. Following the redistribution of parliamentary seats, this was the first time that Hyde had been a constituency in its own right and both Charles and I were delighted that Ashton was duly elected as our first Member of Parliament. It seemed to us both that at least some of the values of the Chartists were beginning to be acknowledged. However, neither Charlie nor I were less than dismayed by the events in London over the following six months. I remember the pair of us – and anyone else who cared to contribute – spending teatimes at several cricket matches discussing not the opposition's bowling attack but the ructions caused by the problem of Irish home rule. Mr Gladstone's Liberals had won the election but had no overall majority and the Irish issue was set to tear the party asunder.

"It's as clear as day what's goin' to 'appen," said Charlie on one such afternoon in early June, frustrated by having bowled too many loose balls and being smacked to the boundaries as a consequence.

"Them that's for keepin' th' Irish locked in our system won't stand much longer for Gladstone's Home Rule Bill. An' I'm talkin' about Liberals, not just Conservatives."

"You're probably right," I agreed, "and it's foolish to carry it forward if he's not got his party behind him."

"The Irish'll vote with him," suggested Frederick Ashton.

"Some of 'em will."

"Most of 'em will."

"There's a Cath'lic majority," explained Charlie, "but t' Protestants'll vote wi' t' Tories."

I was always so impressed with his grasp of the facts, his understanding of complicated situations.

"It all comes down to religion," declared Robert Howarth, greengrocer and wicket-keeper, who happened to be standing by our table.

"Religion an' money," he was saying. "Without religion an' money you'd not have no political arguments. You'd not 'ave no politics at all."

We waited for him to expand on his theory but nothing was added. He wandered off, possibly unaware that he had silenced us all with something of a *non sequitur*.

My own feelings were, and remain, that we British had plundered Ireland for too long. The Irish M.P.s were too small a body to effect change even in their own part of the kingdom. I believe that Britain, prosperous beyond expectations earlier in the century and dominant in trade and influence across the world, could now afford to be generous with our neighbour. Living on an island apart, the Irish must have many concerns particular to themselves and, to my mind, deserved a little autonomy in dealing with them. Whatever I felt, whatever any of us felt, the issue overrode any other in the nation at that time.

A week or two later we were debating the outcome of the bill's fate in a parliamentary vote and its repercussions. True enough, unionist Liberals broke away in large enough numbers from those loyal to Mr Gladstone and the bill was defeated. The rupture in the party, much to Charlie's disgust, caused a realignment of M.P.s and a loss of confidence in the government.

"There'll 'ave to be another election," he said, and I remembering him breaking a teacup as he crashed it down into his saucer.

It was inevitable, of course. Mr Gladstone was unable to hold his M.P.s together and the government's business, Ireland included, was brought to a standstill.

Later that summer, throughout the month of July in fact, a General Election was held. Once again, only seven months after the first time, I cast my ballot for Mr Ashton, the Liberal. It was quite alarming how the tables had turned. In such a short space of time he lost his sizeable majority to his Conservative rival, Joseph Sidebotham, a colliery owner, and Hyde had a new Member of Parliament. Nationally, from Charlie's point of view, the picture was worse: the unionist faction of the Liberal Party had joined forces with the Conservatives and Mr Gladstone's rump were summarily defeated, support from the Irish Parliamentarians notwithstanding. The United Kingdom had a new Prime Minister: the Conservative aristocrat Lord Salisbury.

Although I shared Charlie's disappointment, I found our conversations oftentimes more relaxed if I steered away from wider politics towards a more personal sphere. Surprisingly for a sportsman he had little interest in the town's new football club. He told me he spent much of his spare time during the winter months in the reading rooms of the Manchester Free Library. He mentioned becoming restless in his work at the post office and had an unpleasant disagreement with his superior. Somewhat surprisingly, it seemed to raise his spirits describing it; each utterance was accompanied by hearty laughter. He confirmed that he was actively looking for alternative work. His new lodgings, meanwhile, were very much to his liking. He rented an upper room in a family home at the top end of Henry Street and he confirmed that I was welcome to pay him a visit there at any time.

It was by no means guaranteed that I would be able to avail myself of enough free time, even when the schoolroom was closed, to take a short summer holiday. For one thing it was expected of me that I offer an hour's Sunday school after chapel, and that for every week of the year. On several occasions over the years Frederick Ashton has offered to replace me in that role and for his kindness I have been most grateful. For a second thing, and despite a reliable income, I was never extravagant by nature and am indeed predisposed to thrift. As a result, the extent of a holiday might be taking advantage of an empty week in August to catch a train and go walking in the Derbyshire Peaks, perhaps, or visiting my sister's family on their farm in the hills above Oldham.

We were born a single year apart, Esther and I, and as children we were friendly and close. Rather than a sister, rather than a girl at all, I thought of her as a slightly smaller, a slightly weaker and therefore a less clever version of myself. She has remained slightly smaller but it is debatable which of us is the cleverer. I suppose it would depend on whom one asked. Doubtless her husband has the highest opinion of all her strengths; he is a sheep farmer and for twenty years she has embraced his uncompromising way of life on the weather-beaten uplands edging Saddleworth Moor. They have a pair of energetic adolescent sons and each time I visit them at Diggle Top I find a warm welcome waiting for me in the bosom of a loving Christian family.

In August of 1886 I decided I would invite myself once

more to their homestead and profit from Esther's hospitality. As I had done before, I made an unsatisfactory attempt to assist with shepherding. The boys enjoyed kicking a football around and were surprised that I followed them into the fields with stories of my support for the football club in Hyde. Briefly, and much to their amusement, I joined in with their game but unhappily I had neither the coordination nor the correct footwear to make a positive impression. More successful was my participation in evening games of cards and draughts and Jackstraws. In the long empty days, under a great wide sky lit by shafts of sunlight, I took great pleasure in walking the moors alone; I spotted kestrels and hawks in the air and an abundance of wild flowers and mosses on the ground. One day I might be buffeted by a westerly ruffling the grasses, even troop home soaked by a rain shower, the next I could be baked by a midday sun that embraced the slopes with its generous warmth.

There have been times in the past when, content in my own company, I have wallowed in the solitude of the moorlands: with soaring birds and darting butterflies as my silent comrades I would wander for miles from valley to peak, crossing shimmering carpets of heather and cotton grass, following paths that ran by trickling streams, skirted soft bogs of peat and lead me to gritstone crags – grey shelves of rock worn smooth by the winds and rains of centuries past. Here before me were views of endless open country, wild and barely touched by man. Suddenly, a curious red grouse, a moorcock. A little basking lizard. Less common a bounding hare. Above me the vast, ephemeral sweep of sky. This was God's place, an elemental space of untamed earth, of water and of air. Here, if anywhere, was surely where Mr Blake's "Countenance Divine" had shone forth. It was upon these very "clouded hills". It was on these forsaken, meandering ways that Christ's feet did tread "in ancient times", it was these weathered Pennine crests He had climbed. I felt His presence surround me and was unfailingly gratified, nay, elevated by its grace.

This summer there was something different about my wanderings. My spirits were still lifted by the majesty of my surroundings but, more alert to my loneliness, I felt a stab of deprivation. Day by day it seemed to press ever deeper. I sensed a longing to communicate, not in prayer, but to converse, to share the experience with another living soul - and thus multiply my joy.

Meanwhile back at the farmstead, with my aching feet on a cushion and with a pot of tea at my elbow I spent hours talking to my sister, many of them filled with reminiscences.

One day Esther and I walked down into Lees and stood outside the old parsonage, taking in for old times' sake the dependable stonework and the upper windows where our bedrooms used to be. Our parents had both died prematurely, within a year of each other. I was at college in Manchester at the time. Esther was still living at home and suddenly found herself evacuated to an aunt's house in Oldham.

I was reminded of the parsonage each time I stepped into the parlour at Diggle Top. Over the fireplace, in pride of place, Esther had hung a large rectangular cross-stitch sewn by our mother. Protected by polished glass and framed in cedarwood, it was an intricate representation of Noah's ark. The both of us can remember her working in the light of a pair of gas lamps during long winter afternoons when we were little. Mirrored to the left and right sides of the ark, itself something akin to a Viking longboat, were a giraffe, a lion, a crocodile, many other smaller beasts and what I used to think was a unicorn. *There are no unicorns in the scriptures,* our mother would say, laughing at me, *nor anywhere else for that matter, our Walter, except in fairy tales.* She insisted it was a zebra with a parakeet perched on its head.

Just as painstaking as the illustration, at least to my eyes, was the biblical reference, the coloured words stitched above (*Genesis 7 verse 8*) and strung below as an inscription: *duo et duo ingressa sunt ad Noe in arcam masculus et femina sicut praeceperat Deus Noe.* The whole effect was a work of art, a labour of love. I produce the verse above without call for reference; it is embedded in my memory. Ever the pedagogue, my father insisted I learned the Latin text by heart before he consented to translate it for me: *There went in two and two unto Noah into the ark, the male and the female, as God had commanded Noah.*

The most precious artefact I had rescued from the parsonage was a clock that for many years had sat on the raised ledge of the writing desk in our father's study. It is ticking still and now has pride of place on the mantelshelf in my sitting room. The circular face is fashioned from ivory, as wide as my palm, its numerals Roman and etched in black. Set in an ornate surround of mahogany wood, with two carved human figures reaching out over the top to shake hands, it has, at the base of the frame, an inscription, also in Latin, briefer than the verse from Genesis: *SEMPER AMICIS HORA EST.* It is always time for friends. *Rather there is, Walter. There is always time for friends,* I can hear him say. *Or better yet, there is always time for friendship. Remember, translation is more than a transposition of words, Walter. It is a transference from one language to the other of what those words represent.*

To be sure, friendship was important to my father. Indeed it was in some respects the lifeblood of his ministry. Social gatherings of one kind or another were regular and well enjoyed at the parsonage and since those days I have discovered my own life to be rather less sociable.

Father was an ardent lover of what he called the wisdom and dignity of classical texts. He was disappointed, nay, vexed, that the grammar school I attended did not offer both Latin and Greek. Latin alone was more than enough for me. Although I later came to appreciate its structural clarity, lessons were fraught with trepidation, for we had an irascible old teacher. Ancient is a more appropriate description; with his wispy white hair and his wizened grey countenance, we pupils believed he could be speaking to us about the Roman invasion of Britain from personal experience.

As I have suggested, our mother's greatest skill was with a needle and thread. She oftentimes would salvage clothes, with the permission of the relatives of course, from the wardrobes of the locally deceased. From the discarded material she would refashion new items, designing and creating unique articles of clothing that she would inevitably give away to the poorer children of the parish. Our parents' lives ended too soon. Those days of life and laughter, of conversation and creativity, they ended all too abruptly.

I might add that Esther too is a clever seamstress. Surrounded by a family of menfolk, she confided to me once that she wished she'd had a daughter, not only to make dresses for but also to teach and pass on our mother's gift. It is a truth that I inherited in the main the traits of our father: an indisputable likeness, a studious nature, a love of books and a readiness to inform – that is, to be informative – even if uninvited. From my mother rather less: perhaps her warm heart, her patience and her most steady temperament.

# Book the Third
# Season 1886-87

# Chapter 1

In the summer months of 1886 Blackburn Rovers was the most famous football club in not just the north of England but in the whole of England. Formed in 1875 by a group of wealthy and well-educated local businessmen, the club gradually became the principal force amongst the Lancashire teams, being the first to exploit the pool of talent available in Scotland, where professionalism was banned. In 1882, wearing their distinctive blue and white quartered jerseys, the Rovers were the first northern club to appear in an F.A. Cup final, thus loosening the grip on the competition that had been exerted by aristocratic amateur teams, the so-called gentlemen's sports clubs. Since its inception in 1872 the trophy had been won exclusively by such clubs, notably the Old Etonians, the Wanderers and the officers of the Royal Engineers. Blackburn Rovers narrowly lost their first final but within two years they had once again progressed to the Kennington Oval, the traditional venue for the showpiece occasion, where they claimed their first F.A. Cup final victory. They repeated the achievement the following season and then once again in 1886, setting a stamp on the competition: the Rovers began the 1886-87 season as triple F.A. Cup winners. It may well have raised a few eyebrows therefore, that for the club's first match of the new season, Blackburn Rovers accepted an invitation to play against none other than Hyde F.C. on the windswept Ewen Fields.

It was a most audacious move on the part of the Hyde committee and Edward Berry assured me that a good deal of money was spent on persuading the Rovers to travel south. Nevertheless, and it mattered little that the esteemed visitors left a number of their more valuable footballers at home, I can say that I was in attendance, part of a large crowd on that September afternoon, thrilled to be watching our players compete with some of the best in the land. The result was a surprise to nobody – a somewhat demoralising eight-nil defeat – but, according to Berry, the committee felt that their temerity had been rewarded. The club's profile had been raised and at a meal at the Norfolk Arms after the match the Blackburn contingent had nothing but praise for the progressive Hydonians and generously declared that they showed great promise.

What was beyond dispute is that the substantial defeat at the hands of the F.A. Cup holders did next to nothing to dent the confidence of the members of Hyde F.C. – the players, the committee and the general supporters. With a team fashioned around stalwarts such as Drinkwater, the Hall brothers, Hurst and Pollock, they embarked on a fine run of results up to Christmas of that year. Will Chatterton had been missing at the start of the season but even his most fervent supporter did not believe he would have been able to influence the Blackburn result. A fine footballer, he was an even better cricketer and he spent the summer months playing professionally for Derbyshire. From October onwards, Hyde beat teams from Stretford and Oldham away from home, and on Ewen Fields beat Marple twice and, with Chatterton re-established, overcame Greenhays from South Manchester. Needless to say I found time to attend the three home matches and in doing so renewed my friendship with the Berry brothers.

The days of easily finding a place to stand on the sidelines were already coming to an end. On the Saturdays of matches the designated playing area, selected on the least uneven expanse of the fields, was surrounded on four sides by a waist-high barrier of rope and cinders were scattered along the touchlines to help keep the increasing number of spectators' feet dry. The club rented the pitch for its exclusive use from Mr Oldham the landowner and had formalised an arrangement with the Bankfield Hotel on Mottram Road for use of rooms in which to change and prepare for games. At some point in the autumn of that year collections were taken by volunteers with buckets, encouraging spectators, in lieu of a fee to watch the match, to donate a little of what was in their pockets to the club's coffers. It was evident to all concerned that the project had become more structured, more formalised, and for that we had to thank the members of the committee who were more determined than ever that Hyde F.C. should make its mark.

Edward Berry was not acquainted with every member of the committee, and in any event its membership was rather fluid, but he was close to the Horsfield family who were indeed owners of Slack Mills and therefore his direct employers. As a result I would regularly find him in conversation at the end of a game with gentlemen of a certain influence within the club. After one match – I believe it was the excellent four-nil victory over Marple – Berry introduced me to Frank Hibbert, Fred Perrin and Joseph Maloney who were all three soon to become important members of the club's governance. I was not surprised to find them in high spirits. They were about to join the players at the Bankfield for a celebration.

A supplier of machinery to the mills, Hibbert had a heavy, dark moustache turning ash grey at the edges. He lived a short distance from the hotel in a large property named Brookbank with a wife, two children and two lodgers. Both fellows had been at the match, he said, and pointed them out to us on the far side of the pitch wandering off towards Ridling Lane. Perrin looked a year or two younger than Hibbert, was smoking a pipe of tobacco and thus spoke rather less. Berry told me later that he believed he owned the iron foundry on Norbury Street. Of the three it was Maloney who made the most favourable and, as it transpired, the most lasting impression on me. He was short of stature but beneath a tweed cap his eyes blazed with life and his cheeks were glowing pink. Not yet thirty, married with two infant children, he conceded his thwarted desire to play football himself for his hometown team.

"No, I did not take part in the trials, Mr Rowbotham," he replied when asked how close he had come to realising his ambition.

"I know my limitations," he added, smoothing down his wispy moustache. "Of course, I attended one or two of the trials. As an observer, nothing more. I was curious to discover if the standard of the players was such that I might stand a chance of achieving it. Alas, the standard left me quite at a loss. Let us say, I once thought I was a better footballer than I actually am!"

"And so you bring your other talents to the service of the club, don't you, Joe?" said Berry, patting him on the arm.

"If you say so, Edward."

They exchanged a friendly smile. The pair had obviously met before and were on affable terms.

"Mr Maloney here is standing for the position of club secretary," Edward said, addressing me. "Which will give him a say on recruitment of players and even, I dare say, the selection of the team."

"That's quite a responsibility," I said. "Good luck with your candidature."

"He'll be successful, no question," said Berry.

The crowd was thinning out, the players had disappeared down past the paddocks and volunteers were pulling up the corner flags and collecting stray footballs. It became clear that Maloney was heading in a different direction from Edward and me.

"Before our paths diverge," he said, "I have a proposition for you, Mr Rowbotham."

"A proposition?"

"Indeed."

I looked at Berry whose half-smile betrayed a knowledge of what was to come.

"Since the start of last season," continued Maloney, "that is to say, since the very start, I have been keeping records of the club's matches. The opponents, the venue, the date and of course the results, the lists of players, the scorers of goals and so on."

He paused but I let him catch his breath and proceed without interruption.

"As club secretary, I shall have to do a great deal more than keep records, as you can imagine, Mr Rowbotham. I shall have fixtures to arrange, travel, accommodation. Players' contracts, employment and the like. Suppliers to deal with, contractors to engage, lawyers to consult, oh, I could go on and on."

"Quite."

"And he does have an occupation," interjected Berry.

"I'm a compositor at the printworks," he said before I had framed the question. It occurred to me that in the business of dyeing and printing finished cotton cloth, the two men at my side had had many dealings in the recent past.

"So, my proposition," he went on, again running his fingertips over his moustache, "and this is based on a recommendation of the highest value, is that you, should you agree, assume the responsibilities of keeping the club's records in my stead. Dates, opponents, results, as I described."

He looked at Berry before facing me.

"Edward suggested you, Mr Rowbotham."

"I told him how meticulous your cricket scoring is," said Berry. "I hope you don't mind, Walter. You are far more scrupulous than any of the dozens of the clerks we have in our offices at the Mills."

"Of course, you needn't say yes," said Maloney. "It's entirely up to you. You'd be doing the club a service, I must say. I'm afraid it would be unpaid, if you were at all wondering, but as I say, it would be a service. A great service. As you know, we are largely supported by volunteers…"

"You need say no more," I broke in. Indeed, the decision was one easily and swiftly taken. "I will gladly do it. It is certain that I cannot contribute in respect of the football, but I would be happy to help keep a written record of those that do."

"Splendid," said Maloney, gripping my hands with enthusiasm. "I was going to suggest that you come to my office at Newtonbank and we can discuss everything further but no, you are doing me a favour, and I will make the journey to you. Edward tells me you live in the schoolhouse by Hyde Chapel?"

"That's right."

"Well, I don't know it but I believe my wife does. She was a Gee Cross girl. And it can't be hard to find. They reckon the Chapel has the tallest spire in the borough, don't they? So, shall we say one evening the week after next?"

# Chapter 2

At the start of every new school year I have the same unremitting sense of anticipation. It centres on the prospect of spending the weeks and months ahead with both familiar pupils now one year older and also the most wide-eyed of all, the new arrivals, the six-year-olds blessed with an unblemished enthusiasm for the novelty of the classroom. The other side of the coin, one might say, is the feeling of regret for scholars past: those who have recently moved on to the next stage of their lives, the July leavers, boys and girls for whom bells and schoolbooks are already mere memories. In the first days of September I always miss seeing the faces of the pupils I had come to know and care about as if they were my own children. This year it had been those like the scruffy-haired Danny Harrop: lively, eager, inky-fingered scholars who were suddenly scholars no more.

Most find employment quickly. Gee Cross remains a thriving community with a good number of shops and manufacturing businesses, not least of which are the two enormous cotton mills, set quite out of sight save for their plumes of coal smoke, at the bottom of Apethorn Lane. A few children might apply for work in Hyde where there is an even wider range of opportunities, albeit with more competition for each one. Meanwhile farmers' children would inevitably be given duties on the land.

I concede that my heart sank a little when Daniel Harrop told me that he was planning to find a job at Apethorn Mill. His father's footsteps – years of breathing in cotton dust in the carding room – were surely not ones he wanted to follow in. He assured me he would be working in the weaving sheds, which, to my mind, was no compensation. He was an able scholar, he had a sharp mind, a facility with numbers and a sense of responsibility. He had initiative. I told him, of course, and although I had to explain what the word meant, I sensed his heart swelling with pride to hear my praise.

He allowed me to write a letter of recommendation, a sort of reference to his qualities. I knew how to frame such a statement, having done so before in support of previous pupils of mine who I felt deserved more than menial work. My letter received the blessing of Mr and Mrs Harrop, and happily was considered favourably by the employers at the mill. The boy was granted a position in one of the teams of machine menders: he was an apprentice, he would learn the skills of maintaining and repairing the machinery without which no cotton could be carded or scotched, nor spun or woven into cloth.

I saw him rarely in those days, understandably. Twice during the autumn we met at football matches, for he maintained his interest in the team and his admiration for Will Chatterton. He was fourteen years old, had a group of his own friends and no further need of me to escort him down Hyde. As I have mentioned, the crowds at matches in this second season were more substantial and there was no guarantee we could stand together, but if he did notice me (or more likely, in the first instance, the taller figure of Edward Berry at my side), he would push his way through the throng and make himself known to us. On one occasion the wiry figure of Toffee Mellor appeared in his wake, dark eyes twinkling, his head covered in a woolly hat.

"Hello, Mr Rowbotham," said Danny, tapping me on the shoulder. "You likin' t'match?"

"Hello, Mr Rowbotham," echoed Toffee, mischievous smile in full glow.

It was almost half-time and soon we had the opportunity for a short conversation. Danny reported that his work at the mill was hard but he was learning plenty.

"There's a bit o' bullyin', but I were expectin' that. Seein' 'ow far they can push t' new boy, I suppose. I just ger on wi' t' job, Mr Rowbotham. They'll soon see I can take their jibin'. An' then there's t' women – mitherin' an' snipin' an' makin' all sorts o' improper remarks."

Was the lad exaggerating? He seemed genuinely offended even now but I fancied he would enjoy at least being noticed by the lasses. I couldn't be sure. I had quite forgotten what it was like to be a fourteen-year-old and in my case at that tender age, marooned in a boys' boarding school, any female company beyond my own sister's was unimaginable.

Mellor, now fifteen, had left his work at Slack Mills during the previous summer.

"I were too big for a piecer but they just 'ad me sweepin' an' fetchin' an' carryin'."

"Dogsbody work," said Danny.

"Aye. I got taken on at t' pit. I'm minin' coal now."

"On Manchester Road?"

"Aye. They've got me way cleanin' an' waggonin'."

"So you're underground?"

"Underground? Aye, course I am. It's proper coal minin'."

"Tough work."

"It's tough an' dirty work, Mr Rowbotham, but a sight better paid."

"You dunna mind getting' mucky, do you, Toffee?" said Danny, laughing. "Coal dust dunna show up so much on your face, any road."

"Shut your trap, chalky boy!" came the riposte from the other, as he clipped his pal's ear.

The pair also spoke of the prospects of a junior football team being organised by some of the volunteers at the Hyde club. Berry had told me that there were considerations of matches for a second eleven – a team of reserves. Clarence was involved, apparently, not so much in the role of a player but as a trainer. Even Edward, however, was unaware of a junior team. If such a plan came to fruition, Toffee was more than enthusiastic about a trial. Danny said so too, but I had the impression that he was more hesitant, perhaps less confident in his ability.

I knew the number of amateur teams in the town was multiplying but I had little idea to what extent. Having said that, indications were all around us on Saturday afternoons. Surrounding Hyde F.C.'s pitch were many others: not so flat, no so well marked and not even of uniform size but pitches nonetheless with white goalposts and a scuffed centre spot, played on week in week out by teams of varying standards – by now I could discern that myself. There were teams from pubs and churches, from cotton mills and even separate sheds from within those mills. There were teams representing the dye works, the gasworks, hat works and ironworks, and all manner of civic works at the corporation. There were matches without umpires, without strict adherence to the rules and oftentimes, it seemed to me, with unmatched sides of different numbers of players per team.

What was clear was that of all the emerging leisure activities, more than cricket in the summer and undisputedly much more than rugby, football – association football, to give it its proper name – was easily the most popular. Both as players and as spectators, this was the sport that the young men of Hyde favoured, and in large numbers. Even when Hyde F.C. had a match themselves, Berry told me that somebody from the club would be scouting these peripheral games, hoping to cast eyes on a player who might be a useful addition to our roster.

The subject was one which Berry and I discussed on our way up Back Lane towards Gee Cross. It had become something of a ritual that I was invited into the Berry family home after a match to rest my legs and take refreshment. As a rule I would gladly accept the invitation as the reception at Osborne Road was uniformly warm. The younger members of the family were not always in attendance but Mrs Berry, Mother Mary, was a constant. Indeed I believe that though the words were mouthed by Edward, the invitation came originally from her.

"Mother has a gift for you today, Walter," he told me enigmatically on one such occasion.

"A gift?"

"I apologise. I mustn't raise your expectations. It's a jar of honey."

"It's a jar of honey," Mrs Berry confirmed on our arrival, greeting me in the drawing room with the gift. For some reason she had chosen to wear a pair of pearl earrings and a matching necklace.

"From the lady up at Clough Fold," she elaborated. "You know, the piggery. Where Mr Berry used to get most of his pork. The lady up there keeps bees. Perhaps you might know her, Mr Rowbotham. I believe she supplies one of the groceries up Gee Cross when she has sufficient stocks."

"I certainly know the piggery," I conceded. "I can smell it each time I walk in that direction. As for the lady's honey, I cannot say I have ever bought a jar."

"Well, now you can try it. It has a distinctive floral flavour. Most palatable, I find, on a toasted crumpet."

"That's very kind."

Edward suggested making a pot of coffee and he disappeared into the back of the house. I remember finding the place unusually quiet and could not believe that the young boys at least would not be home on a Saturday evening. Perhaps they were being given their tea in the kitchen by one of the sisters. Here in the drawing room Mrs Berry suddenly rose from her seat and asked me a direct question:

"Mr Rowbotham," she said, offering me a hand, "would you care to come upstairs with me and see my late husband's Lovelock?"

I was quite taken aback and hesitated in my response.

"Don't look so horrified," said the woman. "It's quite harmless if you keep your fingers out of it. Follow me."

And with that she stepped out of the room and I had no choice but to obey her. I found her already halfway up the staircase, heading towards a wide, carpeted landing where an oak chest of drawers regally stood.

"Here we are," said Mrs Berry as I reached the spot. "Not every guest to Osborne Road gets to see this."

She was pointing to the large polished artefact sitting in pride of place atop the chest: on closer inspection it appeared to be a sausage machine.

"Impressive, isn't it?"

"It looks brand new," I suggested. "As if it were never used."

"Quite right, Mr Rowbotham. It's the machine Mr Berry ordered the week before he passed on, bless the man's soul. It arrived on the day of his funeral. We sold all of his other equipment but I wanted to keep this. As a memento."

She was gently touching the rim of the funnel with its milky white enamel interior. The rest of the object was in cast iron: black and highly buffed, and the handle of the turning grinder looked like polished, flat-grained ash. At its base the words *Lovelock of London* were embossed in silver paint.

"None of the boys showed any interest in butchery," she went on. "I know Mr Berry had hopes of our Clarence and then latterly our Charlie but the boy was only ten years old when he lost his father. I think it was too much to expect a ten-year-old to set his heart on being a pork butcher, don't you, Mr Rowbotham?"

"I'm sure you're right," I said, examining the shiny accessories lined up at the side of the great device.

"Charlie was Mr Berry's favourite," she said, playing with the largest of the pearls strung below her throat. "He wouldn't mind me saying so. Our Blanche says it's quite wrong to have a favourite child, or at least to make it so very obvious. Mind you, she's training to be a teacher, as you know, so she's speaking from that perspective, no doubt."

"She's right," I acknowledged. "Schoolteachers should be impartial, although it's quite natural, quite human, I would add, to like some scholars more than others. Discretion is the key, I have found."

"I see you are admiring the attachments," Mrs Berry noted,

lovingly picking up the largest piece. "They screw on to the out-pipe over there. The beauty of the Lovelock is that it is adjustable in so many ways. There's the lever around the back, see. It chops, it shreds, it minces coarse and fine. This appendage is for coarse-grain mince – pie fillings, if you will. The others are for sausages, thick and thin."

I noticed the Liverpudlian traces in her manner of speaking becoming more pronounced as her excitement grew.

"I see."

"It's a tragedy that Mr Berry never got to use it. It's a Mark III, see the little badge. *The best sausage machine you can buy*, he said. It's the least I could do to keep it here, right outside our bedroom door."

"Indeed."

I could smell coffee brewing downstairs and suggested we regain the ground floor.

"Is that a new necktie you're wearing, Mr Rowbotham?" the woman asked once we had resumed our seats in the drawing room. "It's such a fetching colour. Cornflower blue, would you call it? It almost matches your eyes."

For the briefest of moments I tried, in vain, to conjure up my reflection, seen once in the mirror that morning.

"It was a gift from my sister," I said.

The details of my limited family provided material for further conversation over coffee as the light beyond the window faded. When it was time for me to be on my way Mrs Berry scurried off to the scullery and returned with a second jar of honey.

"Take two home with you, Mr Rowbotham," she insisted with a breezy smile.

"Don't worry, I have plenty left. I'm sure you'll agree that it is so very delicious. And you do look like a fellow with a sweet tooth."

At this time two stiff-backed notebooks were to be found in my study, recent additions positioned for ease of access on top of my old piano. Once confirmed as the club secretary, Joseph Maloney had arranged for a delivery boy to leave them for me at the school room along with instructions, or, more accurately, suggestions. The printworks compositor was not pernickety, he insisted, when it came to the presentation of the match records: *We can trust you to come up with a system, Walter.* Nevertheless, as a template, he had dispatched both the first book – Hyde Football Club Season 1885-86 – with all relevant details displayed in his own flowery hand, and also the second, the current record which I would inherit from the end of November 1886. I had no argument with Maloney's record-keeping and indeed the names and figures I wrote in his stead were no more nor less comprehensive but I must say that the design I settled upon was an improvement in respect of clarity. It would be false modesty to say otherwise. I also took the liberty of including, where known, a brief weather report.

Until Christmas the team played a series of matches away from Ewen Fields, meaning that the information regarding players from both sides, the score, the scorers and so on was sent to me on separate sheets of paper and in a variety of script. It was my job to decipher these scribbles and produce a legible account. I dare say there are mistakes in the spellings of the names of some of the footballers that Hyde came up against but I did my best in the circumstances. I have seen handwriting so shoddy I am certain my eight-year-olds could have produced neater work. Home games were easier as the chances were that I would be in attendance and thus able to confer with the opponents' record-keeper if necessary. By and large it was not such an onerous task and as the weeks went by, as the list of completed fixtures lengthened, one elegant page after another steadily became a most satisfying body of work.

Late one afternoon in December, Daniel Harrop appeared at the door of the school room, out of breath and still in his oil-stained working clothes. The last of the embers were glimmering in the brazier as I came through to answer the knock. There he was, standing in the dark street, under what was the first flurry of a snow shower.

"Danny! Come inside," I insisted. "What brings you up to Chapel Street?"

"They're 'avin' a trial at t' weekend, Mr Rowbotham," said the lad, gasping out his words. His face and hands betrayed the greasy residue of a day's labour.

"A football trial?"

"Aye, for t' juniors. Hyde juniors. There's a lad in t' weavin' shed knew all about it. Anyone can come, well, anyone younger than sixteen, I think he said."

"Come in properly, Danny. Sit yourself by what's left of the fire. It's raw outside."

I closed the door firmly and joined him in the centre of the shadowy classroom.

"So, you'll be going, will you?"

"I reckon I might. See 'ow I get on."

I noticed that he had chipped one of his front teeth; no doubt the result of an accident at work. Set in his grubby face, I thought how it made him look older, somehow less of a child.

"Well, I hope it goes well for you." I said.

"I were wonderin'," he continued after a moment, "well, I were 'opin', Mr Rowbotham, well, I were wonderin' if you might, if you might want to come an' watch?"

"Me? Really?"

"If you've nowt else to do."

I stood up, opened the grate and poked a glow into the dying coals.

"I've got plenty to do here, Danny, what with Christmas coming. But I'm not saying that to make excuses. You know what I think, honestly?"

"Honestly? What?"

I looked him directly in the eyes. I wanted him to see my sincerity.

"I think that if I'm on the sidelines you'll have one eye on me instead of concentrating on your game. Better off that the only folk watching you are the trainers, don't you think?"

I gave him a moment.

"Suppose."

"You can come back here afterwards and tell me it went ever so well and they invited you to be captain!"

"I dunna reckon that's gonna 'appen," he said. "Not if Toffee Mellor turns up."

He shifted on his little seat and I sensed his disappointment slowly melt away in the face of my reasoning. We sat for a moment staring at the orange nuggets flickering in the ash.

"I hear your father's a bit better," I said presently.

"Aye, he is. He's on 'is feet more. Still coughs like a dried up old boiler. He were on about goin' down to t' mill an' seein' if they might have owt for 'im."

"Not in the carding room, surely?"

"No, not there. He thought 'appen they might 'ave summat for 'im in t' stores."

"That would be good news. Well, if he's strong enough. Can he walk far? It's a steep pull back up to the Gerrards from the bottom."

"He's gettin' stronger, I reckon. He walked up to t' pub last night. He might leave it a week. That's what me mother said, any road."

"Stay there, Danny," I said, getting to my feet.

I walked into the study, leaving him sitting quietly in the gloom, in the familiar classroom where he had sat as a scholar until six months ago.

A minute later I reappeared with a jar of Clough Fold honey.

"Is your mother still putting honey in his tea?" I asked.

"When we have any, she is," he replied, straining his eyes to see what I held in my hand.

"Here," I said, offering him the jar. "Give her this. With my compliments. I hope it does your father some good."

# Chapter 3

Derby County F.C., formed in 1884 as an offshoot of the county cricket club, had a fast-improving team and tasted success in the F.A. Cup in only their second season, beating the well-established Birmingham club Aston Villa on their way to the third round. For a prestigious game to mark New Year's Day in 1887, Derby County were invited to be guests on Ewen Fields, home of Hyde F.C. More than a publicity stunt, which most interested parties would admit was the reason behind the match against Blackburn Rovers four months earlier, Derby were chosen in part to gauge how much progress the Hydonians were making in what some would consider their first full season.

It was a splendid occasion which I remember vividly.

Over one thousand spectators jostled for space on the touchlines and although the club officials tried to encourage payment, I am quite sure that most folk enjoyed the spectacle for free. Played on a frosty Saturday afternoon under a clear blue sky, the match finished with the visitors winning by five goals to two. As with Blackburn before them, the players and staff from Derby were complimentary about Hyde's team and congratulated the club on its development in such a short period. I recall speaking with the County recorder at the conclusion of the game and listening to his enthusiasm for our centre forward Will Chatterton, who had excelled. Of course he was a player some of the Derby contingent knew well as he still had a contract with the county cricket team.

The results in January and February were uneven. It was appreciated that our team were confronting opponents of a higher calibre than a year earlier but there was disappointment amongst some on the committee that Hyde were unable to sustain a run of victories. I restricted myself to home matches and as a consequence I was absent from defeats which took place in Denton, Gorton and against a Manchester Association XI. The games on Ewen Fields were more fruitful and the fair-sized crowds were sustained. To take advantage of local interest there were rumours that the pitch rented exclusively by Hyde F.C. was to be fenced, so that access for spectators could be managed at certain lockable points of entry.

I remember such hearsay being confirmed at an impromptu gathering directly after a 5-1 victory over Stretford F.C. towards the end of January. Once I had said my farewells to the visitors' match recorder I would invariably head off home, more often than not accompanied by Edward Berry. On this occasion I discovered Edward and his brother Clarence in conversation with Joseph Maloney. The club secretary, in buoyant humour after so resounding a win, invited the three of us to join him at the Bankfield for celebratory drinks.

Drinks, celebratory or otherwise, implied alcohol. Although the non-conformist ministry is associated in most people's consciousness with temperance in this regard, I must mention that its target as a social scourge has long been the consumption of alcohol in its purer and more virulent forms, notably gin, rum and other spirits: those whose addictive nature can become ruinous once a weak soul is entrapped. More diluted varieties, namely beer or cider, are far less frowned upon. Even in some religious circles a well-brewed ale, produced from fresh stream water and hops and barley of good quality, is considered nutritious, refreshing, and harmless at worst. The health benefits are not overtly advertised but neither are they much disputed. As for me, I am not especially partial to beer and the notion of drinking in excess appals me, but I can appreciate its quality as an accessory to lively and friendly intercourse and I am not a man given to condemning others for such a minor foible.

I was gratified to have been invited and together we walked down the slope towards the hotel where numerous young fellows had already assembled. Maloney told us that the owner of the playing fields was demanding an increase in the rent, and charging spectators a small sum to gain access to the pitch side was a way of offsetting costs. He insisted it was unavoidable. For the comfort of the supporters there were plans to lay cinders and sawdust to stand on to prevent the ground becoming a quagmire after heavy rain.

Encouraged by the contents of a bottle of whisky which was circulating amongst a few of the gentlemen present, the diminutive Maloney became ever more loquacious. I have no reason to believe that anything he told us was confidential but I sensed that he relished the thrill of disclosing restricted information. The committee had decided several weeks ago, he said, that the team was competent but in need of strengthening. He asked us rhetorically if we hadn't noticed the poor decisions certain players were making, how this one was incapable of running hard for more than half a match, how that one was hesitant in a physical challenge. He confided that three or four new players would be joining the club before too long.

"Stronger lads," he told us, emptying his whisky glass and sucking the dregs from the bottom of his moustache. "There's a pair we've spotted from round here, and a couple from further afield – lads we've had good reports of. I've got to sort out work for them in Hyde before they sign on, of course. We can't be paying them to be sitting on their backsides when they're not kicking footballs for us."

"Any names?" asked Clarence.

"As long as you keep them under your hat, Master Berry," answered Maloney, tapping the side of his ruddy nose. "The lad Morledge'll be staying, we hope. The lad in goal today. We reckon T.H. has had his day, harsh as it may be."

There were raised eyebrows. I was under the impression that Drinkwater had been missing for reasons of injury.

"The others, well, they're just names. They'll mean nowt to you until you see 'em. Wilson, Bowers – a big Derbyshire lad – and, we're hoping, a fella who's been playing in Shropshire or Stafford, somewhere down south – name of Pressdee. We'll have to see if they'll agree to our terms, of course, and, when it boils down to it, if they want to live in Hyde."

"Can't imagine anyone not," said Edward. "Can you, Walter?"


Daniel Harrop was overjoyed to have been selected to play in the first match of Hyde F.C.'s junior team, a side chosen from the best of the boys (all aged fifteen years or younger) who had attended the recent trials. So excited was he that he called in at the schoolhouse on his way home from the final practice; the team was to play the following Sunday morning, kick-off at eleven o'clock on Ewen Fields – *one o' t' bottom pitches, Mr Rowbotham, not where t' seniors play!* – against Godley Boys.

"You'll come an' watch, won't you?" he begged, eagerly expecting an affirmative and yet quite forgetting the fact that

114

my Sunday mornings were invariably consumed by chapel and Sunday school.

"It's impossible, Danny," I said. "You know exactly where I'll have to be on Sunday morning."

"Here," he said, crestfallen.

"Here indeed."

A short silence fell as he hoped that somehow I would be able to change my mind.

"But remember what we agreed the last time, Danny," I resumed. "The time you had the trials. And on Sunday you'll be wanting to give everything to the match, won't you? To your own performance. You'll be needing to focus on that and nothing else. Certainly not on looking out for an old schoolmaster standing on the touchline."

"Suppose."

"There's no suppose about it, lad. I'd be a distraction and no mistake. You go and have a wonderful game and you can come back and tell me all about it afterwards."

The Sunday of the match was a day of overcast skies but with little threat of rain. The Reverend Dowson seemed somewhat distracted and the morning service was over earlier than usual. Back in the school room I found a depleted class of scholars (so many children had coughs and colds, it appeared) and I decided to curtail the lesson without scruple. The time was just after eleven and my mind was already made up. I would walk down to the fields and as discreetly as possible would arrive at the junior match in time for the second half.

That I missed the kick-off was quite deliberate, but the number of spectators (parents in the main and a few trainers and volunteers) was small and my appearance on the halfway line was impossible to disguise.

I recognised the Hyde boys as the team in the royal blue shirts provided by the Hibbert family. Godley were less well equipped: a majority wore white jerseys borrowed, I later discovered, from the men's team from Highbank Mill and a few of the lads looked lost in apparel several sizes too large, habitually worn perhaps by an older brother or father. Three or four made do with plain white cotton vests, already smudged with grass stains and dirt.

Danny, who was playing as a right full back and, as it happened, close to my side of the pitch, spotted me immediately and gave me a shy wave. I nodded cursorily and glanced away, following the ball. I noticed that Clarence Berry was one of the trainers. I heard his voice, his encouraging words, his instructions carrying across from the opposite side of the field. Later on I recognised the man standing by his side with an even louder voice as Tom Harry Drinkwater.

The Hyde team were winning, already three goals to the good at the interval. The game was rather different from the senior confrontations I was accustomed to. In some ways, being less brutal, it was a more pleasing spectacle.

This in spite of the larger proportion of the boys skidding about in working boots; few wore proper football boots and those that did looked to have borrowed battered old pairs two or three sizes too big, tied up with long laces wrapped around the soles. There were plenty of mistakes from both sets of players, not to mention a general reluctance to head the ball, but I discerned, at least from the Hyde team, attempts to pass the ball between them, to produce patterns of play and progress up the field in that manner rather than in marauding knots of hard running and brute force, which categorised much of the senior team's approach.

Danny seemed to have little to do, so ineffective were Godley's forwards. A quick-footed winger burst through near the end of the match but Harrop was in position to make a strong tackle and the advance was halted.

"That's it, son!" cried Drinkwater.

"Well done, Danny, lad!" I shouted, unable to stop myself.

I noticed him smiling but his eyes were firmly on the game. He was smiling to nobody in particular or perhaps it was a private little smile just for himself.

It was interesting to watch Toffee Mellor. He was by no means the most influential player – that would be a burly centre forward who looked older than fifteen and who had scored all of Hyde's goals – but the young pit-worker had an array of skills which kept opponents kicking out at thin air. He loved to dribble the football but I could see, and indeed hear, Drinkwater's frustration as he would eventually be ambushed by a pair of chasing defenders. Mellor needed schooling in team play but if the trainers could harness his ability he would be an important component in the future. With only moments to go before the end of the match, he found himself close to the goal with the ball rebounding in his direction. Without hesitation he controlled the ball and kicked it hard past the Godley goalkeeper for his goal: the lad's day was made.

Hyde won by six goals to nil and as the players took pleasure in their moment of victory I decided it was time for me to sidle away. It was important for Danny, tousle-haired, red-cheeked and as muddy as the rest of them, to share the satisfaction of the result with his new friends.

# Chapter 4

Of Bowers and Wilson, the two new players who arrived at the club in March, it was the former who made the greater impression on me and, in some respects, I on him. Both players began their careers with Hyde F.C. in a five-nil win against a Manchester Select. Chatterton had a field day and scored four goals but Bowers' own performance was not to be overshadowed. He was a sturdy, fair-haired fellow with thighs like steel but, if he was able, he preferred to eschew the physical approach for a more cerebral manner of play. I noticed how he readily surveyed the whole pitch and with a mighty swing of his right leg he could send the ball great distances left and right into spaces which the opponents were ill-prepared to cover.

Harry Bowers was a young man from Derbyshire, an apprentice engineer by trade whose confidence on the field of play belied a more reticent character off it, at least in his early days as a Hydonian. A large part of his hesitancy had its roots, I believe, in a poor education and a crippling unease with reading.

I was introduced to the man before the Manchester match as the club's record-keeper: *Rowbotham, the fellow with the ink pen and ledger,* if I remember Frank Hibbert's words correctly. At the end of the game Bowers approached me again, smiling as I made reference to the swelling on his cheekbone – the result of a collision with an opponent's elbow which would certainly become discoloured overnight.

"It's all part o' t' game," he laughed. "At least we won."

He gently pulled me away from the knot of people I was

standing close to and began to speak quietly. He wondered if I could help him. He explained that he had been presented with two contracts to sign: one for the football club and another for employment at Goodfellow's Works (Mechanicals) on Mottram Road. He was reluctant to bother Mr Maloney, knew no lawyer and hoped that I, as a literate man associated with the club yet somewhat independent (he had made such a judgement in the intervening ninety minutes while dominating a football match!) would do him the favour of reading over the documents and offering advice. I saw no reason to refuse.

"Come down an' 'ave your tea wi' me one night this week," he said. "I'm lodgin' at t' Moulders on John Shepley Street. Mrs Calland does a tasty beef an' carrot pie, so 'er 'usband says."

I agreed that it sounded like a fine idea.

"Then, Mr Rowbotham, I can let you read what they're askin' me to sign."

The Callands had been managing the Moulders Arms for many years and had a regular drinking clientele composed in the main of employees at the sprawling Goodfellow's Works across the road. There was one upper room available for rent and it was this space that Maloney had secured for Bowers. On the evening of our meeting the public bar was smoky and noisy with men released from their toils. I caught Calland's eye and asked if he would summon Bowers from upstairs. I bought a glass of cordial and stood waiting, listening to the conversations that filled the steamy air around me.

Bowers joined me promptly and we found a space on a bench where we could talk. Presently the room quietened as a good half of the drinkers departed in dribs and drabs.

Mrs Calland served us a bowl of broth and a plate of meat stew with boiled potatoes, and my companion persuaded me to try a glass of ale to accompany it. Our conversation was convivial. He was from Chesterfield, he told me, born in Dove Holes in the Derbyshire Peaks, which I knew. He was eager to learn more about Hyde and questioned me on my own contribution to the town. All the while a shaggy-coated cocker spaniel, russet in colour and relaxed in demeanour, lay by the glowing hearth, its thoughtful eyes locked on the pair of us. From time to time it was briefly distracted, as was I, by a self-assured tabby cat that prowled silently through the shadows like a marauding tiger cub.

When it came to the contracts Bowers wished me to peruse we concluded that the light was too poor and the pages too numerous for me to complete the task comfortably there and then after all. I offered to take the documents home with me and return on the morrow.

"Let me walk with you part way," he suggested as I finally stood to take my leave. "I've been takin' Calland's dog out for a late walk these past couple o' nights."

The spaniel was already on his feet, sniffing at Bowers' legs in anticipation.

"You ready for a stroll round t 'streets, Whisky, then?" said the footballer, lovingly rubbing the dog's head. The cat meanwhile was nowhere to be seen.

I found it dispiriting that the fellow had not had the confidence to try to make sense of the detail in the contracts. Although I encountered an amount of unnecessary legal obfuscation, in the main the contents were predictable and quite undemanding of a competent reader. The only concern I had on Bowers' account featured in the Goodfellow's contract which rather than stating the maximum number of hours he should work per week (generally twenty-five according to Maloney) stipulated instead a *proportion* of a full-time fitter's obligation, in this case fifty per cent. I alerted Bowers to the possibility in the future of a mandatory increase in working hours which could affect him adversely without recourse. I suggested that he speak to the management at Goodfellow's and have his maximum clarified.

Twenty-four hours later and for the second consecutive evening we were seated at a table in the dimly lit taproom of the Moulders each with a glass of ale at our elbow. Bowers had insisted that he paid for this and the next one, so grateful was he for my solicitude on his behalf. In the event I should have been equally willing to stand the round, for half an hour earlier I had found myself in need of assistance of a quite different kind.

By the time I had completed my perusal of the contracts, scribbled a note or two, eaten a quick meal and prepared the classroom for the morrow, it was seven o'clock and under a starless sky darkness had long since fallen over the town. The March air was cold and still, and I met barely a soul on my path from Gee Cross village. As I was passing St Thomas' Church, only five minutes from my destination, I heard footsteps on the cobbles behind me and, sensing them approaching, I turned around. Before I knew it I was being accosted by two young ruffians; pushing me from the left then the right, they demanded I pass over to them whatever money I was carrying on my person. I had barely a shilling or two to give them but instinctively I resisted their unseemly threats and tried to dart away in escape. They had me again in no time, one fellow striking me hard across the cheek while the other snatched the leather satchel which contained Bowers' documents. Still they had not finished with me. Once again money was demanded and, quivering with fright and with the taste of blood on my lip, I was resigned to unbuttoning my coat to find something to placate them. Just at that moment I heard the insistent barking of a dog, then the rapid patter of the animal racing up Lumn Street. I saw the alarm in my assailants' faces and, before they could make a decision, the dark shape of the cocker spaniel was flying at them, snapping at their ankles and followed in no time by the brawny figure of Harry Bowers, who with harsh words and forceful clouts saw them off. By the time he had dusted down my coat for me and picked up my bag from the gutter the two miscreants had disappeared like squealing rats down a shadowy ginnel. A few yards away Whisky stood panting, her tail quivering, ears pricked, staring wide-eyed into the darkness, assuring herself that the threat had passed.

One evening a week or two later, I decided to wander down past the cricket field towards Knott Fold. When the conditions were opportune I liked to watch the sunset from that place, with its prospect of the last rays of sunlight glinting off the roof tiles of the streets of Hyde and further to the west, the wide span of a dusty crimson sky darkening over the distant smokestacks and the familiar shapes of Manchester. That evening I added a pleasant mile to my walk and steadily climbed back into the village along the wooded tracks by way of Cheethamsfold and past the old mill house in Gerrardswood. At last I was approaching the schoolhouse when I noticed a short figure emerging from the chapel yard. It was late, I considered, for visitors to family graves. The hour was well past seven o'clock and the daylight had faded. Looking past the human shape towards the Chapel I saw a lighted window in one of the side rooms.

As our paths inevitably crossed I realised the person was a woman, her head covered by a dark scarf. An instant later I recognised Martha Harrop. Caught in the gaslight of the nearest street lamp her lined face looked ghostly, her expression distraught. She glanced up and, seeing me, was the first of us to speak.

"Oh, it's you, Mr Rowbotham."

Her voice was subdued but she had more to say:

"I'm glad I bumped into you."

"How are you, Mrs Harrop?" I asked, filled with apprehension.

"I've been to see t' Rev'rend Ashton," she went on, ignoring my question. "He were very kind. He knows what's to be done."

"What's to be done? What's to be done about what, Mrs Harrop?"

"About t' funeral. It'll be a small affair."

There was no necessity for me to ask whose funeral she had been discussing in the side room. I placed a comforting hand on her arm and let her talk.

"John died this mornin', Mr Rowbotham. He died in 'is sleep."

"I'm so very sorry."

"He'd been workin', you see. He were determined to get back to it. They'd given 'im mornin's in t' stores. Just tidyin' up, shiftin' things about."

She stopped, as if she were in a play and had forgotten her lines. Then she suddenly resumed her narrative.

"I told 'im to stay away from liftin'. *You dunna start liftin' no 'eavy loads*, I told 'im. *I won't, Martha*, he promised me. *I'll not be doin' owt daft.*"

Again she paused, looked me in the eye and took up my trailing hand in both of hers, raising it to her chest. I could feel her heartbeat, I could see the glistening in her eyes.

"I believe he kept 'is word, Mr Rowbotham," she said. "It were that 'ill that killed 'im. Them that found 'im said he'd collapsed 'alfway up Apethorn Lane. By t' barns. Some lasses found 'im gaspin' for breath. They reckoned he'd breathed 'is last there an' then."

"But they brought him up to the Hollow?"

She heard my question but took a moment to utter a reply.

"They put 'im on a passin' cart. One o' t' lasses, a farm girl, I think she said, stayed with 'im. Fetched 'im up to our doorstep. He were still livin' but barely. Between us we got 'im inside an' a neighbour sent for a doctor. Nob'dy came till this mornin'. He coughed an' coughed all night long, he did, poor man, weaker an' weaker. Coughed up blood at first, brown blood, dark an' thick as slutch, then thin like rusty water. I 'ad a cloth for 'im to retch into. Then he were croakin' up spittle, gluey an' grey. Then he were done. He'd coughed up t' life out of 'im."

Her voice had trailed to a whisper. I released my hands and wrapped my arms around her poor, shivering frame.

"It's a relief, Mr Rowbotham," she said. "That's what t' Rev'rend Ashton said, an' he's right. My John's 'ad no life these past three year."

"Remember God is with you, Martha," I whispered. "You'll not be alone."

The woman was breathing hard, fighting for her words, but I felt a strength within her.

"I'm glad I bumped into you," she said once more, a faint, stoical smile forming on her lips.

"It's better you know from me. I know our Danny would feel he 'ad to come an' tell you 'imself. He's fourteen but he's just a little boy at 'eart. It's upset 'im an' no mistake. Nob'dy slept last night, Mr Rowbotham. He watched 'is father pass away. Poor lad, he'd not want to be lettin' you see 'im cry. You know that, I'm sure you do. That's t' last thing he'd want."

# Chapter 5

It was a matter of agreement amongst the majority of their supporters that the impetus of Hyde's new players came too late in the season to be judged an unqualified success. Hibbert talked of a *period of adjustment*, Hall was encouraged by the promise of a more cultured method of play. Berry bemoaned the paucity of fixtures in March which meant that activity wound down just as momentum was building up.

Nevertheless, in late April at the club's annual general meeting which I attended, the consensus was that Hyde F.C. had indeed made considerable strides in eighteen months. The team had markedly improved, there had been some success in early rounds of local cup competitions and in the series of regular matches, both at home and away, notable victories against more established clubs had been achieved. Frank Hibbert, revelling in his new position of club chairman, highlighted recent wins against Gorton and the narrow loss at the hands of Derby County Wanderers, a select XI who had been invited to Ewen Fields for an Easter fixture. The occasional defeats through the season, the Blackburn Rovers match notwithstanding, had all been narrow and hard-fought. No team had enjoyed an easy ride against Hyde. *No-one has even come close to embarrassing us*, he maintained. We were a match for anyone. There was not a gentleman in the room who could dissent from the statistics, least of all myself, the provider of a consummate written record of the season for the benefit of one and all.

If Hibbert's aim had been to bring a note of optimism to the proceedings, he did that and more besides. As in his turn did the pipe-smoking Fred Perrin, duly elected as the club treasurer. In spite of spending large sums on ground rent and the fencing of the pitch, on guest opponents, on new contracts for players and on other sundry expenditure (*accounts available for scrutiny for all those interested*), he declared that the club had made a healthy annual profit of fifty pounds. This figure, he stated, had comfortably allowed the committee to agree to the laying of wooden boards around the perimeter of the pitch for the convenience of spectators at the beginning of the following season.

It was left to Joseph Maloney to offer a word of gratitude to local boy Will Chatterton for all his endeavours on behalf of the club since its beginnings. The player had earned a move to Derby County, a sports club where he could combine his talents in scoring both goals in the winter and runs in the summer. The much-admired player spoke briefly in response and was given a loud ovation.

If that was a sad moment, Maloney was quickly able to restore some cheer to the room. More new players would be sought, he announced: indeed, the club was close to adding two more signings which he expected would be finalised during the summer. Secondly he reiterated the plans to face a higher standard of opponent in the coming season; he was already working on an enlarged list of fixtures. The first of these, he said, to herald our new season, would in all likelihood be another home match against one of the prestigious Lancashire clubs. He gave a glance over to Perrin who nodded theatrically as if to confirm that, yes, there were funds in the bank to secure such an undertaking.

Finally, and with grudging reference to our more illustrious neighbours from Ashton-under-Lyne, Maloney was excited to inform us that following in the footsteps of Hurst F.C., and in the hope of emulating that club's success in the competition in three recent seasons, the committee, on behalf of Hyde Football Club, would aim to raise our profile to a national level by applying to take part in the 1887-88 F.A. Cup.

It was a few weeks later, when my thoughts had turned away from football, that I received a letter from the District Committee of the Unitarian Church. This was not such an odd occurrence in itself as this body, my direct employer, was in contact with me by mail from time to time. The longer I was established at Hyde Chapel, however, it seemed that I was bothered less and less frequently. My work was assessed every two or three years by a Church inspector – these assessments being less rigorous with each inspection – and any routine concerns were cordially addressed by the Reverend Dowson. In brief, I had been happy in my work at the Chapel school from the very start and had no indication in all that time that my employers were in any way less than satisfied.

I recall opening the envelope during the children's playtime. I had made myself a cup of tea which had gone cold by the time I remembered to drink it. For the letter, an ominous, single folded page, consumed me for many minutes once I had digested its contents. It was a most strange feeling for there was nothing in those words which deliberately aimed to unsettle me; any threat therein was purely in my imagination.

The secretary of the District Committee expressed the hope that the school year, now approaching its conclusion, had been a productive one so far. Social niceties aside, he went on to advise me, in a sentence of sheer functionality, that I was invited to attend a meeting with members of the Education Committee at the Church's headquarters in Cross Street, Manchester, at 11am on Saturday 21st May. My presence was expected without equivocation. The import of the secretary's words was unquestionable, his signature utterly illegible.

In the days before the appointment my mind was filled with musings, mainly of a dispiriting character. Occasionally I had been to Cross Street for a conference or a meeting of some kind in which I was a minor player. I had not been summoned in this way since I was appointed to the post at Hyde Chapel seventeen years earlier. I approached the Reverend Dowson for his perspective on the matter but he was adamant he knew nothing and assured me there was no cause for concern. I did wonder about the value of his reassurance if, as he said, he had no information on which to base it.

The day arrived swiftly and my misgivings remained. I dressed as smartly as I was able and left Gee Cross in plenty of time to catch an early passenger train from Hyde into the city. I had not been instructed to bring any documents to support my work and for want of knowing what pieces of evidence might bolster me most effectively, I resolved to take with me nothing at all. With my satchel left behind in my study and without a thing to carry I felt oddly uncomfortable. I purchased a newspaper for the journey, both for entertainment and companionship. As entertainment I found it rather lacking and so spent half of the time blankly staring out of the compartment window as the drab buildings slid past or else lost in my own thoughts, rehearsing my lines.

Redeploying me would achieve nothing, I would argue.

Surely I was too old to have the energy to establish myself successfully in a new environment? I was content in my work and that in itself was a key to a fruitful outcome both for me and for my school. I had chosen a metaphor but was unsure if I had the courage to employ it. It is easier to uproot a sapling, I was of a mind to say, as it takes so little effort, so little inconvenience, to release the vigorous, youthful roots from the soil. Once a tree is established, however, then its removal is twenty times the effort. And not only are the roots likely to be damaged in the lifting, the earth itself is disturbed more deeply, more widely and may never recover its vitality. A tree, in such balance, in such harmony with the local soil may never establish itself elsewhere for want of the suitability (I had considered *the embrace*) of a new anchorage.

In the event I said none of this. What I did say implicated me even more embarrassingly if only for the reason that it was *not* rehearsed; it came from some deep, instinctive source I imagine I had been subconsciously burying.

I was directed to a sparse, draughty room on the first floor where I was introduced to three members of the Education Committee, all gentlemen of a certain age, all bloodless in countenance, all dressed with little regard for colour.

I recognised none of them and my eyes were drawn to the enormous, unvarnished wooden cross hung precariously on the wall high above their heads. They sat opposite me along one side of a long table, empty but for a sheaf of papers lying directly in front of the bearded central figure. In a friendly tone he firstly introduced himself as the Chairman, Mr Primmer, followed by the others and yet was the only one of the trio to speak to me for the entirety of the interview. The man to his right, the only one wearing a clerical collar, smiled at me slightly more often than the man to his left: here was a fellow with wire-rimmed spectacles and a constant sniffle who looked mildly bored throughout.

"We see that it was in 1870," Mr Primmer was saying, looking down at the top sheet of paper in front of him, "that you were appointed to the position at Hyde Chapel."

His words earned a slight echo in the stark, high-ceilinged space.

"That is correct," I said, unnecessarily.

"It has been a satisfying experience, would you say, Mr Rowbotham?"

"It has been, sir, and continues to be."

"All our records do indicate positivity, both pastorally and scholastically."

He paused to stroke his beard and engage me with his rheumy eyes.

"So, Mr Rowbotham, we congratulate you and we thank you."

Had I imagined a note of finality in his voice?

"And so we come to the next chapter," he continued. "*Your* next chapter."

"I hope you have no plans to move me, sir?" I interrupted. "To remove me from Gee Cross?"

I paused, waiting for a reaction, but his look invited elaboration.

"With respect, Mr Primmer, I would say that I am most reluctant to leave the village, or even Hyde more generally."

He raised a hand from the table to suggest I stop.

"Mr Rowbotham," he said, "our proposal to you is more nuanced."

"I am engaged to be married," I stated quite suddenly, rather loudly and without warning to anyone present, not least to myself. The sniffly man took off his glasses and blinked at me.

"Engaged to a local lady, a Gee Cross lady," I bumbled on. "My fiancée is an only child, sir. She is extremely close to her parents. It would break her heart to have to move away from them. Theirs too, it most certainly would. Her mother is a mainstay of the Chapel, a lay reader, a great support to the ministry. The Reverend Dowson will vouch for her, and for her daughter, I have no doubt."

I noticed that Mr Primmer's frown had become a smile. The other gentlemen adjusted themselves on their seats and coughed simultaneously.

"Mr Rowbotham," said the Chairman, "firstly I must confirm that there are no plans to remove you from Hyde Chapel. No plans at all."

I must have breathed a sigh of relief as his smile grew a little wider.

"And secondly, well, I suppose I must congratulate you on your engagement. It's lovely news to have for one so late in life."

I nodded and tried to imagine where on earth the origins of my lie had sprung from.

"We have been looking at the reports from the Reverend Dowson," he went on, "not to mention those of our inspectorate. The popularity of the school is on the increase, as you are obviously well aware, being at the heart of it all. I dare say you sigh rather each time another child is squeezed into your little classroom."

Another nod.

"The school is in need of expansion, Mr Rowbotham, and we are in a position to instigate one. An expansion without any more delay."

Mr Primmer shuffled his papers and found the relevant page.

"The school body will be divided. Divided into two parts. We will call them the Infants, the children between five and eight, perhaps nine years old and then the Juniors, the others, the ten to thirteen-year-olds."

"Then you'll need two teachers, sir," I interjected. "And ideally two rooms."

"Of course. Two teachers, two classrooms. We will provide both, have no fear. The Reverend Dowson has an outline of our plan and he will ask you to help add the detail according to your recommendations."

"*My* recommendations?"

"Well, of course, Mr Rowbotham," he said, rubbing his hands together. "If we cannot trust the man *in situ* to have something useful to say, then whom can we trust?"

"I am much obliged, sir."

"Acknowledged."

With an indication from the man at his right he pulled out another sheet of paper from the pile. They mumbled a few inaudible words and then Mr Primmer looked up at me once again.

"There is something else, Mr Rowbotham."

"Something else?"

"If you are willing to accept it. We believe that if you assume responsibility for the Juniors you will find yourself with the smaller of the groupings. It will mean a little less teaching for you, I assume. A narrower curriculum, and so on. Am I right?"

"Yes, I suppose it would amount to that."

"Then perhaps you would entertain our invitation."

He covered his mouth to cough lightly and retrained his eyes on mine.

"One of our school inspectors is retiring and we are looking to replace him. We need a man of experience, of insight, of integrity. A communicator, a mentor to new schoolteachers. We can think of no person more appropriate than you, Mr Rowbotham."

I was taken aback. It took me a moment to respond:

"That is very kind of you."

"And the division is most suitable," said Mr Primmer, lifting the page in his hand. "You would be responsible for schools in the division of North-east Cheshire. They are listed here. The travelling would not be so onerous. We believe somebody like yourself would be able to combine the task with their own teaching perfectly comfortably."

I realised that the three committee members were all staring at me in anticipation.

"So, Mr Rowbotham. Do you need some time to consider it all? You may feel we have ambushed you with not one but two changes to your *status quo*. We do apologise for that. Please, take a moment. I do not believe that any one of us in the room is in a rush this morning. Shall I send out for some tea and biscuits?"

Henry Dowson apologised for having kept me in the dark. It was not in his gift, he insisted, to reveal the plans of the Education Committee. On the other hand, nobody was more generous in their congratulations on my promotion. I had not considered it as such, concerned more with doubts over my ability to do two jobs instead of one, but, on reflection, a promotion was exactly what it was and the Reverend, as with most things, was right to say so.

As Mr Primmer had suggested, I was consulted to a degree on the changes to the fabric of the school, and Frederick Ashton and I worked closely for the remaining weeks of term on our preparations. The appointment of a schoolmaster for the Infant class was beyond my responsibilities; Mr Dowson assured me that the selection process was already in train and all efforts would be made to find me a most suitable colleague.

Work on the schoolhouse was to begin on the first day of the summer holidays. My study would be transformed into a classroom for the Juniors. My ground-floor living space was to become a new study area for both teachers to share. On the upper floor my bedroom was to remain fundamentally unaltered and new living quarters were to be built in what was previously a little-used storage space under the rafters. As a result the new occupant would be a first-floor dweller: living upstairs and working below. I say *new occupant* because it quickly became evident that I would no longer be expected to live at school. This was to be quite a shift for me, so used was I to having my life encompassed in one convenient arena. At first I was loath to accept the idea of a move elsewhere but after consideration I came to realise that a new separate abode would give me more independence and thus the impetus to extend my experiences. My interest in the football club had already broadened my horizons in so many ways and yet I sensed that leaving the schoolhouse could be the start of an even more fulfilling chapter in my life.

Through the Chapel's contacts with the property-owning Ashton family (much of the western end of the village was theirs, not to mention Apethorn Mill), I was allowed to rent an empty cottage in Jollybant Row, towards the bottom end of Gerrard's Street and a mere five minutes' walk from the school. The moment I set eyes on it, I knew it would suit me perfectly. It offered a good deal more space than I was used to, had a proper scullery and a coal shed and privy in a flagged yard at the back where I might take an armchair and sit out in the sun on a summer's afternoon. Best of all, the window in the back bedroom offered a view of the shallow vale of knotted woodland and beyond it the rough, grassy slopes of the high hills.

As it was likely that the summer months of resettlement would find me occupied with one chore or other, Mr Dowson promised he would refrain from burdening me with the task of keeping the scorecard for the Chapel cricket team.

"I'll have a word with our Mr Ives," he told me. "He's a little out of practice, but recording an innings on a scoresheet isn't something a man ever forgets how to do, is it now?"

# Chapter 6

Apart from the short reign of William IV during the hazy years of my early childhood, only one other monarch has occupied the throne of the United Kingdom during my lifetime. On 20th June 1837 Queen Victoria acceded as an eighteen-year-old and she has remained our sovereign ever since. How our country has changed for the better in those fifty or so years.

In celebration of her Golden Jubilee a banquet was held at Buckingham Palace to which were invited fifty kings and queens, princes and princesses, dukes and duchesses, counts, countesses and maharajas. The following day she took part in a procession in an open-topped landau from the palace to Westminster Abbey, escorted by the Indian Colonial Cavalry and cheered the length of the route by thousands of jubilant well-wishers. All across the land parties were arranged, services of thanksgiving took place and even the humblest of her subjects raised a glass to Her Majesty's good health.

Victoria's supporters in Hyde were no exception. The twentieth was a Monday and declared a national holiday. The previous week school time was dominated by a celebratory flavour to the lessons to such an extent that even the youngest, most inattentive child could remember who Prince Albert was and all were able to point without a second's hesitation to India on a map of the world. The Chapel services of Sunday the nineteenth were devoted almost exclusively to the Queen. We prayed for her, we listened to a sermon about her, we sang hymns for her. Certain members of the fellowship stepped forward to read letters to her (self-penned but never sent) singing her praises. A lady even chose to recite lines of fawning verse (someone less charitable than myself might have called it *doggerel*) composed in her honour. There was a moment in the midst of all of the jubilation when I was forced to ask myself whether we were dealing with a human being or a deity.

On the Monday there was no hammering of anvils, every shuttle designed to rattle back and forth across a weaving loom was motionless and not a single nib of an office clerk's pen was dipped in ink. Classroom doors across the land were locked. Union flags were flown from prominent buildings. Folk had time to meet their friends, families took leisurely picnics in the shady woods or the sunlit meadows, and the alehouses of Hyde sold more beer in a day than they would normally sell in a fortnight.

Meanwhile the Reverend Dowson invited a favoured selection of friends and acquaintances to the parsonage for an afternoon garden party. I was gratified to be included on the guest list. It was a fairly intimate gathering of no more than forty at an estimation, and yet as I arrived the combination of chatter and laughter, the chinking of glassware and the tinkle of cutlery had risen to a considerable volume. Mr Dowson was sporting a sand-coloured sunhat, a relic, he informed me, from his days as a student in Heidelberg. He was rearranging furniture on the lawn and I gave him a helping hand.

I spotted Thomas Ashton, the former mayor, the Reverend Frederick Ashton and various other ladies and gentlemen whose faces I vaguely recognised. A pair of younger fellows stood smoking cigarettes at the top of the path which led to the tennis court. A few of the guests were prominent members of our church, including Maria and Jesse Thornley, dressed in their Sunday best, whom I found in conversation with the widow of a processing manager at Apethorn Mill; recently bereaved, she was nevertheless in good spirits, buoyed no doubt by the jollity of the occasion.

The garden was decorated with bunting, a piano had been trundled outside on to the paved patio, available to anyone who felt inclined to play, and the air, heavy with the scent of early season blooms, rang with merriment and good cheer. A long trestle table, bedecked in startlingly white linen, was laden with plates and dishes of food, and our glasses were filled at intervals by none other than Henry Dowson himself. He offered ginger ale or fruit cordial but made an exception for a special toast to Her Majesty by serving a fizzy Rhineland Sekt to those who had no objection to a modicum of alcohol.

"It is preferable to champagne, I'm sure you'll agree," he announced, topping up the glass of Thomas Ashton, a fellow Teutonophile. "And perfectly appropriate for the occasion, bearing in mind our sovereign's German heritage!"

I noticed Mrs Dowson sitting in the shade, sipping from a glass of lemonade and resting her feet on a cushion. I enquired as to how she was and if she were managing to play much tennis this year. She sighed, smiled wearily and whispered that she would rather be playing that very afternoon than having to play hostess to so many guests. *No disrespect to Her Majesty, you understand, Walter.* The woman often looked worn out, I thought, either at chapel or in her own home. She had produced eight children, from Miss Margaret to the seven-year-old Oscar, and, the contribution of nursemaids and domestics notwithstanding, I could only imagine the weight of responsibility on her shoulders. The younger children and their friends were having their picnic on a blanket in the shade of the fruit trees, fussily supervised by a pair of younger women, one of whom I recognised as Louisa Thornley.

I spoke briefly to her parents. From beneath a flamboyant, wide-brimmed hat Mrs Thornley dominated the conversation with talk of how much her dear mother had always admired the Queen and what a splendid job the gardener had done at the parsonage since the spring storms.

"I take it you have visited before, Mr Rowbotham?"

"I have, Mrs Thornley. On numerous occasions, in fact."

"I am a regular visitor," she stated. "Myself and Mrs Dowson have so much in common, you see. And it's always a privilege to have the ear of the Reverend. Have you tried the salmon? You really must, before it disappears."

The woman knew of my impending move out of the schoolhouse.

"Of course, it will be quite an adjustment for you, Mr Rowbotham," she was keen to inform me. "You'll have a little more space, I should hope. Well, thank Heavens for that. I cannot imagine how you could have lived for so long in those tiny accommodations afforded by the school. I understand some other poor soul is moving in to help you with the scholars in September. Is that really necessary? Have you met the fellow, by the way? What is he like? Young and handsome?"

I had to disappoint her with the paucity of my information. I turned to her husband and asked about the current state of the ironmongery business. The poor man answered in the briefest of sentences. For some reason he had chosen to wear a worsted suit and a high collar and was sweating uncomfortably in the intense sunlight.

By and by I was introduced to the other guests. I had a pleasant conversation with a physician who mentioned that he had been engaged by the football club in Hyde in a consultancy capacity.

"I have developed a variety of drills to improve physical endurance," he said, selecting the largest slice of fruitcake from the display. "I believe I have seen your face before, Mr Rowbotham. Do you attend matches from time to time?"

I assured him that I did.

On the far side of the lawn Louisa and her friend had gathered the youngest of the children in a circle. They were told to sit close together on the grass and a game of Pass the Parcel was about to begin. The Dowson children's German governess, Frau Loewe, sat herself down at the piano and played the melody of *Twinkle Twinkle Litte Star*, stopping at random intervals so that which of the ever more excitable children happened to be holding the bulky parcel had time to tear off a layer of its wrapping. Once or twice a boiled sweet in a paper twist would fall out as a little bonus. Several interruptions later the pianist progressed to a broken version of *Alouette*, and as the squeals and shouts of the children grew louder, more adults were drawn to watch the game's conclusion, struck, as was I, by their offsprings' wide-eyed impatience for the prize. In the end a Fry's chocolate bar was raised into the air by a delighted little boy as he tore away the last flimsy layer of paper to general applause.

For much of the afternoon I chatted amiably with Frederick Ashton. I had always found him easy to talk to. We found a pair of chairs in the shade and for a while the Chapel cricket team was a topic between us. Devoted as he was to the Chapel choir, he went on to describe his musical plans for the rest of the year and, not for the first time, vainly attempted to persuade me to join. We discussed the building work at the schoolhouse, the specifics of the amended curriculum and the expectations of the new teacher. In short, it was the sort of rambling dialogue we could have had at the chapel gate on any day of the week.

Without warning one of the young women took herself to the piano and started to play: it was a waltz by Strauss, as I remember. I wandered into the shade cast by the house to listen. Presently I realised that I was standing by the French windows which led into Mr Dowson's study. Instinctively I tried the door handle but found it to be firmly locked. No matter. I peered through the glass into the dark room whose walls I knew to be lined with bookshelves. I had always considered the collection of reading material a little dry. The Reverend was largely a reader of academic works: historical, philosophical, educational and, of course, religious.

"Has something in there caught your eye, Mr Rowbotham?"

A woman's voice made me spin around in surprise.

"Oh, Miss Louisa."

"I've brought you a glass of ginger ale," she said, smiling.

"That's most kind. Thank you."

Carefully I took the glass from her hand. It was a tall flute, filled to the brim.

"Mother said I should help with the service."

"But you've been busy enough all afternoon, as far as I could see. Helping with the children and such."

"I suppose so. Actually I'd rather do that anyway. Rather that than make conversation with most of the adults here."

"Really?"

"Not you, Mr Rowbotham," she giggled. "You are exceptional."

"I'm pleased you think so."

A few bars of the waltz, disappointingly played without the required vitality, filled a moment while we seemed to gather our thoughts. I took a sip of the drink. Louisa's hair was drawn tight and tied in a white ribbon. She wore a dress of pale lilac which accentuated her narrow waist. The lace in her sleeves matched the adornment of a parasol which she held in one hand. With her other she attempted to push open the French windows.

"They're locked," I said redundantly.

"A pity."

"Are you curious to see Mr Dowson's collection?"

"I was looking for a little indoor shade. And I've heard Nellie playing this piece before. She never gets any better!"

Her bright blue eyes blazed mischievously.

"Mr Dowson has mainly academic material," I said at length. "As you might imagine."

"Then I dare say I would be bored within five minutes."

"What do you like to read, Louisa?"

She paused to consider an appropriate reply to satisfy a schoolmaster.

"Stories," she said. "I like stories. And a little poetry too."

"Mr Wordsworth, perhaps?"

"Oh yes, I like Mr Wordsworth very much."

"And novelists? Mr Dickens?"

"Dickens? I once read *David Copperfield*. I believe it was a children's edition. It was very amusing, I remember. No others, however."

"You ought to read more. I may have some you could borrow."

"Really?"

"Well, of course. Or perhaps something dramatic by Mr Hardy. Do you know Hardy? He has some splendid female characters. Tales of country folk. A little *melodramatic*, some might say. I don't expect you'd find anything by Mr Hardy in the Reverend's library!"

She laughed and looked past me through the glass into the recesses of the room.

The music had stopped. Suddenly her mother's shrill voice broke through the subdued applause.

"Louisa! There you are!"

Maria Thornley purposefully approached the pair of us. I took a gulp of the ginger ale.

"Gather up your belongings, darling," she said. "It's time to go. Your father says he is feeling a little poorly. Come and say thank you and your goodbyes. Come along."

"Goodbye, sir," said Louisa, facing me. "I did enjoy our little talk."

Then she obediently drifted away from my side.

"And goodbye to you, Mr Rowbotham," said the mother. "I do hope you are very happy in your new home."

Rather abruptly she turned and walked away. I noticed that her husband had already gloomily made his way to the gate. I remember feeling nothing but sympathy for the fellow.

I first set eyes on Benjamin Lloyd sometime during the last week of July. When he introduced himself I recognised the name: Mr Dowson had mentioned it several weeks earlier when reporting that the man tasked with the job of imparting the ABC to our school's youngest learners had been chosen. He showed me a copy of the fellow's letter of application, his certifications and his references.

"Lloyd, Benjamin Tertius. Unmarried, like yourself. Have a read, Walter."

All seemed in order and I said at the time that I should look forward to meeting him and subsequently working alongside him.

"You'll have seniority, Walter. That goes without saying," the Reverend had said. "He's a youngish gentleman, as you'll have noted. He will defer to you. And I should expect he will learn from you. That'll not be a problem, will it now?"

I had walked up from Jollybant Row one morning to collect some books from school. At this stage I was not entirely ensconced in my new dwelling, reckoning that I had the whole of August to empty the schoolhouse of my personal belongings in dribs and drabs. Having no word of warning about my new colleague's arrival plans, I had not expected to meet anyone else in the building.

Before I saw the man's face I heard evidence of his presence in the form of music, for as I entered the classroom I caught sight of the back of a figure seated on a stool fingering the strings of a large harp with some dexterity. He was playing a melody which I knew as the *Old Hundredth,* one that was familiar to our congregation as the hymn *All People That on Earth Do Dwell.* I halted my approach to allow him to finish his piece undisturbed. The instrument was very fine, its swooping triangular shape fashioned from highly polished, smoky brown wood, perhaps walnut. Finally he stopped, solemnly pulled his hands away from the strings and then, on sensing my presence, swivelled around on the stool to face me. I apologised for startling him.

"Oh, hello," he said, standing up. "I'm Benjamin Lloyd."

He was a tall man with a long face punctuated by a thick black moustache, a boyish fringe of straight hair and narrow, dark brown eyes.

"Welcome to Gee Cross," I said, offering him a hand to shake. "I had no idea exactly when you'd be arriving. My name is Walter Rowbotham. Delighted to meet you."

"Ah, Mr Rowbotham. My fellow schoolmaster, I believe. The Reverend Dowson has had plenty to say to me about you, sir. I'm pleased to meet you indeed."

I detected an accent to his diction that was foreign to our corner of northern England. It was a surprise at the time as I remembered that his application for the position had been sent from an address in Stockport, just five miles distant.

"I've never heard a fellow from Stockport speak in the way you do, Mr Lloyd."

"You must call me Benjamin, please," he said. "You are right to notice that I am not locally born. In fact I am not even an Englishman. I was born and grew up in Wales. You have heard of Wrexham?"

"I have heard of it. I have never set foot in the place."

"And Gwersyllt?"

"I beg your pardon?"

"Gwersyllt?"

For the briefest of moments I thought he was choking.

"Gwersyllt," he said once again. "That's my village. Well, it was until we moved to England."

"I see."

"I was ten years old. That's long enough to make a Welsh accent permanent, it turns out."

"Did your family move directly to Stockport?"

"Yes, we did. My father is a Methodist pastor. He fell out with the Welsh ministry. We've lived in Stockport for twenty years. I've been teaching in schools in the south side of Manchester since I qualified. Mill schools and chapel schools like this one."

A Welsh heritage aside, it struck me that he had followed a similar path to my own, even down to having a father in the ministry.

"You play very nicely," I said, pointing to the harp.

"It's my passion," he replied.

"You'll have noticed the piano over there. I have my own, an old one in the other room."

"The one here is the better of the two?"

"Infinitely. The school bought it not so long ago."

"Then you should move it into your classroom. It rolls along on wheels, doesn't it?"

"Well, yes, it does. Are you sure?"

"Please. Take it. I rarely play the piano. Everything I need to play, I can play on the harp. It's just as versatile as any piano. From hymns to shanties and all manner of instrumentals."

I was expecting a smile of pride but in truth he had already given me the impression of being a serious fellow who was not prone to joviality for its own sake. I decided to change the subject.

"Has Mr Dowson invited you to play this coming Sunday?"

"Play? On Sunday?"

"Yes. I'd be surprised if he hasn't asked."

"The harp? You mean in chapel?"

"No!" I laughed. "I'm sorry, I meant cricket. On Sunday afternoon. You do play cricket, don't you? I imagine it was at the top of his list of criteria when selecting you for the position here."

"Cricket?"

"Do they even play cricket in Wales?" I asked, wondering at the same time if irony was an accepted form of humour in that country.

"We play everything in Wales, Mr Rowbotham," he stated. "Everything. And to a very high standard, I might add."

# Chapter 7

Nobody needs to have two pianos. Not even a professional pianist needs to have two pianos.

Once the space formerly used as my study had been transfigured into a prospective classroom for the Juniors, there was sufficient room to be found for the larger school piano. My old tinkly one, bought second-hand from a curiosity shop on Manchester's Deansgate, was carried out into a back corridor to await its fate. Of course I knew there was only one possible destination for it and that was against the partition wall in the parlour of my cottage in Jollybant Row.

Transporting a piano, however, was not such a simple process. Benjamin Lloyd volunteered to help but the schoolteacher was still dividing his time between Stockport and Gee Cross and was vague about his availability. Realising the task would require a third party, not to mention a cart of some kind, I was obliged to make arrangements to engage an additional pair of hands. Happily I needed to look no further than across Knott Lane. Mr Ives, the Chapel groundsman and formerly my instructor in the science of cricket scoring, was an amenable sort of fellow, I had always found, and once I approached him with the offer of a small removal job – yes, of course I was willing to pay him for his time and trouble – he patted me on my shoulder and offered me his near-toothless smile.

"Just say t' day, Walter," he said, "'an' I'll sort out me schedule to suit you."

Even more conveniently, and as I was hoping he would,

149

he offered the use of his cart. It had sturdy handles and was comfortably long enough, being the one used not only to carry heaps of horse muck to the rose garden but also to ferry coffins from the Chapel altar out to the graveyard.

"It's gor a rickety wheel, but it'll get your piano down t' street, no bother," he assured me.

After consultation with Lloyd I picked an early evening in August for the endeavour and prayed that the rain would hold off.

Less than fifty yards from my front door and set back somewhat from the road stood a wide-fronted house. It attracted visitors, or rather customers, wishing to buy goods ranging from pork chops and packets of tea to balls of string and pints of beer. It was a most curious establishment, the home and business premises of the Emery family, incorporating a butchery, a grocery and an alehouse. I was told that in the middle years of the century it had even housed a rudimentary village school. These days its most prominent business was done in its taproom, for in spite of the competition in the village, the place attracted a good proportion of the local drinkers. It had even given itself a name – the Cheshire Cheese – no doubt a reflection of the variety of its wares. By my estimation (I have never set foot on the premises, not even to purchase a quarter pound of cheese), the drinking room must surely be of limited dimensions. For that reason, on a summer's evening the landlord provided a pair of wooden tables and an arrangement of benches and stools at the front of the building where his thirsty customers could spread themselves more comfortably in the warm air.

The rumbling approach of Ives' cart, laden with the roped-up piano and cautiously manoeuvred down the slope by myself, a panting Benjamin Lloyd and the aforementioned gravedigger, inevitably attracted the attention of the dozen or so men gathered to sup ale in the slanting evening sunlight.

"If you three want to be thievin' a pianoforte, you should be doin' it after dark!" cried one man, standing up and waving his tankard at us.

We reached the assembly and halted our course as the laughter petered out.

"It's the schoolmaster from the Chapel," said someone to his pal.

"Mr Rowbotham," said another. It was Quigley, the Irish shoe mender.

"How do, Mr Ives," said another, addressing our wagoner. "You stoppin' off for a pint, then?"

"That looks like thirsty work," said a rotund fellow in a straw hat.

"Goin' far, are you?" asked his neighbour, an older man, grey-whiskered and with a sun-weathered scalp.

"Happen they've got a concert goin' on down in th'ollow," suggested a youth leaning against a window ledge.

"That's not a bad idea," said Lloyd to me.

"What's that?" I asked, one eye on the piano, still wobbling in spite of Ives' efforts with the knotted cord.

"Stopping for a drink."

"The house is yonder," I insisted. "Just past the stables. You can see it from here. Two minutes more. Let's get the thing inside and come back for a drink after."

"Give us a tune, mister!" shouted the youth.

I ignored the remark and looked over to Ives for support.

151

"Give us a nice old tune we can sing to," said the man in the hat, "an' we'll stand all three o' you a glass o' beer."

"Come on, Mr Rowbotham," said Quigley. "We could do with a bit o' music, so we could, after the day some of us have had!"

There were cheers of encouragement from almost every man present.

"I need to get this cart back, Walter," interjected Ives. "I can't be 'angin' round 'ere suppin' ale."

"Tell you what," suggested the young man, who had wandered over to the cart. "We'll untie t' thing, ger it down for you, an' Mr Ives can take 'is cart 'ome. Then we'll 'ave a song, shall we? Is that alright, Mr Rowbuckle? Summat to cheer us all up a bit. An' dunna fret, there's enough of us 'ere to get a little piano up an' over your threshold, no bother. Did I 'ear you say it's one o' them cottages on Jollybant?"

At the time I wanted simply to get the job over and done with, without a song for an audience of drinkers, without recompense tapped from the barrels of the Cheshire Cheese. Upon reflection, however, I was gladdened that I had been persuaded to perform: not only did I create a good impression of myself on folk who largely were to become my neighbours of sorts, but also, to my surprise, I enjoyed the sociability of this impromptu occasion.

Four sturdy drinkers effortlessly set the piano between the tables, the old man drew up a stool for my use while the round-bellied fellow reappeared carrying glasses brimming with ale for Ives, Lloyd and myself. The clouds had long since drifted away to the east, the sun was setting and Gerrard's Street was bathed in a pale orange glow, falling in strips on the ground between the lengthening shadows of the houses.

Once they heard me tuning up the old instrument, passers-by paused to listen and more curious folk from within the hostelry appeared on the roadside. I took a sip or two of ale and just as I was composing myself I became aware that the attention of certain members of my audience had been diverted.

"Cripes! What's that I'm seein'?" shouted one of the drinkers, looking at the half-empty glass in his hand as if for an explanation.

"You've not seen a bicycle before?" asked his companion.

"A bicycle? Is that whar it is? Wi' wheels that size?"

I looked across to see a colourfully-dressed man in a flat cap carefully directing a shiny black bicycle into a narrow space by the tables. I recognised Robert Howarth, the greengrocer's son, the cricketer, and bringing the machine to an unsteady halt he recognised me. He offered the slightest of nods in acknowledgement.

His contraption was one of the new Safety bicycles I had seen advertised in the newspapers. Unlike the old boneshakers, it had two wheels of equal diameter and, set between them, the pedals propelled the rear of the two by means of an ingenious mechanism driven by a slim chain.

"That's a fine toy, so it is," shouted Quigley with a grin for his friends.

"It's more than a toy," laughed Howarth. "I can travel for miles around on this. You lot havin' a party, are you?"

"Mr Rowbotham's givin' us a recital," said the grey-whiskered man, making himself comfortable on a bench.

"Well, much as I'd like to join you," the cyclist said, "I'm not stoppin'. I'm plannin' to ride down to Bredbury an' back before it goes dark. Enjoy your music!"

We all watched as he mounted his saddle and, pushing off the ground with his left foot, pedalled away from us down the street towards the Stockport turnpike.

"That fella's done well for 'imself," said the old man.

"Aye, with a leg up from 'is father," said somebody else.

"Them bicycles'll cost a few shillin'" added another.

"What I dunna understand," said the large man, scratching his chin, "is 'ow he manages to stay upright on two wheels an' not end up in t' gutter on 'is arse."

"It's the laws of dynamics," I offered, having overheard the fellow's query. I knew a little about physics and could not help myself.

"Gyroscopic dynamics, to be accurate," I added.

A look of bewilderment descended on several of the faces of those waiting for me to play a tune. My explanation, admittedly lacking elaboration, was as nothing. I might as well have been speaking to them in Ancient Greek. Which, on reflection, was exactly what I had been doing.

"That's enough o' your teachin', schoolmaster," shouted one impatient fellow. "Give us a tune, like you promised!"

I chose to play an easy melody by Beethoven, *Für Elise*, which was tolerated respectfully by my audience. Lloyd, standing by my side, encouraged applause as the final note died away.

"What about summat we can sing to?" called out a drinker.

Suggestions came thick and fast but most were unknown titles to me. At that moment I caught sight of a slender young woman leaving the building with a cloth bag full of provisions. It was Louisa Thornley, shielding her eyes from the last low rays of sunlight. She was wearing a dress of pale violet and her shoulders were covered by a cardigan of purest white. Surrounded by the dusty menfolk she looked like an orchid blooming in a field of chaff. She smiled as she recognised me and raised her free hand in a little wave.

We decided on *The Poor Cotton Weaver*, whose first verse I played without voices. I noticed Louisa had perched on the end of a bench and was settled there to watch my performance. The choir of drinkers found their voices one by one and as soon as I brought the song to its conclusion they insisted we repeat the whole piece from beginning to end.

Ives had finished his drink and was ready to take his leave. Lloyd offered to help him steer the cart back up to the Chapel. I thanked them both and with Louisa still present and now engaged in conversation with a woman I took to be Mrs Emery, the landlady-cum-grocer, I had no compunction in playing on.

I rehearsed the opening bars of *John Brown's Body* and set about the verse to a ripple of applause; it was the rustic sort of music my old plinky-plonk piano was best suited for. The chorus of *Glory, Glory, Hallelujah!* was most heartily rendered by a growing number of singers and once again an encore was demanded. Next somebody suggested *The Wild Rover*. It was a song I grew up with and one I ought to have proposed myself. I had not played the melody for some years and yet, from some deep recess of my memory, my fingers knew exactly which notes to play and with the young mill worker taking a verse solo, we charmed the entire congregation. I have to concede that he provided a surprisingly melodious vocal.

My confidence growing, I improvised a little while more drinks were served. To the tune of an old sea shanty I had learned as a student one of the fellows stood up from his stool, found himself a wide flat flagstone and set about dancing – tapping and clacking his hobnailed clogs on the ground in time with the rhythm, raising sparks and shouts of delight from his admirers.

Folk were patting me on the back after each performance and another glass of ale appeared on the piano top. I heard my name being shouted from more passers-by across the street. A wagon driver and his mate halted their horse in the road, stopped their jabbering and listened to the music in delight. At one point I picked out Daniel Harrop and his mother standing transfixed in the twilight. I cannot remember when Louisa Thornley disappeared but by the time I began playing the opening bars of *Onward Christian Soldiers* her seat was filled by an old man and Mrs Emery had gone back inside.

I did not recognise a single one of my raucous supporters from the regular Sunday congregation at the Chapel and my choice of a modern hymn as a finale was a risk but it seemed that even if the words were unfamiliar at the outset, the chorus was an easy one to pick up. In addition, the tune lent itself to alternative lyrics and at one point some wag at the tables turned it into a song about our football team. The single word *Onward* had been adopted as the motto of Hyde (the town, not the football club), and as we sang and then sang again the final chorus I thought that, with or without the Christian Soldiers, this town, with progress at its heart and branded on its new coat of arms, was where I felt most at home in all the world.

The cheering and clapping finally ceased. I had provided almost an hour of entertainment and indeed had been thoroughly entertained myself. For the drinkers, and for some of those who had appeared later to swell the ranks, the evening was just beginning but the men were as good as their word. Under the supervision of the old boy with the grey whiskers who was by this time starting to slur his speech, three of the strongest picked up the piano, carefully transported it those fifty yards to my new address and lifted it over the threshold as if it were a sack of cotton lint.

The upper-story window at the front of my home offered a prospect of the terrace of cottages edging the opposite side of Gerrard's Street. Beyond them, to my left, as the contours of the land fell away, I could see deep, dark-leaved thickets of trees and from their tangled midst, on cooler evenings, fingers of blue coal smoke rising into the sky from the partly hidden chimneys of the old dwellings in the Hollow.

It did not take long for word of my new address to reach the ears of Daniel Harrop. One evening after his shift at the mill he knocked on my front door and in an altogether adult manner asked me how I was settling in and was there anything I needed. His offer made me smile. I invited him inside and we shared a bottle of sarsaparilla. The light was already fading yet I noticed the shadow over his upper lip and saw that what I had in previous days taken to be a smear of engine grease was in fact a faint line of downy growth.

It was just him and his mother at home now but together they had quickly grown used to living without an invalid.

"Truth be told, Mr Rowbotham," said the boy, scratching his head through the mop of hair, unbrushed as ever, "me mam's got more time to 'erself now. I try to be at 'ome so she's not so lonely. We're managin' alright."

I was reluctant to mention the tenuous situation regarding their renting of the cottage, strictly tied as it was to employment at Apethorn Mill. I assumed that Danny's job would give no such guarantees as, moustache or no moustache, legally he remained a child. The last thing they needed was an eviction order.

"Mother's lost 'er job at Quigley's, you know," he suddenly said and my heart dropped. "He told 'er he were sorry to let 'er go but it were a family thing. An Irish thing. He's taken on some distant cousin from over in Haughton Vale. She needed work, he said. He'd no choice. She's already lodgin' with 'im up t' road."

"I'm sorry to hear that. Your mother liked working in the cobbler's place, didn't she?"

"It were a job," he said, pausing to finish his drink. "Any road, Mr Rowbotham, dunna look so glum. She's done better for 'erself. Better than bein' a shoe mender's errand girl."

He grinned and I caught sight of that broken tooth.

"Better?"

"They found summat for 'er at t' mill. Mr Roscow's known 'er a while now. You know, since me father 'ad 'is sickness."

"Who's Mr Roscow?"

"He's an office manager. Dunno which one – one of 'em. He wears a suit an' everythin'."

"And he offered your mother a job?"

"Aye. He knows she can read an' write well enough. He's got 'er in an accounts office. Accounts? Is that right?"

"Dealing with payments and wages?"

"Aye, summat like that?"

"Full-time?"

"No, it's only afternoons. For now, any road."

"But you say you're managing?"

"Well, I've got me wages too, Mr Rowbotham. We'll not starve."

When he left I came to a decision with little hesitation.

The following afternoon I made my way down into the Hollow and startled Martha Harrop by knocking on her door when she was in the scullery in the middle of peeling potatoes. Inside the cottage hung a faint smell of boiled cabbage and although all the windows were fastened shut, the place felt as cold as morning dew. I was not intent on staying for long but the woman insisted I sat at the table while she stood listening to what I had come to say. Making mention of my new responsibilities as a class teacher *and* a school inspector and the time and energy they would demand of me in the coming months, I offered her the opportunity to assist me with my domestic arrangements. Pulling a loose strand of hair away from her face and wiping both sides of a wet hand on her calico apron, she shook mine to confirm the agreement. For a generous sum Mrs Harrop gratefully accepted my offer to visit Jollybant Row on two occasions per week: once on a Monday to clean the cottage upstairs and down, and once on a Friday to occupy herself with the delights of my laundry.


The weather during August of that year was disappointingly inconsistent. Along with afternoons of scorching sunshine there were heavy skies, days of drizzle and even chilly evenings which brought to mind the football season. The old season already seemed an age ago and I had not seen my friend Edward Berry for some weeks. I knew his whole family was taking a summer holiday together in a hotel on the Lancashire coast. The new season was still one month away. Joseph Maloney's plans to invite a prestigious team to Ewen Fields revolved, so I remembered him telling me, around a date in the middle of September.

I recognised the sense of anticipation I felt before the start of every school year. Now it was creeping up on me with a double impulse. The prospect of the new football season, beginning at the same time of the year, was producing the very same effect: the eagerness to make a start, the hopes, the doubts, not knowing whether expectations would be joyfully realised or simply turn to dust.

I knew that some of the older children in my class would be sharing these feelings. The exploits of Hyde F.C. were widely known and talked about in the village. Some of the scholars' fathers walked down to watch the matches. Some even took their sons along with them.

My record of the 1886-87 season was complete. Maloney had borrowed it, copied some notes and then returned it to me for safe keeping and as a reference for the next year's fixtures. Sometimes on a quiet evening I would take it down from the bookshelf and revisit all those recent matches in my mind. I reread the dates, the opponents, the players' names, the results. It seemed that the allure of this game had captivated me like a magician's spell. From being immune to its appeal not so very long ago, I was now in danger of being enthralled by it. The results mattered to me in a way I could not have begun to understand a year ago: a win for Hyde and I walked with a spring in my step for the rest of the weekend, while a defeat felt like a personal setback.

Casting the partisan element to one side, there was so much to admire about this simple game. There was a nobility to the physical challenge. I had marvelled at the players' bravery and speed and all manner of athleticism. There was an intelligence to the tactician's cunning and in those whose decisions were made a fraction of a second ahead of the rest. There was a grace in the moments created by the most skilful of players – those dancing ball-spinners, those whose feet possessed the deft touch of an artist. Not to mention the agility of those most courageous of individuals, the goalkeepers, diving this way and that across a bone-hard pitch, regularly launching themselves into a hacking crowd of boots. They brought to mind a heroic fellow I once saw in the streets of Manchester's Ancoats district, a delivery lad who, with little regard for his own safety, dived in front of a trotting horse to grab hold of a distracted infant who had wandered blindly into its path.

Above all I have witnessed a mutual respect amongst the players and officials, indeed the manners of gentlemen, even after the roughest of roughhouses, once the final whistle was blown. Footballers know that without an opponent there is no game. And without the umpires there is no order to the game.

Each of the Hyde players I had come to know was a personality in his own right. Observing these characters develop and interact fascinated me, the dynamic of the chosen eleven subtly different from match to match but sewn together with a common thread of comradeship which I found quite inspiring.

At the end of the season I had given Clarence Berry a contribution of a few coppers for an old football that the club had no further use for and I hid it in a cupboard in the classroom. One fine afternoon back in June, once the lessons were concluded and with an hour to fill, I decided against imposing yet another hymn practice on the children. Instead I produced the shapeless pudding of leather and, to howls of excitement, inflated it to an approximation of the correct pressure and suggested we adjourn to the cricket field down the lane and have a little match with it amongst ourselves.

"Keep off the square!" I remember Frederick Ashton shouting from the chapel yard gate as he watched us head off down the slope.

So popular was that sporting interlude that I repeated it twice more before the end of term as a treat for good behaviour. Several of the boys loved to talk to me about the game. I encouraged the conversations and, in an attempt to introduce a more spiritual element, I once asked the question: *if Jesus had been a footballer, which position on the field would he have taken?* It did not take long for a lively discussion to ensue:

"We call 'im Our Saviour, so he'd be t' goalkeeper. Just as he saves our souls he'd save th' opponents' shots on our goal."

"No, he'd be t' centre half, at th'eart of t' team, like we find 'im in our own 'earts. He gives us direction, like Harry Bowers does on a Sat'day."

"He'd not be a footballer at all, Mr Rowbotham. He'd be an umpire. We follow 'is rules, he sets us right when we trespass."

"No, that's not right! Jesus *forgives* us our trespasses. An umpire punishes us with a free kick to th'other team."

"You're all wrong! Jesus is the timekeeper, the referee. He tells us when our time's up."

"You mean when we die?"

"Aye, that. Jesus tells us when our time is done. Don't he? Or is that God, Mr Rowbotham?"

# Book the Fourth
# Season 1887-88
# As Far as Preston

# Chapter 1

In the second week of August I received a short letter from Joseph Maloney, secretary of Hyde Football Club, inviting me to attend a training session for the players on Ewen Fields on Saturday the twentieth. I would have the opportunity, he wrote, to renew old acquaintances, meet the new players and discuss the club's ambitions for the coming season. He also intended to pass on a pristine notebook for me to use in the coming months to record the details of what was to unfold on the pitch.

It was gratifying to be included in the preparations even to a limited extent and the sense of excitement springing from his handwritten words made my heart beat a little faster. The season was approaching and advertisements had been appearing in the town in recent days, posted on noticeboards, in shop windows and in the local newspaper, announcing that Hyde's first match was to be played on 10th September and the esteemed visitors were to be Bolton Wanderers.

One of the very first things that Maloney told me when I met him was that the club had spent twenty-five pounds to secure the appearance of the Wanderers, a team that had an F.A. Cup pedigree and great ambitions of their own. The Lancashire club was established ten years earlier than ours and had already gained a most progressive reputation; they were determined to challenge the formidable pair of Blackburn Rovers and Preston North End, less than twenty miles up country. I was interested to discover that in the club's first four years they had played their matches on three different grounds and the original Christ Church Bolton F.C. had thus adopted the nickname *the Wanderers*.

The practice session was notable as a contrast to the one I had witnessed almost two years earlier. Some faces were the same (the Hall brothers still took an active role, for example, and it was T.H. Drinkwater who directed dedicated training activities with the goalkeepers) but the drills were more structured, more seriously followed and, I dare say, altogether more professional. There were clear objectives to the physical conditioning, I sensed, and individual skills such as running with the ball, shooting, passing and tackling were practised with a proper sense of purpose. I would have much to report to Edward Berry when next I saw him.

During a short interval most of the players trotted over to the side of the pitch where we were standing.

"I can't be doin' wi' all these calistatics, Wally," muttered Robbo Robinson between gasps.

"Calisthenics," I replied, offering an uninvited correction.

"Aye, them an' all," said the inside forward, searching for a bottle of water.

It was good to see Harry Bowers again. Like all the rest, he was breathing heavily and dripping with sweat, for we were still in the summer and the afternoon air was humid. In between long draughts from a water bottle he told me he had enjoyed a productive break. He had spent a week in Derbyshire and seen his parents. He had done some training out there on the fields alone or with his friend Arthur Hopkinson from Chesterfield who had joined him at our club earlier in the month.

"He's over yonder," he said, wiping his brow with his shirt sleeve. "Skinny lad talkin' to Joe Hall. There's not much of 'im but he's quick as a whippet. A useful winger, is Arthur. I 'ope he makes t' team. I'll introduce you later, Wally. Oh, an' I tell you what else – I've been doin' a bit o' gardenin' for Mr 'Ibbert over at Brookbank. Lovely spot. He knew I were int'rested in plants an' that an' he offered me a few 'ours extra work tidyin' up."

Before the training resumed I was cursorily introduced to two more new players. Firstly to James Pressdee, the inside forward Maloney had mentioned back in the winter: he had agreed to sign on providing the club could find him work in a large grocery as that was his trade. He wore his hair cropped and his eyes sparkled with vivacity. He was not a large fellow but his leg muscles were impressive and I had already noticed his uncommon acceleration and powerful shots at goal. He told me he was very satisfied with his colleagues and the situation the club had secured for him as an assistant to Mr Smethurst in his emporium on Reynolds Street. He had lodgings on Cheapside which was convenient for both the football fields and the Moulders Arms.

Secondly I exchanged a few words with a chirpy young man named Charles Bunyan, a goalkeeper brought in from Chesterfield Town. As we watched him returning to the group, physically imposing and bubbling with confidence, I scarcely believed Maloney when he told me that the lad was only eighteen years old.


It was time to admit to myself that I was infatuated by Louisa Thornley. The moment that she appeared so close to me by the Dowsons' French windows, offering me a champagne glass overflowing with ginger ale, I knew that it was unquestionably she who was the mysterious fiancée that I had even described so preposterously to Mr Primmer and his Education Committee in their high-ceilinged upper storey conference room.

I had shocked myself at the time. Matters of the heart have been like a foreign currency for most of my life: I was aware of their existence but had no practical experience of them. I have always considered myself to be a measured man, someone for whom extravagant emotions were to be, if not avoided, then at least reined in, and especially if women were involved. Whatever it was I felt for Miss Thornley, before my desperate attempt to thwart the Committee's wicked ambition to redeploy me – and then just as suddenly afterwards – those feelings were buried. They were part of my subconscious, I believed, surfacing for that one moment of panic, only to slip back rapidly into the dark recesses of near oblivion. The identity of my illusory fiancée, however, was in truth never so much of a mystery: I had even described her mother, for goodness' sake.

I rationalised that my life had changed in the past year even if my character fundamentally had not. My studious, introverted nature had not disappeared – it was part of me forever – but I had allowed myself to draw open the curtains a little, more willing was I to challenge myself with new experiences and new people. My involvement in the football team was not entirely the reason but this unearthing of a hitherto undiscovered enthusiasm was at least part of what I might call my psychological development. I was starting to believe that I was what a botanist might describe as a late bloomer.

Moreover, now I was obliged to leave the confines of the schoolhouse for a home on the village street with passers-by and neighbours who were neither teachers nor clerics – neighbours who might knock on my door to borrow an egg or crave a meandering conversation over the wall that divided our yards, or even invite me to stand with them in the Cheshire Cheese and take a glass of ale. My cottage itself called out with an opportunity and I heard its call: it was warm and homely with space not just for a single, middle-aged bachelor, but for two, indeed (did I dare say it?) for a man and his wife.

I told myself there was no good reason to keep my emotions submerged, to chain my impulses to the dungeon floor; I wanted to feel at liberty even to act out of character, no matter how fraught with confusion that might be.

Louisa was as beautiful a young woman as I had ever set eyes on. Her own shone blue like the midsummer sky, each of her smiles melted my heart a little more and her slender waist mesmerised me. I felt no embarrassment in admitting that I dreamed about passing my hands around her and drawing her closer. She was perfect. She would make me the perfect wife. In those days after the garden party I felt as I imagined a young man might feel having fallen in love for the first time.

*You are exceptional.*

Her words, so sweetly spoken, echoed in my memory.

*You are exceptional.*

And so was she. Her pretty fingers had caressed the glass just as one day she would, I hoped, caress my cheek. Slowly I was beginning to understand the power of emotions and the desire to make sense of the inexplicable, of the irrational act. For it was nothing short of irrational for me to leave the party with that very glass concealed in my pocket, to fetch it surreptitiously to my parlour and place it –nay, parade it – unwashed, on the mantelshelf by my father's old mahogany clock. If that was not out of character then I didn't know what was.

I had read enough novels and followed the fortunes of enough courtships to know that the pathway to love was neither smooth nor straight. Was I talking already of love? Really, what did I know about love? Nevertheless, an opportunity to take a step along that twisty byway came to me by chance on a Friday afternoon in the middle of August.

I had been getting to know my new colleague Benjamin Lloyd rather better but, truth be told, he was a guarded sort of personality and, though genial enough in his own way, I found it hard to connect with him as a friend. It went without saying that we had plenty to discuss in the realm of education, and I had no doubts about his sincerity and his suitability for the work he had ahead of him.

One day we had been speaking about the American Civil War and the emancipation of the slaves in the South. I had been musing as to whether it would be suitable, in a simplified form, to introduce some elements of this momentous story to the older scholars. Lloyd was enthusiastic about the idea. Indeed he told me he had some useful notes for lessons which he had used in one of the Manchester schools to mark twenty years since the Lancashire cotton workers had supported Lincoln's blockade of the Confederate ports in spite of the penury it brought them. He believed they were in a box somewhere in his new garret apartment and so would search for them and leave them out for me on my classroom desk.

The structural work on the attic was all but completed and there had been some nights recently when Lloyd had slept under its reconfigured roof. For the next few days, however, he confirmed that he would be absent: it was his mother's sixtieth birthday and he would be spending the weekend with his family in Stockport.

Towards the end of the Friday afternoon, a little after five o'clock, I was finishing my preparations in the schoolhouse when I remembered the conversation we had had about the United States. I ferreted amongst the papers on my desk (clutter would be a better word) but failed to find what I was looking for. I guessed that with the important family reunion on his mind Lloyd had forgotten his promise to bring the materials downstairs; it was annoying as I had planned to read through them over the weekend.

I climbed the staircase to the upper floor. The bedroom he had arranged on very spartan lines: perhaps he had more still to do to make it more comfortable. The connecting door to the living area was closed but, as I discovered, unlocked. I had been inside once before, a fortnight or so earlier, when the builders were at work. Now it seemed to me that the jobs were finished. I had a cursory glance across the man's table but there was no sign of any teaching materials concerning Abraham Lincoln. Rooting amongst his drawers was plainly out of the question. While I was up in the room, however, I did take a moment to study the embellishments. The walls had been rendered and the rafters painted but the most impressive new features were a small fireplace (a foot or two of brickwork had been removed from the chimney breast and a little hearth had been built) and an elegant skylight. Although small, this had been cleverly conceived: neatly fitted into the roof, it provided some natural light and gave a narrow prospect to the north. I peeked out and over the lane I could see one flank of the Chapel and an expanse of the graveyard. I remained there for several moments, transfixed, for the longer I looked the more certain I became that the distant figure I could spy standing between the headstones was that of Louisa Thornley. There was nothing I could do to still my racing heart.

I ran from the rooms, down the staircase and out through the study into the street. With blood rushing into an empty space where my brain should have been, I crossed the lane and strode towards the very patch of grass I had surveyed from above. Louisa, for it most certainly was she, was moving away from the graves and on to the path, heading towards me. Her hair was loose this evening, she wore a dress of sky blue and her shoulders were covered with a woollen shawl of rich purple.

"Why, Mr Rowbotham!" she said, as if I had startled her.

"Oh, good evening, Louisa," I replied, regaining a steadiness to my breathing if not my composure. "I was just on my way to the vestry. How are you?"

"I am very well, sir," she answered. "I was visiting my granny's grave."

She turned her face back towards the granite headstone as if to invite me to look.

"Mrs Gledhill," I said, almost to myself.

As Louisa retraced her steps, I found myself following her graceful movements. She stooped to reposition a vase of fresh flowers for a final time. I could tell it was an arrangement of her own creation: mainly wild flowers in a certain colour palette, the blues and pale purples of verbena, honeywort and catmint.

"One thing I have learned about you, Louisa, is that these are your favourite colours, are they not?"

"You are quite right, Mr Rowbotham," she answered with a

little giggle in her voice.

I wondered if my remark had crossed some line of intimacy for I fancied she was blushing slightly.

"I come here every Friday at this time in the summer months," she said after a moment, standing tall and making to walk away. "Earlier in wintertime, of course, if it's not too horrid."

"Are you heading home directly?" I asked.

"Mother will be expecting me."

We wandered towards the gate together in silence. On reaching the lane, she turned and said goodbye.

"Before you leave," I stuttered, having had a little time to form a question, an invitation of sorts:

"When you come back, when you come back next Friday, I will make a point of meeting you here. If you do not object, of course. And if you agree, I would like to accompany you up Joel Lane afterwards. If you agree, of course."

For a second or two the young woman hesitated, tightened the shawl around her shoulders, looked up the lane and then back to me. I dared not breathe. My heart dared not beat. My eyes dared not blink.

"I should like that, Mr Rowbotham," she said at last with the hint of a smile. "We can talk about poetry perhaps."

"Indeed. It will be my pleasure."

"And shall I see you in chapel on Sunday?"

"I am certain of it," I said, and smiling with relief added: "but I shall be occupied with the demands of a dozen Sunday scholars. Next Friday will be far more agreeable, I am sure!"

Like a hawk I had spied and recognised Louisa Thornley from a distance of a hundred yards from the roof window of the schoolhouse, but I had to concede to myself that in these past twelve months my capacity to see closer objects had steadily diminished. Reading and writing, the very essence of my profession (and indeed much of my leisure time) had become increasingly troublesome. I blamed fatigue, poor light or an inability to concentrate, so reluctant was I to accept the inevitable: my old spectacles, somewhat bent yet so faithful and seemingly indestructible, were no longer practicable.

Mr Dowson recommended an ophthalmic optician in Hyde who, he said, would set me right. There were some fashionable designs available these days, he added.

"Buy yourself a modern pair, Walter," he suggested. "They'll make you look ten years younger!"

I readily decided that the moment had come to spend some money on my appearance and to rescue my failing eyesight at the same time. I made a point of striding into town on the Monday morning and while I was there I would buy a small gift for Louisa. Nothing ostentatious. A book. A book of poetry would be perfect, perhaps something modern such as Steeples' *Reflections*.

I called in to Mrs Beech's shop on the way, but she could not provide a suitable article.

"If there's a market on you might be lucky," she said. "There's a fellow on some days with a stall full of second-hand books. They're in a good state as a rule. They have to be, I suppose, or he'd not sell them."

Indeed there was a market on and indeed I was lucky. The bookseller had no poetry but amongst the pamphlets and periodicals he did offer a fair selection of well-known novels. Finding something appropriate for Louisa took me some time but the fellow was patient and had few other customers to serve. Disappointingly he had neither Hardy nor Austen. The Brontës were well represented but most were in a poor condition. In any event I did not enjoy them and could not in all conscience recommend them to a novice. My choice was reduced to Dickens. Louisa had found Dickens amusing, she said. I found a copy of *Bleak House*, a book I loved but it was long, complex and perhaps too demanding. Alternatively there was *A Christmas Carol*: an old edition but a shorter, accessible story and an easier subject for a discussion. I chose the latter, overlooking a number of folded pages and pencil markings, and probably paid the seller more than I ought.

Following a successful consultation with the optician, I proceeded back up Market Street, stopping to buy a length of lilac coloured silk ribbon and two squares of tissue paper of the finest quality in a pleasant shade of primrose yellow. I spent much of the afternoon erasing every pencil mark I could find in the pages of the Dickens and flattening each of the meddlesome folds. When it came to the wrapping I was all fingers and thumbs. I made several failed attempts to produce a tidy parcel that was attractive to the eye. Martha Harrop, sweeping out the scullery at the time, overheard my wails of exasperation and saved the day.

"That's a very thoughtful gift, Mr Rowbotham," she said, examining the cover. "Is it for a niece? It's a favourite o' mine, to be truthful. Poor Mr Scrooge," she laughed to herself. "How they do torment 'im!"

I could only stand aside and admire the woman's dexterity as she carefully folded the tissue this way and that, secured it with the ribbon, lined top to bottom and side to side in the neatest of crosses, and then finally tied the ends together for me in a perfect bow.

When Friday arrived I was again grateful for the visit of Mrs Harrop to my cottage; her presence in of itself and her quiet, unfussy attention to my laundry was a welcome distraction to me, wrapped as I was in uneasy mental preparations. At the top of Joel Lane as the road ran south-west along the rim of Werneth Low, there was a public house which called itself, in rustic tradition, the Hare and Hounds. I had passed by the place on rambles across the hills, oftentimes with eyes fixed on the shifting patterns of the clouds, on a circling bird of prey, but had never paused there for refreshment. Nevertheless it had always struck me as a pleasant spot, especially in the summertime with wooden benches arranged in its modest garden and views to the west of the distant rooftops of Hyde and the hazy expanse of Manchester towards the horizon. I resolved to walk with Louisa as far as this place, confident that in spite of my age, my healthy constitution would permit no embarrassment on the steep incline.

Thankfully it was a dry afternoon with no threat of rain and the temperature was gentle. I chose to wear my favourite necktie – *cornflower blue, would you call it?* – and made my way up to the chapel yard shortly after five o'clock. From the gate I caught sight of Louisa kneeling between the headstones: her hair was tied back with a white ribbon and she wore the same purple shawl as before. As she stood I recognised the pale lilac dress she had worn at the parsonage garden party. Was it a special one she had picked out for my pleasure, I wondered.

Presently she moved away from the graves. This time my appearance did not surprise her. She smiled as she noticed me and we greeted one another politely with a delicate handshake.

"I have brought you a little gift," I said, offering her the book, wrapped in its tissue and ribbon.

"Whatever for?" she asked, unexpectedly.

"As a token of our friendship," I replied. "I suppose."

She took it from me and traced a pretty finger along the ribbon.

"You chose the colour deliberately?"

"Well, yes. Yes, I did. And you can guess what the tissue conceals, I imagine."

"Indeed. I can feel the shape of a book. But the mystery is, which book?"

"Will you open it to find out?"

"No, I shall wait. It is my birthday on Sunday and I shall open it then. Thank you, Mr Rowbotham. You are most generous. Now, let us walk."

Before I had the chance to say anything more she had turned and was several paces ahead of me, her slender waist as hypnotic as ever.

The young woman was a brisk walker in spite of the climb. There were several fellows sitting at a table outside the Grapes Inn sharing a large jug of ale and conversing loudly. I thought that some comedian might make an impudent remark as we passed but I was mistaken. Once we had crossed into Joel Lane we settled into a steadier stride which allowed for conversation. Louisa was eager to talk about her day: she had been horse-riding with her friend Nellie and had much to say about the stables and the choice of ponies. Duchess was her favourite: a three-year-old grey with the sweetest of temperaments. I had little to add to the topic but took pleasure from the sound of her voice. I was about to introduce the idea of walking on as far as the Hare and Hounds but, almost without pausing for breath, she had already begun a story of her mother's convoluted arrangements for Sunday and a special birthday tea party. I listened politely but my interest in the singular fussiness of Maria Thornley had its limits. We passed the lane cottages and the grassy embankment of the reservoir and as the track veered towards Arnold Hill, her family home came into view. To my surprise she slowed her pace and presently came to a stop outside the painted gate.

"Well, thank you, Mr Rowbotham," she said, slightly out of breath. "Here I am. Safely returned."

"But, but wouldn't you like to walk on, walk on a little further?" I stammered. "At least to the top, to the top of the lane? I had a longer walk in mind. We could take a drink, perhaps, at the Hare and Hounds?"

"Oh no, Mr Rowbotham, that would never do. If I were to enter an alehouse with an older gentleman, I cannot imagine what my mother would say!"

She laughed as if the idea was so preposterous it was almost comical.

"Well, at least let us stride on together and take in the view."

"I had enough of the view on horseback this morning."

There was a moment when no word passed between us. I could think of nothing to say to rescue the situation.

"Good evening," Louisa said eventually. "And thank you so very much for the book. I shall spend all day tomorrow guessing at its title!"

She had already pushed open the gate. She was disappearing down the curving pathway before I called, a little desperately:

"Goodbye, Louisa. It was a pleasure to walk out with you. Shall I see you in chapel on your birthday?"

There was no answer to my question. Only her fluttering white ribbon was briefly visible above the bushes and then, suddenly, all sight of her was gone.

# Chapter 2

There was a great deal to preoccupy me in the following days, not least the establishment of the Welshman Benjamin Lloyd as a permanent resident in the schoolhouse and our preparations for the new term, both in conjunction one with the other and in my own separate projects for the Junior class.

My brand new reading spectacles arrived and made such a difference to my ability to see tiny print that I quietly cursed myself for not having discarded my old pair months ago. They were in a modern styling, having oval shaped frames in blued steel. The Reverend Dowson was the first to compliment me not only on my good sense but also on the strikingly handsome effect they made on my appearance.

In spite of this trivial boost to my confidence, I remained anxious about the progress of my courtship of Louisa Thornley. The Sunday of her birthday passed without a glimpse of her. When I enquired of her mother in chapel as to her unexpected absence I was told that she had a slight chill and, with so many guests invited, had much to do at home in preparation for her birthday tea. I recognised the setback as one of the bumps in the road I had been expecting and resigned myself to patience and perseverance.

On the following Sunday morning Louisa reappeared by her mother's side but cast barely a glance in my direction. It was the eve of the new school year and the Sunday scholars were restless and required much attention, and I missed the opportunity to approach her at the conclusion of the service. No matter that the school was brimming with life once more and the demands on my week were considerable, I resolved nevertheless to place myself at the chapel gates on the Friday afternoon at five o'clock and face her again. At the very least I would ask her if she had started the Dickens.

If I had been residing a quarter of a mile closer to Apethorn Mill, for example beyond Gerrardswood, there is no doubt that I would have heard the sound of the dreadful explosion that filled the valley on the Wednesday evening of that week.

I was quite unaware of the commotion until the following morning as I made my way to school. The street was busier than usual, there were mill workers I rarely saw at that time of the day, some walking up the hill with their children, many gathering in groups discussing an event that had passed me by. Outside the dairy shop I noticed Mrs Hill standing with young Jack and a gentleman I knew to be an overseer in one of the weaving rooms. I approached them and quickly discovered that there had been a calamitous explosion in one of the boiler houses. The main boiler had shattered into fragments which were sent flying far and wide; one fractured end was resting in the canal. The secondary boiler was also buckled beyond repair.

"Was anybody killed?" I asked.

"Mercifully not," replied the man. "At least that's what I've been told. It happened after most folk had gone home. General operations have closed down on that site a while ago. They're gettin' ready to start back up an' the boilers were bein' cranked up again, I suppose. I've heard them on an' off, blowin' steam these past few weeks."

"You've been told to stay away for now, have you?"

"For today, aye. There'll be tons an' tons o' rubble to shift. The south mills are untouched but they dunna want swarms o' folk down there. It sounds like a right chaotic scene. The canal's blocked for a start so the water traffic'll be stopped an' all."

At dinnertime the rumours were embellished by Daniel Harrop who, having an unexpected day of freedom, appeared in the schoolyard looking for me. He was not especially concerned at the prospect of a lasting closure of the mills. Instead I found him bubbling with excitement.

"It 'appened on t' north site, Mr Rowbotham," he said. "They were gettin' ready for reopenin'. There'll be even more work for t' likes o' me, what with all t' repairs. All th' other sheds'll be runnin' tomorrer, I reckon. Or if not, on Monday mornin'."

I offered to make him a cup of tea but he had more to say first.

"I wanna see it for myself. See what t' damage is like. They reckon it's a sight to behold. How about me an' you takin' a wander down there later? After you've done with your lessons? Shall you call for me about five o'clock?"

I was worried that the site would be unsafe but I admit I was most curious to witness the scene and agreed to accompany him as close to it as we would be allowed.

As we descended Apethorn Lane later that afternoon I noticed Danny grow quiet the closer we came to the corner where it was said his father had collapsed. It must have been quite a cross to bear for the boy to pass this spot twice a day but the work at the mill suited him and he was not of a mind to give it up.

In the event it appeared that a good deal of clearance work had been achieved and the waterway was already partially reopened. The towpath was generally accessible and along with other groups of spectators we managed to get a comprehensive view of the devastation. Danny spotted a couple of work pals and took a pride in introducing them to me. Across the canal men with horses were still dragging wreckage into a yard. The boiler house was utterly destroyed and amongst the great piles of bricks and dust and split timbers and shards of bent metal lay ripped lengths of twisted piping and curved flanks of iron. I spoke to a man in overalls who was holding court to a gaggle of youths who were as fascinated as we were. No blame had been attached to anyone at this stage, he confirmed, but an enquiry would be set up, of that there was no mistake.

It was a miracle that of all the workers on the site at the time only one man, a fireman named William Shore, was seriously injured. It appeared that he was wheeling a barrow into the boiler house at the moment of the explosion and the force blew him out the way he had come. He was discovered buried in debris but protected by the wheelbarrow, which had landed on top of him upside down. He suffered severe bruising but was carried away alive.

To my dismay the female figure I observed a day later stepping away from Mrs Gledhill's grave was not the deceased's granddaughter Louisa but her daughter Maria. Instinct encouraged me to hide behind the gatepost like an outlaw but the sharp-eyed woman had already spotted me and was heading in my direction with a resolute expression on her face.

"Mr Rowbotham!" she shouted. "Don't you dare disappear! I need to speak to you."

She lengthened her stride and reached me within half a

minute. I had not moved an inch. I waited for her to catch her breath.

"I am glad I have you alone," she said at last. "What I have to say to you, sir, should be spared the ears of a hundred curious souls at Sunday chapel."

"Say what you must," I retorted. "I was hoping to speak with Miss Louisa this afternoon. It is her habit to visit her grandmother's grave at this time, I understand."

"What I have to say to you concerns Louisa directly," she said, staring hard into my face with eyes as piercingly blue as her daughter's. "You have no idea how much you upset my child a fortnight ago."

"I upset her? My intentions were quite to the contrary."

"The very idea of walking out with her! At your age! You must realise that you are old enough to be Louisa's father? What were you thinking?"

"The very idea of a walk together was appealing to her. She was most heartily in agreement, Mrs Thornley, I assure you."

"You can assure me all you like but I won't believe a word of it. She's an agreeable young lady. It is in her nature to please. You took advantage of her, Mr Rowbotham, there's no two ways about it. She said you even had designs on sitting in a dusty alehouse with her at your side. It's grotesque."

The woman's face was becoming quite red.

As it seemed fatuous to insist that I would never have entertained buying her daughter an alcoholic drink I remained silent and let her words assault me further. For indeed, after a deep intake of breath she had much more to say:

"And on top of all of that you attempt to buy her affections with a book. How very sordid. For a man we all trusted, a schoolmaster, a member of our Chapel, how thoroughly sordid. And a second-hand book, to boot! A grubby little dog-eared second-hand book! *A Christmas Carol.* What sort of book is that to give as a birthday gift to a young lady? A story of ghosts and destitution and bitterness, if I am not mistaken. And in August? A Christmas book in the month of August? No, sir, it will not do. You will stay away from my daughter henceforth."

"Mrs Thornley, I am sorry you feel this way but I do believe that Louisa likes me. I respect your point of view, of course, but…"

"Henceforth, Mr Rowbotham, henceforth. Otherwise I shall be obliged to take the matter to the Reverend Dowson. And all the way to Manchester, all the way to the District Committee, if I must."

# Chapter 3

It was both a relief and a pleasure to be once again part of a large, boisterous crowd of football enthusiasts. The pitch was in a fine state of repair and the bright blue flags rippled in the breeze at the four corners as the spaces by the touchlines filled up with hundreds of excited supporters. A temporary raised enclosure had been erected along a portion of one side of the ground for the occasion. Folk who were prepared to pay an additional amount of money were allowed into it, along with officials from both clubs and sundry special guests.

Edward Berry and I found a convenient place to stand close to a corner flag, from where we could see something of a commotion within the enclosure as a fellow sitting in a wheelchair was introduced. He was readily surrounded by well-wishers who wanted to meet him. Someone near us recognised him as William Shore, the fireman injured in the Apethorn Mill boiler explosion. From our viewpoint I could discern the poor man's legs, motionless and heavily bandaged. He did seem to be in good spirits, however – at the centre of attention and evidently delighted to be a guest of honour at such a prestigious match. A few boys came asking for his autograph and I watched him signing one after the next with a theatrical flourish, revelling in his unexpected celebrity. Standing directly behind him and manoeuvring the convalescent's chair into a comfortable position I noticed the physician I had met at Mr Dowson's garden party.

Twelve months earlier Hyde F.C. had been thoroughly beaten by Blackburn Rovers. On this day there was a similar outcome but everybody I spoke to was of the opinion that the performance of the Hyde players was much more promising. Bolton Wanderers, playing in their splendid stripes of red, white and blue, gave their hosts a lesson in keeping the football away from scurrying opponents and won the game by eight goals to one. Poor Harry Bowers, for all his endeavour, had very little opportunity on the ball to show his worth. Several other Hydonians were making their debuts: the goalkeeper Bunyan, the winger Jimmy Wood (from round the corner in Godley) and the stocky inside forward Pressdee who scored our consolation goal. The supporters standing around me, including Berry, were prepared to put the defeat down, at least partly, to so many of the players being unfamiliar with each other's games.

"It's too early to judge this team," said Berry somewhat disconsolately. "Let's wait and see how they do when they get to know one another a bit better."

The two of us walked back together towards Gee Cross. The familiarity of the even rhythm of our steps and the spontaneous bursts of dialogue were reassuring. The new season had begun; I would be a part of it and it would be a part of me. Now that the Bolton fixture was done with, the regular series of matches, of winnable matches, could start. Teams like Bolton Wanderers were out of reach at this early stage in the development of Hyde F.C. but Maloney's list of matches included an intriguing array of opponents against whom we could realistically judge ourselves: Eccles and Denton, for example, Gorton Villa and Wigan, not to forget Hurst F.C. from Ashton-under-Lyne.

I was not inclined to break my homeward trek at the Berry family home on Osborne Road but Edward insisted that his mother had another gift for me; she would be more than disappointed if I did not show my face at the door.

"Walter! It's lovely to see you again," said Mother Mary as I stepped over the threshold.

"You too, Mrs Berry," I replied, gently shaking her hand. "I'll not stop, if you don't mind, but I couldn't walk past your road without bidding you all a good afternoon."

I noticed she had called me by my Christian name. I was not at all offended by her informality but I did wonder what had happened in the months since we last met. Back in the springtime I had been Mr Rowbotham.

"Mother," intervened Edward, "don't you have a little gift for my friend?"

"Indeed so. Thank you for reminding me. Blanche!" she called down the hallway. "Blanche! It's Mr Rowbotham. Can you fetch that jar from on the kitchen table? And didn't you have a question for him?"

I was intrigued.

"Come inside properly, Walter," said Mrs Berry.

"I'll wait here, honestly," I insisted. "My boots are very muddy. They've put boarding around the pitch but you still have to walk over the fields to get to it!"

"Very well. Blanche! Blanche, hurry yourself!"

The daughter appeared presently with a kiss on the cheek for her older brother and an unlabelled jar of something pale and indistinct for me.

"It's apple sauce, Walter," explained her mother. "Freshly made, and from our own apples. We planted the trees in our garden over ten years ago as Edward has perhaps told you."

From the corner of my eye I could see her son shaking his head.

"My late husband wished to produce a special compote of home-grown fruit to complement his selection of pork products. The crop remains small but the flavour of this year's vintage is highly intense. Please, Walter, take it."

"Thank you kindly. I do appreciate a fine condiment."

"Who doesn't, Walter? Who doesn't? Now then, Blanche, what did you want to ask our experienced schoolteacher?

The young lady held an opened notebook but seemed rather embarrassed to trouble me with it.

"It's just a matter I was unsure of, Mr Rowbotham, sir," she said. "I've been working on these little exercises for my class. As you can see, rhyming words. I wondered if you thought they would be appropriate for seven-year-olds."

I smiled, lifted the book from her hand and put on my spectacles to peruse the content. The work seemed fairly challenging and I suggested a couple of ways of simplifying it. Blanche listened intently and as I returned the book to her she thanked me graciously.

Edward listened less intently and smiled to see his friend tutoring his dear sister.

Mary Berry listened hardly at all but I sensed that her sharp eyes were watching me as I pointed out a detail here, a detail there to her dear daughter.

"Are those new spectacles, Walter?" she said excitedly when the consultation was over. "Blued steel, if I'm not mistaken. Oval frames. My goodness, Walter, they're very modern. Very fashionable. And yes, they really do suit you, I must say. Don't you agree, Blanche? They make you look such an intellectual, if you don't mind me saying so. Like a proper handsome professor!"

It is true that I am partial to a good, sharp apple sauce. Pickled red cabbage remains my favourite accompaniment to a meal, however, and strangely enough, it was this latter comestible that took centre stage in the little drama that unfolded a fortnight later.

It followed indirectly, I suppose, from a conversation on a train on the last Saturday of September. Hyde F.C.'s second match of the season was an away fixture against Greenhays. Filled with early-season enthusiasm, Berry had suggested we went to the match; it was to be my first game away from Ewen Fields. It did not require much persuasion for me to accept his invitation. I was eager to see the new players in action again and the journey was not so onerous: the passenger train from Hyde into Manchester stopped at Ardwick and from that station it was a walk of no more than a mile through the grimy streets to the Greenhays pitch.

The day was damp and dreary but we were rewarded by an entertaining display from both teams. Harry Bowers' friend Arthur Hopkinson was chosen to play his first game for the club and indeed he caught the eye in a victory by two goals to one. At the end of the match and in my capacity as official record-keeper, I became entangled in a tortuous conversation with the host club's secretary and Berry and I found ourselves leaving the ground at the same time as some of the players. In fact we sat in the same compartment on the train back to Hyde as Bowers, Hopkinson and James Pressdee.

I spoke quietly to Harry about aspects of my summer, notably my change of dwelling, but it was the footballers, energised by their winning performance, who were by far the more talkative. Harry encouraged his friend to ask me if

I would run an eye over the paperwork the club had expected him to put his signature to. Suitable part-time employment had been secured for him at an iron foundry but, like his fellow Derbyshire man, the winger had difficulty understanding the specialised language and abstruse formulations of legal documents. I agreed to help without hesitation.

Bowers himself was more enamoured of his voluntary work in the gardens at Brookbank than his paid employment at Goodfellows. When I described the tiny yard I had at the back of my cottage he was dismayed that I had so far done nothing to embellish it with plant life.

"I'll get 'old o' some cuttin's for you, Wally," he enthused. "Hibbert'll not mind. Buy yer sen a big stone pot an' fill 'er up wi' compost. You'll 'ave a bit o' colour by next summer. What d'you fancy? Clematis? Azalea? How about a little hydrangea? Sturdy an' fast-growin'?"

"A hydrangea would make a nice bush. That's very kind, Harry. Pink or blue?"

"That depends on you, Wally. Well, it depends on t' soil you use."

"I think blue. Blue for the football club!"

"Then you'll be needin' acidic earth. I'll bring you a bag o' sulphate. You can keep 'em blue by diggin' in yer fruit peelin's, yer eggshells, coffee grains and such."

"He knows his stuff, Mr Rowbotham," said Hopkinson. "You should see 'is father's place back 'ome."

Pressdee was listening to the horticultural advice impatiently; I could tell he was eager to take over. An effervescent presence on the football pitch, he was just as lively off it. Quick-witted and with a most expressive face, once he hit his stride he made for an engaging travelling companion. For the final ten minutes of our ride into Hyde the only voice we heard was his. He loved working for Mr Smethurst, he told us, turning at that moment to Edward – because he was trusted.

"It's essential in a workin' relationship, Mr Berry, is trust."

Pressdee had been in the old grocer's employ for less than a month and already he had been given the responsibility three times a week of managing the market stall on his behalf. Meanwhile he had licence to process his speciality pickles in the back room at the shop.

"Just one taste, just one little mouthful, that's all it took. Mr Smethurst says to me: *That's grand, lad, most delicious. My customers'll love this.* And they do. I can't make enough of it!"

The mention of marinated red cabbage made me salivate. There were onions he did too, and gherkins and beetroots and even hard-boiled eggs.

"It's a secret Shropshire recipe," he said with a wink.

"An' so what's yer secret, Jimmy?" asked Bowers as the grocer's assistant finally paused for breath.

"You're not listenin', Bowers," he said, breaking into laughter. "I said it were a secret. Don't you know what the word *secret* means, you great lump?"


Edward Howarth, the owner of the best greengrocer's shop in Gee Cross, had reached his middle sixties and with each passing year he receded further and further into the background. While a successful and lucrative business flourished around him, these days he was far more likely to be found reading a newspaper or, scratching his bald head, puzzling over a hand of patience in the storeroom at the back of the shop than standing behind the counter weighing out sprouts and runner beans for customers. The man had worked hard to establish his business and at this stage in his life he felt entitled to step back from the heart of the operations.

I knew a little of the man. He was the youngest son of a farming family who to this day work the land and rear cattle at Clough Side. Of all the brothers Edward was the one who precipitated a diversification to vegetable crops. Beginning as an independent market gardener, he expanded into retail operations by renting a market stall in Hyde and gained a reputation for the quality of his produce. When a premises became available on the main street of the village, he could afford to buy it with an inconsequential loan and for many years since that day Howarth's has been the first port of call for a large proportion of the women of Gee Cross responsible for feeding a family. A part of the attraction was the fellow's geniality which he maintained even in the face of his wife's death ten years ago.

It was a shame (and this opinion is by no means mine alone) that Edward's son Robert, who to all intents and purposes managed the business these days, inherited none of his father's generosity and charm. Perhaps it was unfair to blame him entirely when the shop announced it would no longer allow credit; it might have been a decision arrived at between father and son, but it was one that alienated several of the poorer families I knew, especially in times of unemployment or similar crises. What was clear to all was that no excuse to raise prices was ever missed, and with the explanations and expressions of regret came an underlying surliness. Robert knew he had the best produce in the village and as far as he was concerned his customers were free to shop elsewhere. Of course he would never be so explicit; he would never say the words *take it or leave it*. He would smile, apologise and repeat his recommendation that his fruit and vegetables were beyond compare.

I was an irregular customer myself, partial to the summer fruits, the pungent onions and Edward's home-made pickled red cabbage. As chance would have it, on the Monday after the match in Greenhays, I called in at the shop to refresh my larder with potatoes, pears and aforementioned pickle. Alas the younger Mr Howarth, who was lately in the habit of wearing his cricket cap indoors, informed me that there was not a single jar of the pickle left on his shelves. It had been a poor summer for cabbage, he reported, especially the red variety. He hoped to replenish his stock with the help of another supplier but he could not promise when. Finally he offered an apology. On my way back home I visited Mrs Emery's shop at the Cheshire Cheese but she could not oblige; she'd not had any pickles other than onions on her shelves for weeks.

Remembering the effusive words of James Pressdee, I considered the notion of calling in on the Tuesday afternoon training on the fields and requesting a jar of his Shropshire special. Was I so desperate for a helping of pickled red cabbage with my tea? When the following day dawned bright and mild, and when the lessons were over and I had a few empty hours ahead of me, it was as much for the exercise, for the chance to watch a little football and to chat with a player or two as it was to complete my grocery shopping that I decided to stride out down the hill towards Hyde.

I found the players reaching the end of their afternoon session. It was evident that they had been drilled hard for when Jos Hall, who was directing the final part of the exercise, blew his whistle, many of the men dropped to the ground and sat where they landed, motionless save for their heaving chests. They looked to me like wounded soldiers scattered across a battlefield.

Little by little the chattering resumed. I quickly realised that the subject of their conversation was not the weekend fixture against Halliwell, but news of the F.A. Cup first round draw: Hyde had been paired with Preston North End. Some of the players seemed dispirited but most were excited at the prospect of playing against one of the best teams in England. Preston was a well-established club, the peers of Blackburn Rovers, who had regularly performed well in the Cup, often giving lesser teams a mighty hammering. The previous season they had reached the semi-finals. Not only would they be a formidable opponent, to compound the difficulty the draw had given Hyde the away tie: we would have to travel to play against Preston on their home turf.

For once Pressdee was too exhausted to have very much to say on the matter. I managed to pull him to one side and, apologising for the triviality, asked him if he could guarantee me a jar of his pickled red cabbage. He listened to my tale of frustration at Howarth's greengrocer's, laughing all the while. After a moment his expression changed and I could tell that he was hatching a plan. Ever the entrepreneur, he presented me with the spontaneous idea of wheeling a barrow load of produce up Gee Cross the very next day.

So it was that when I absented myself from the schoolyard, leaving Lloyd to the Wednesday dinnertime duties, I headed up to the junction at the bottom of the old Mottram turnpike where the young grocer's assistant had promised to be. I found him directing a shop boy to position his handcart at a certain angle to the footpath then to arrange the display of goods.

"Here's your cabbage, Wally," he said, handing me a jar. "No charge. If this afternoon goes as well as I think, then it'll be me owin' you."

A passer-by or two was already attracted to the cart.

"Don't be shy, ladies," Pressdee called out, a glint in his eye. "Gather round! You'll not regret it, not if it's a little treat for your taste buds you're after."

The boy was sent away with a fistful of flyers to post around the village advertising the grocer's wares.

"Wally," he said, "could you catch up with Alf? Take him round the village for me? Show him the best spots for the notices."

When I saw him again, later in the afternoon, the barrow was all but empty. Lloyd accompanied me and bought the very last jar of pickled gherkins. It appeared that a jar or two of cauliflower florets were all that remained.

"I told you I'd sell out," said Pressdee, beaming. "The lad can take the barrow back down Hyde an' I'll treat you to a glass at an alehouse of your choosin'. They do say this village has a good selection."

"Who's this?" said Lloyd suddenly.

We looked up to witness the approach of a bicycle in the fading light, piloted by the only bicyclist in the village, Robert Howarth the greengrocer.

"What's been goin' on here?" he shouted.

"Do you need to ask?" replied Pressdee. "There's flyers all over the village."

"This is illegal!" blustered Howarth, his face becoming ever redder. As he halted his machine a gust of wind blew off his cap and for the first time I saw the extent to which his hair was receding.

"You can't just pitch up an' flog stuff on the side o' the road," he went on.

"Can't you?" asked Pressdee mischievously.

The shop boy was hiding a smirk behind his hand.

"You know damn well you can't. It's in the by-laws. You've no licence to trade here, have you? If I see you here again or anywhere else in Gee Cross I'll have the constable after you an' no mistake."

Pressdee said nothing.

Howarth turned his gaze to me as Lloyd graciously returned his cap.

"Are you owt to do with this lawlessness, Mr Rowbotham?" he said.

"I'm just a customer," I replied. "One of many, it would appear."

"One of his last in this village," harrumphed the cyclist, pushing off and rolling away into the twilight.

"Healthy competition," smiled Pressdee, tapping a bulging money pouch at his waist. "Some folk can't be doin' with it but I say it makes the world spin around."

"That's summat I dunna get," said the shop boy, looking confused.

"What's that?"

"How a fella can sit on a two-wheeler like that an' not fall over."

I was about to launch into an explanation of gyroscopics but suddenly thought better of it. That Pressdee interrupted me in any event was probably for the best.

"Alf, lad, you don't need to worry yourself about such matters. Get this barrow down to Reynold Street for me before it gets dark, will you? That's a good lad. I'll see you right in the mornin'. Now then, Wally, come along, show me where you like to sup. An' your friend, will he come too? The more the merrier, I'd say."

# Chapter 4

Was it as a consequence of the F.A. Cup draw that the footballers of Hyde F.C. seemed distracted when they competed with Halliwell F.C. on the first day of October? This was a question Edward Berry and I (and many scores of other supporters, no doubt) had on our minds as we tramped home after a frustrating defeat by three goals to two. The Hydonians' second-half performance was at the root of the disappointment. Jimmy Wood had played wonderfully in the first half, his trickery on the ball and his readiness to take a fast shot at goal had caused misery to the Halliwell defence; he score two rattling goals to give our side a handsome lead.

The suspicion was that after the interval, thinking the game to be done and dusted and with an eye on the imminent match at Preston, the home team players relaxed. Whether they felt the game was already won or for fear of an injury that would prevent them from playing in the Cup tie, the result of such a loss of intensity was that the visitors were allowed back into the match. Some lackadaisical defending from Hyde and Halliwell's renewed confidence produced three second-half goals to turn the game on its head. For all Hyde's late, desperate flurry of attacks the equaliser would not come.

The grumbling amongst a section of the crowd had begun as soon as the impression took root that a few players might be "going through the motions", as Berry described it. Spectators were entitled to complain, having paid their entrance money and, of course, I had heard rumblings before when things were going badly: colourful criticisms directed not only at the players of both teams but also towards the match officials, whose eyesight and sanity were regularly (and humorously) brought into question. It seemed that for some supporters there was nothing more satisfying than sniping from the sidelines like an irritable Greek chorus.

"We'll have to play a sight better in a fortnight," muttered Jos Hall to a couple of his teammates as they plodded past on their way down to the Bankfield.

I had spoken to Harry Bowers before the kick-off but now he was in no mood for a chat. He was already disappearing down the slope towards the paddocks, his arm around the shoulder of Hopkinson as if offering his friend some advice. I caught sight of Bunyan and Pressdee, two of the most vivacious characters amongst the players but they too were trooping away with the rest of the disconsolate bunch, barely a word exchanged between them.

Joseph Maloney spotted us and wandered over to greet us.

"Well, that wasn't what we were hoping for," he said, smiling through his regret. "Not much of a fillip to our confidence before Preston, was it? Mind you, I'm certain that damned referee had it in for us from the very first whistle."

"I'm sure we'll see a great deal more determination up there," said Berry, the eternal optimist. "It'll be our opportunity to let the rest of the country know that Hyde has a fine football team. Not a single one of our lads is going to waste it, I'm sure."

"I hope you're right, Edward," said Maloney, lifting his tweed cap to scratch the top of his head.

"The match is definitely on the fifteenth, isn't it?" asked Berry. "I heard a story that Preston wanted it changed."

"Oh, it'll be the fifteenth alright, don't you fret. We've seen to it. That's the date the Association set for the first round and Preston can chunter about it all they want but we're not moving it."

I asked what the problem was.

"It's not a problem, Walter," insisted the secretary, taking a deep breath. "Preston had already arranged a fixture on that date and they wanted to play it. They asked the Association, and by extension us too, if they would be prepared to allow our match to be played in the middle of the following week. Our committee didn't give an inch, I tell you. Our players have their work commitments for a start. We weren't shifting for nobody. Proud Preston, they call themselves. Well, no-one's prouder of their town and its football team than a Hydonian. We'll be at nobody's beck and call, believe you me."

I smiled at the passion in the man's argument.

"You'll be going to the match, will you, you two?" he asked.

"Aye, and no mistake," replied Berry. "Biggest game in our short history? I've got to be there to see it. Walter too."

We had discussed arrangements on our way down Back Lane earlier that afternoon. There was nothing could stop us making the journey up into north Lancashire and Berry agreed to investigate our travel options.

"There'll be special trains running from Manchester, as far as I know," said Maloney. "Well, at least some extra carriages, I expect. The railways know there'll be a demand for seats."

"Leave it with me, Walter," Berry smiled. "I'll see to it we have a ticket each."

"Wally!" called a voice from the far side of the slowly thinning crowd. I turned around and recognised Harry Bowers.

"Wally! I've got yer plants!"

Some of the supporters had words of commiseration for Bowers, others patted him on his back as he walked towards us, still dressed in his dirty football clothes. In each hand he held a sack, weighed down by what appeared to be a spade or two of earth.

"Here you go, Wally," he said, grinning. "A pair o' healthy hydrangeas. An' there's a bag o' sulphate in wi' one of 'em."

"That's very kind," I said, taking the bundles from him. "I only asked for one."

"Well, I got yer two. Ask yer friend 'ere to carry one 'ome for you if you can't manage 'em both."

Berry obliged straight away by relieving me of one of the sacks. Curious, he unrolled its neck and peeked inside.

"You've got two colours there," added Bowers, returning his concentration to the plants. "That 'un's a pale blue like you wanted. An' t' other's a rare beauty. It's a deeper blue, like a royal blue, you might call it. So if you feed 'em right you'll 'ave two shades, just like this 'ere shirt I'm wearin'!"

"A proper loyal blues supporter, eh, Walter?" suggested Maloney.

"Indeed."

"How are the lads, Harry?" asked the secretary.

"Oh, you know. A bit flattened. We let 'em back into it today. But dunna worry, Mr Maloney, we'll not be makin' t' same mistake in a fortnight. Preston'll not know what's 'it 'em, I guarantee!"

Some time later as we trudged away from the ground, weighed down by our horticultural offerings, Berry mentioned that his mother was feeling under the weather and would not be receiving visitors. He apologised on her behalf.

"I know she looks forward very much to your little social calls, Walter," he said before changing the subject. "Listen, it's a pleasant enough evening. I'll give you a hand with your plants all the way up Gee Cross, if you like."

"In that case you must come inside and I shall make a pot of coffee for you for a change."

The conversation returned to football soon enough. Neither of us truly believed that Hyde would cause Preston North End too many problems, but we were hopeful that our players would at the very least give a good account of themselves. What we did not want, we agreed, was to witness a humiliation. We decided to take the earliest train north and in that way we might travel with the team. Clarence and his friends were also planning to make the journey but more than likely they would catch a later service.

"Have you been to Preston before?" I asked.

"As a matter of fact I have. Only a few months ago, as it happens. Our train to the coast began there. We travelled up to Preston and then had to wait there for half an hour or so. We never left the station so I couldn't say I know the town. The only thing I do know about it is that they say that since they signed up half a dozen of Scotland's finest, their football club has the best collection of footballers of any town in England."


Shortly after three o'clock on the following afternoon the Reverend Henry Dowson coughed loudly to attract attention and bring silence to the function room at Hyde Chapel. We had gathered to mark the imminent departure of his assistant

Frederick Ashton, who had been appointed as the new minister of the Fitzalan Street Chapel in Glossop, seven miles away over the Derbyshire border. We were sad to lose him but heartened that he had been able to step out of Mr Dowson's shadow and secure his own ministry. He reluctantly agreed to cooperate in the arrangements, modest fellow that he was. He had insisted it was not to be a lavish affair and so, up to a point, the organisers' committee acceded to his wishes.

There were no more than thirty people in the room, mostly belonging to a certain grouping of ladies of the Chapel membership who liked to be associated with the leaders of our ministry. Notable amongst them, pillars of the choir to a woman, was Mrs Maria Thornley, who had taken a primary role in the organization of the party, which meant that coordination of the decorations, the arrangement of the furniture and the choice of refreshments had been assumed by her alone. As for the invitations, I dare say Frederick himself may have been at least cursorily consulted; this could have been the only reason that I found myself on the ladies' guest list.

Mr Dowson gave a short, complimentary speech about his dear colleague's sterling qualities, wished the man every success in his new role and proposed a toast to his good health. Within five minutes he had apologised and departed; his wife Lucy had a fever and he was concerned about her.

The centre of attention passed to Benjamin Lloyd, who had arranged for his harp to be transported across the lane. The chattering of those present ebbed away as the young teacher ostentatiously practised his fingering. Presently he began in earnest and indeed thoroughly entranced us all with a delightful rendition of *Greensleeves*.

During a short lull in proceedings one or two of the ladies searched me out with questions about Hyde's popular footballing grocer.

"When's that nice Mr Pressdee coming back up Gee Cross with his handcart, Mr Rowbotham?" asked Mrs Booth, the baker's wife.

"Such a charming young man," added her friend, cheeks aglow. "We are very much looking forward to casting our eyes over his delightful range of comestibles again."

I placated them by promising to mention their enthusiasm for his wares the next time I saw him on Ewen Fields.

Before refreshments were served there was a presentation to the Reverend Ashton of a parting gift. I was intrigued to see that somebody, presumably her mother, had asked Louisa Thornley to do the honours. She spoke only a single sentence but charmed the room, so natural was her smile. In view of us all, Frederick unwrapped a fine pair of calfskin gloves – a special order, I was told later, from George North's works on Robert Street.

Queuing for tea and cakes meant unavoidable interaction with Mrs Thornley, who was the mistress of a very large teapot. She seemed genuinely surprised to see me when I presented myself before her.

"Oh. Mr Rowbotham. How are you?"

She granted me the shortest amount of time to speak, inconsequentially, of my current health, and continued after the meanest of breaths:

"I hardly expected to see you here. I would have thought that you'd have been far too busy for socialising. Shouldn't you be spending your afternoon correcting pages of your scholars' arithmetic?"

The woman looked around to see if any of her circle of friends had heard her remark and found it amusing. Nobody had.

"As you can see, and indeed as you have heard," I said, "Both Mr Lloyd and I may be schoolteachers but we are not chained to our chalkboards."

"Tea, I presume?"

"Please. And, as I'm sure you'll agree, Mrs Thornley, *semper amicis hora est.*"

"I beg your pardon?"

"It's Latin."

"Latin? Well, that's no use to anybody in Gee Cross, is it now?"

"*There's always time for friends*, Mrs Thornley. And Mr Ashton is a friend of mine."

"Help yourself to a plate. The cakes are over on the far table."

"Arithmetic can wait its turn for a friend's party."

"Wasn't Mr Lloyd's *Greensleeves* divine?" she said, lifting the pot once again.

I was about to answer but realised that she was in fact talking to the lady behind me, the next person in the queue.

I took my refreshments to a seat in the corner of the room from where I could watch Louisa. She was wearing my lilac ribbon in her hair, which I took to be a good omen. She and her friend Nellie were standing in friendly conversation with Benjamin Lloyd, still seated at his harp; the exotic musical instrument seemed to fascinate them. I stood up and caught Louisa's eye. She smiled directly at me and then was distracted by something her friend said. Nellie had her hand resting on the curved shoulder of the harp and I saw Louisa's fingers running lightly along its shiny pillar. Suddenly the young women began to giggle, attracting the attention of a group of older ladies standing nearby, sipping from their teacups. I noticed the harpist himself was not immune; it was quite an achievement of the two friends to make the man smile with such spontaneity.

I did not tarry at the party but Louisa's smile stayed with me for the rest of the evening. It was a smile of warmth, I believed, accompanied by a fleeting sparkle in her sapphire eyes. Or was it a smile of resignation, of apology for her mother's unwelcome intervention? I realised that interpreting a woman's smile was a hopeless task. What did I ever really know about women? Once girls of eleven or twelve left my classroom for the last time I ceased to understand them, how they turned into young ladies and, moreover, I had even less of an idea how they functioned on reaching that hallowed state. They were mysterious creatures, as fragrant and as delicate as almond blossom, so apart from the solidity of men. They shifted in both appearance and temperament with the wind, their behaviour as inexplicable as the most whimsical of genies. Was Louisa's a smile of warmth after all? It could just as easily have been a smile of pity.

No matter. I was not to be deterred. Neither Louisa's ambiguity nor her mother's dismal objections would blow me off course. The crabby rebukes of Maria Thornley were born of ignorance and no little snobbery. They were the irrational ramblings of a sour old woman, the empty threats of an overprotective mother who had lost sight of her daughter's true wishes. They represented no more than another challenge I would willingly meet, another obstacle on the road to rise above.

Standing flat against the wall in the wide corridor of the schoolhouse was an imposing locked cupboard of heavy, dark-stained wood. It was an ancient piece of furniture of no discernible style. On the shelves inside it were stored much of the establishment's valuable documentation, its particular archives in fact, and the notes relating to all of the former pupils since the school's beginnings.

When I had a moment between classes on the following day, I made a point of locating the key to the cupboard and availing myself of the records of those leavers from the summer of 1870, the children who departed immediately prior to my arrival at the school.

I took the dusty file, sat down at my desk with it in front of me and put on my excellent spectacles. Of all the contents alphabetically arranged within it only one subject was of interest to me on that morning: a copy of the final report of Louisa Thornley, aged twelve. The girl was not unknown to me at that time. She had continued to attend Sunday school for two more years and indeed had helped me from time to time with the very youngest scholars. What I now read in her school report from all those years ago confirmed the half-forgotten impression I had of her as an adolescent. A picture of the dark-haired, bright-eyed girl drifted into my mind as I read the cursive handwriting of my predecessor, which formed a neat paragraph below a table of numbers:

*Louisa is polite and generally obedient but can be wilful and short-tempered. She is a self-contained girl with an independent spirit which will serve her well in the modern world. She writes fluently but with frequent errors. She loves to read, both silently and in front of the class. She is averagely proficient with numbers. She draws most imaginatively and has a melodious singing voice.*

I read the words twice. In fact I read the final sentence three times, for it was the nub of a clever idea that occurred to me. I remembered the Reverend Dowson telling me some years ago that Louisa had learned, piece by piece, to manage her father's business accounts at the ironworks but that in the end Jesse had come to value her more for her artistic contribution. It was said that much of the more decorative metalwork commissioned for manufacture – fire baskets, garden gates and such – had indeed been designed by his daughter.

She was an engaging young woman who could both illustrate and sing. What a treasure she might be. How could her mother, steeped in service to the Chapel, possibly object if I, or even better the much admired Reverend Ashton, in a final request, suggested that Louisa become a regular assistant to me at Sunday school?

# Chapter 5

The final over of the cricket season had been bowled many weeks ago but Frederick Ashton had only belatedly got around to emptying out his kit bag and tidying its contents in preparation for the move to Glossop. As the umpire for the Hyde Chapel team he was oftentimes handed articles to look after while the game was in progress; as a rule it was a question of minding something that a bowler did not wish to have jangling about his person while he was running to the wicket. It was not uncommon for him still to have such articles in his deep pockets long after the match had concluded. Coins, spectacles, sunhats and even a pack of playing cards had all been forgotten by this or that bowler over the course of the previous season. Amongst his most recent collection of lost property at the bottom of his bag he had found an old cap with the letters CK inked into the rim, which he recognised as belonging to Charles Knott. As the young bowler had played only once for the Chapel this year, Ashton remembered quite clearly the occasion on which he was asked to look after the cap while Knott prepared to bowl: a home match against Floweryfield, a close victory. Knott took three of the visitors' wickets in a late winning flurry and the consequences were excited celebrations and a forgotten cap.

Umpire Ashton knew that the young fellow was a friend of mine and so, in the hope that I could return the headgear to its owner, he delivered it to my cottage a few days after his farewell party. I had not seen Charlie for some time. Having completed my teaching responsibilities in good time, and once the rain had stopped, I decided to call on him on the Thursday afternoon and renew acquaintance.

His lodgings in one of the tall terraced houses at the top end of Henry Street were easy to find. The landlady of the property, a distinguished, grey-haired lady of about my age, greeted me and confirmed my friend's presence.

"I did hear him step inside," she told me in little more than a whisper. "An hour or so ago, it was. He must have got away from work nice and prompt for a change."

She led me up a narrow staircase to a door on the first floor and knocked gently.

"You have a visitor, Charlie," she said, stepping back on the landing.

I guessed that the young man had been napping for when he appeared in front of me his hair was sticking out in all directions and his eyes were dulled. Nevertheless he was pleased to see me, laughed as he recognised the battered cricket cap I was holding, and quickly regained a brighter mien.

His room, although somewhat untidy, was spacious, comfortably furnished, and the window gave on to the street below. There were newspapers littering much of the floor space and crumpled clothes formed an unruly pile by his bed. He made no excuses for the state of the room, however, and instead offered to make me a hot drink – he had free access to the family kitchen downstairs, he declared – but I declined. He bade me take the empty armchair as he perched himself on the end of his bed and thus we settled to enjoy each other's company.

I spoke to him of the developments in my life: notably my promotion, my new home and my new colleague from

Gwersyllt, a place he thought I had invented to amuse him. I stayed clear of making mention of my feelings towards Louisa Thornley although it was a fact that he knew her, at least by sight, and I would have been curious to know if he believed that she might make me a suitable wife. Such matters had never been discussed between us, however, and I felt it was most wise to maintain discretion. That said, he did surprise me somewhat later in our conversation.

His own circumstances had also changed, he told me. He had left the post office after a series of disagreements and was now employed as a clerk in one of the banks in the Market Place. He liked his colleagues but was unsure if the world of banking would be where he made a career.

"I 'ave me doubts, Walter, you know. We're trained to treat t' customers politely an' all that, but t' bank itself gives 'em nowt. Look at t' diff'rence t'ween t' measly int'rest rate they'll give you for your savin's an' what they expect you to pay them on what they'll let you borrer."

"It's a business like any other, I suppose," I said. "They expect their customers to pay for their services."

"Pay, aye, but not through t' nose! I reckon them mutual societies 'ave a better idea when it comes to lendin'."

I turned the subject to politics but he sighed and declared that the landscape was moribund.

"Rob Howarth were right. Money an' religion is all it is, politics in this country. An' t' consequences o' t' power that money an' religion can give. I'm more int'rested these days in how that power is abused. The morality of supremacy, Walter," he said, pronouncing the words carefully as if he was introducing the title of a pamphlet he had written.

"How did you become so learned, Charlie Knott?"

"Well, my friend," he said grinning, "it were you that taught me to read!"

He spoke briefly of admiring Mr Mill's *On Liberty* but remarked how tame it was (I remember *bourgeois* was a word he used) when compared with what Mr Engels had been writing ten years earlier.

He knew all about the F.A. Cup tie at Preston as football was a topic of interest to more folk than ever in the town since the intriguing draw was made. He was not surprised that I was planning to follow the team to the match yet still seemed amused, if not baffled, by the fact that his stuffy old schoolteacher was so energised by watching football matches.

"One of these days you'll have to come to Ewen Fields with me," I said, "and you'll wonder why on earth you've never been before."

"Happen I will," he conceded.

Fingering the rim of his cricket cap, he explained that he had played so rarely for Hyde Chapel lately because his allegiance was now largely with the team of Hyde St George's.

"You dunna 'ave to be a churchgoer to play for 'em," he said, "an' you can see, well, just about, that St George's is right across from 'ere, just yonder past them 'ouses."

I approached the window and saw that he was right. A strong-armed bowler could throw a cricket ball from his front door and just about land it in the churchyard. I noticed that the rain had started to fall once again.

"It's a good standard o' cricket, an' all, Walter."

"I'm sure the Chapel will miss you."

"Well, aye," he said, pausing before adding, "but there's summat else."

"Oh?"

"I've got myself a young lady."

"Have you now?"

"We've been courtin' these past four month. She'll come an' watch t' cricket, see me play. She belongs to t' church, see, she's a St George's girl."

Invigorated, he straightened himself up and ran a hand through his hair. I could see he wanted to tell me more and so let him speak.

"In fact she's a teacher at their school. I kept seein' 'er of a mornin' as I were leavin' to go down into town. She'd be there, day after day on th'other side o' t' road, turnin' into Church Street. It got so we were smilin' at each other every day. We got talkin', as you do. An' well, I reckon I'm smitten, Walter. She's a lovely, sweet thing, she is, an' no mistake."

His smile was infectious and my heart was warmed by his story.

"What's the lady's name?"

"Blanche, she's called. Blanche Berry. She lives on Osborne Road. Do you know it? Off Hyde Lane, near t' railway line. A big 'ouse – mind you, she's got a big family. One of 'er brothers plays cricket with us at St George's now an' then. Keeps wicket."

One of her brothers? Clarence, of course. A small world. A small town.

"Th'only snag is 'er mother. A bloody funny woman, she is. Asks me all sorts, which I suppose she's entitled to. She knows I'm not struck on bankin' but I get the feelin' she's tryin' to persuade me to take up butcherin'. Pork butcherin'! Can you believe it? I dunna know nowt about belly pork apart from it tastes lovely roasted up with a pile o' taters an' a nice drop o' gravy."

"Do you know you've got a leak in your gutter, Mr Rowbotham?" asked Martha Harrop as she folded the last of my shirts.

I was in the habit of spending my Friday dinnertimes at home, leaving Lloyd to supervise the scholars. In that way I could have a few words with my laundrywoman at the end of her chores and catch up with the news of her son. On this day I had dodged the heavy showers to stride down Gerrard's Street in the drizzle. As I awakened that morning I had noticed that rainwater was gushing against the window pane of my bedroom as if a dam had burst somewhere on the roof.

"At t' back o' th'ouse," the woman confirmed. "I reckon it's either blocked or it's split open. You shouldn't 'ave drippin' like that up there."

"Thank you for mentioning it, Martha," I said, filling the kettle. "I shall see to it, perhaps at the weekend. How's your Danny this week?"

I had spied her son from a distance in the crowd at the Bolton Wanderers football match but since that afternoon our paths had not crossed.

"I'm sure he wishes he could go with you up to Preston, Mr Rowbotham," said his mother, sitting down for five minutes' rest, her tasks completed for the morning, "but o' course he's not got that kind o' money."

"I'll make sure I give him a full and detailed report of the match," I said, setting down two cups and saucers on the table between us.

Since the club had imposed an entrance fee for spectators I realised that for some younger folk, no matter how paltry the sum, it was not an amount they could readily afford. His mother had told me a week or two ago that Danny's new friends at the mill were more interested in fishing than football. He had not been selected for the Hyde Juniors this season, which was a disappointment to us all. Meanwhile I knew from Clarence Berry that Toffee Mellor, now sixteen years old and growing into an athletic young man, had been invited to train with the senior players.

Rain continued to fall through Friday until well past midnight. As I lay in bed I heard the ceaseless drips from the gutter, their liquid monotony eventually sending me to sleep but not before I had resolved to rectify the situation the next day. I had no wish to report the matter to the estate manager and wait an age for a worker to be sent up to assess the problem; another week would then go by before a second worker was sent up to repair it.

Saturday dawned brightly. Preston was one week away, there was no football that day and I had time to perform my reparation. I borrowed a neighbour's ladder and, placing it at an appropriate angle against the stonework above the bedroom window, gingerly climbed the wooden rungs. I was thankful that the winds were light, for the higher I climbed, the more exposed I became to the breeze, the more aware I became of the vertiginous distance I was from the unforgiving flagstones below. For a moment I regretted my decision to leave the estate manager out of the process. I swallowed hard and took two further steps towards the clouds.

Finally I could see into the guttering: the metal was intact but the streams of rain water had been caused by a blockage directly above the window. I had no idea how long ago the gutters had last been cleared but I was confronted with a thick decantation of sodden debris preventing the normal drainage course: clumps of leaves, twigs, grit and at least one bird long since deceased. I slowly descended the ladder – a motion no less precarious than the ascent – and found an old brush handle I could use to loosen and poke away the obstruction. A minute later back at the top of the ladder, slightly breathless and with my heart in my mouth, I dug away into the mess, fetching out handfuls of wet, decaying matter and dropping it with a splat at the ladder's feet. Eventually the open curve of the gutter was as clear as I could make it and I was confident that on the next occasion the rain was torrential, all would be well.

It was at that moment that, from some distance away, I heard a short squeal of laughter. Instinctively I turned my head and once again felt uneasy at such a height; I gripped the ladder ever more tightly. The prospect behind me was an elevated version of that which I enjoyed from my bedroom window: the trees of Sugarloaf Wood in the dip and beyond it the open fields on the northern flank of the Low and the trail of hedges lining the course of the stream from Sugarfield Spout. I peered over my neighbours' yards, then out as far as the stables towards the back of the Cheshire Cheese, but there was no sign of movement. Just as I was about to climb down I heard the same laughter again. It was coming from the woods this time, I was sure of it, and I would swear it was the laughter of a woman.

I took a step back up to give myself the optimum view. I knew these woods. I had led nature rambles through them for the scholars on many a summer's afternoon. I directed my gaze at the points amongst the shadowy puzzle of branches where there were narrow paths and clearings. Autumn had not yet stripped the trees of their foliage, now turned golden and copper-coloured in the main, but I could discern the gaps between them. Suddenly, at a distance of fifty yards or so, I caught sight of movement: a flicker of a shape, a bobbing head of dark hair and attached to it, glinting in the sunlight, a strand of lilac ribbon. The branches about it were disturbed but I was too far away to see or even hear the reason why. The blur of pale purple disappeared and with it much of my rational thought.

It had to be Louisa in the woods. Had she spotted me from the bushes, high up on my ladder? Was she laughing at me or at something else entirely? Was it even her laughter I had heard? My heart was beating rapidly and encroaching vertigo was not the sole reason. I needed to find her, to intercept her, to be with her. For I was certain that her mother would be far from the muddy paths and Louisa would be strolling out alone. As quickly as I could I climbed down the ladder. In my haste, four damp rungs from the bottom, I misplaced my footing and slipped. I lost both my balance and my grip on the rails at the same time, tumbling to the ground and twisting my ankle as I landed. The brush handle bounced on the flags before rolling against the wall. I cursed my misfortune and my clumsiness.

It took me a moment to catch my breath and come shakily to my feet. I put a little weight on my ankle and flinched but there was really no time to lose. I followed a path I knew at the rear of the stables which led over a stile and down into the little valley where the wood began. It was most slippery underfoot and I descended unsteadily until I reached the tangle of trees, heavy with wet leaves and shadows. I directed myself towards the clearing from where the ribbon had flashed into view. Upon reaching the spot I paused, felt a sharp pain shoot through my foot, and listened. I heard nothing beyond birdsong and decided to press on, taking the most obvious path running west towards the edge of the Gerrardsfold plantations. I had proceeded no more than twenty yards, limping all the while, when I heard more laughter: the same voice, the same woman, the same Louisa. Then a second voice, no more than a murmur. I slowed to a snail's pace, wary of announcing myself prematurely.

All of a sudden I caught sight of a white bonnet ducking ahead of me. I stopped in my tracks and hid behind a bush as the movement beyond me also paused. It was Nellie! Louisa had brought Nellie with her, they were walking in the woods together on a sunlit Saturday morning.

I was on the point of showing myself when he spoke. Confused, I leaned into a gap in the dripping foliage to get a closer look. I was a mere ten yards from them, motionless and quite invisible, for they had eyes only for each other. The white bonnet was a cricket cap. I watched dumbstruck as Louisa Thornley, her hair tied loosely with my ribbon, was taken into the brawny arms of Robert Howarth. Their embrace became a kiss – a long, tender, secret kiss. I turned my gaze away, distraught, feeling the blood in my veins grow cold. My throbbing ankle was forgotten for the pain was now all in my heart. I listened but could not bear to look. I heard whispered words of love, I heard promises and prayers. I heard sighs of pleasure as they kissed again, as he ran his fingers through her hair, along her cheeks, tightening his grip on her delicate waist. Then I heard them stand up, I turned to watch as they held hands, looked at each other adoringly and smiled. Again a little squeal of girlish laughter. Then they departed the scene, heading away hand in hand along the path that would take them across the stream and into the open fields.

I waited, feeling the same dizziness I had experienced on the ladder, then, breathing unevenly, made myself slowly walk over to the space between the trees – here a sturdy oak, there a noble beech – where the embrace had occurred. I saw the patch of damp grass, flattened by their bodies, then their footprints in the mud, his and hers, trailing away as if linked together. Finally I saw, to my dismay, hanging limply from a low branch of a hawthorn bush, a fraying length of lilac ribbon, abandoned to the October rains.

The first words Benjamin Lloyd said to me on Monday morning stopped me in my tracks:

"My mother passed away on Saturday."

I was aware she had been poorly but this news, so starkly reported, was shocking. Lloyd was busying himself at his desk as he explained the circumstances, the futile attempts of a physician to save her and the effect it had left on his father.

"And how are you?" I asked. "Are you sure you feel strong enough to work today?"

"I'm fine," he replied, finally looking up at me. "Working is good for me. It gives me something positive to think of. Let me ring the bell and get the children inside."

"What of the funeral?" I wondered aloud.

"The funeral? My father will arrange it. It will be very soon, I have no doubt."

"If there's anything I can do," I said, "please ask."

"Thank you," he answered, turning away to count out a number of samplers. "I dare say I'll manage."

Instinctively I walked towards him to place a supportive hand on his shoulder but halfway across the room I paused. He was already on to another task, quietly comforting himself in the security of his routine. I retreated into the corridor in silence.

We had developed an easy working relationship, the two of us, but it was one which was limited to its functionality. I had come to know the man a little better in the past few weeks but I had not yet warmed to him and was beginning to doubt that I ever would. There were times when I found his a rather leaden, charmless presence. I dare say many folk might regard me as a sober sort of fellow but although not prone to gratuitous witticisms I do consider myself to possess a funny bone; given an excuse I like to laugh freely. I have come to believe in the argument that a lack of a sense of humour can be a person's greatest weakness. That said, I conceded that now was categorically not the time for laughter.

I did not share the pain of my own weekend with another soul. Margaret Dowson had volunteered to help with Sunday school lately and mercifully it was her turn to entertain the children. I deliberately missed chapel: a rare absence which I imagine raised a few eyebrows amongst certain members of the congregation.

I was bitterly aware that the likelihood of Louisa Thornley ever agreeing to become my wife was but a puff of smoke. I also realised that I had been a fool to ever think otherwise.

Self-pity is a lamentable state but for some time on my return from the woods I was held tight in its grip. The very first thing I did was snatch the champagne flute from its place on the mantelshelf and fling it to the scullery floor, where it shattered into a hundred pieces. Later I found myself sitting in the darkness making a fatuous comparison between myself and the greengrocer, the bicyclist, the cricketer, the much younger man set to inherit a successful business and a comfortable home. Howarth's receding hairline was my sole consolation and briefly I smiled to myself in a self-serving sort of way.

The tiny shards of glass were left untouched overnight. By the middle of the next morning I forced myself to sweep up every last fragment lest Martha Harrop spied the smallest speck on the morrow and set about asking herself (and Heaven forbid, asking me) what had happened. The woman must have wondered what an unwashed glass was doing on the shelf since the month of June – I had told her never to touch it – but she was too discreet to ask. Now, as far as she was concerned, the object would simply have disappeared: a far less dramatic conclusion than a floor littered with splinters.

Through it all my ankle was hurting. I remembered my mother's remedy for sprains and bruised bones: she had wrapped my young joints (and those of my sister) on many an occasion with bandages holding boiled comfrey tight to the skin. It was a plant whose restorative qualities she would swear by. She had it growing in wild clumps at the damp end of the garden: leaves of deep green, hairy to touch and as broad as spears, dotted in the summertime with clutches of flowers like little thimbles, the palest of pink, hanging invitingly for the bumblebee. I thought of hobbling back into the woods in the hope of coming across a patch by the stream but considered it to be too late in the season. Instead I made do by wrapping my ankle in a cold, wet cloth to contain the swelling – quite unsuccessfully. I limped from armchair to bed like a wounded soldier and started to worry about the week ahead. Would I be able to walk to school? Would I be able to function effectively if I even arrived? More importantly (yes, it did seem more important), would I be able to make the journey to Preston at the weekend?

There was a little easing overnight on the Sunday. The swelling subsided to be replaced by bruising of cloudy blue. Once at school Lloyd's sorry news of his mother's demise and the demands of my boisterous class of pupils provided me with different concerns and I plodded through the day, and the next one, and the one after that, hoping that I was on the mend.

It transpired that the funeral was arranged for the Thursday. Lloyd duly excused himself from school with my permission. Of course I had no wish to prevent his absence although it necessitated me combining our classes and thus teaching one group of unwieldy proportions. Reluctantly I was planning my strategy when he appeared again at my classroom door.

"Goodbye, Walter," he said solemnly. "Thank you for taking charge of my scholars. All being well I will see you on Monday."

"On Monday?"

My sigh was surely audible.

"Yes," he nodded. "I chanced to speak to the Reverend Dowson earlier and he insisted that I take the Friday as well. He believed my father would appreciate my support for the whole weekend."

"So you'll be absent for two days?"

"Two days, yes. Yes, I will. Thursday and Friday. I realise it's an imposition, Walter, but I hope you know that, in the circumstances, I would do exactly the same for you."

# Chapter 6

The train was decelerating. Below us coursed the grey curve of the river Ribble. Beyond the track there were buildings now, casting shadows: factories, rows of houses, a municipal park, the backs of more houses, street after street. There was a sudden squeal of brakes, metal on screechy metal, and the harshest of whistles ripped into the air. The men around me were stirring, stretching their legs, starting to button up their jackets. One by one they tried to remember exactly where in the racks they had lifted their luggage, one by one they repositioned their caps on overheated heads.

Moments later we were being shunted to a crawl, edged by a wide concrete platform dotted with folk who walked this way and that. Some stood waiting, eyes eagerly following the carriage doors that passed slowly before them. And large black signs with bold white lettering displayed the information that nobody needed telling: we had arrived in Preston.

There were carriers waiting outside the railway station to transport the players and officials across the town to the north side where the pitch at Deepdale was located. For the rest of us lay a walk of over a mile through the lively streets of the town centre. The state of my injured ankle had much improved but I was glad we had taken the early train and thus there was no necessity for speed. Edward Berry was eager to arrive at the ground, set to march purposefully forward. I had to call him back more than once, to demand that he slowed his pace, which he did with good grace in spite of his obvious impatience.

It was interesting to be walking through an unfamiliar environment. The architecture and the arrangement of the buildings was no surprise, however, as Preston, in common with most towns in the county, had developed from a market town into an industrial centre with the arrival of mechanization and the building of textile mills. Berry and I agreed that in some respects the place felt like a rather larger and wealthier version of Hyde.

It appeared that we had just missed the dinnertime closing of the mills as groups of workers were heading off in all directions – to the shops, to the alehouses or home for a wash, a change of clothes and some refreshment, thence many of them no doubt would set out again to the football. As for us, we strode up Fishergate and past the large cotton mill – Yard Works, somebody noticed – whose operations were winding down for the weekend. Soon the high stone walls of Her Majesty's Prison loomed into view on our right; here we had been advised to fork left and take the Deepdale Road. Just beyond the infirmary and over a railway bridge open fields came into sight: rolling parkland to the west and farmland to the east. It was in the midst of the pastures of Deepdale Farm that the football ground had been laid out. Leaving the main road we followed a lane which led us to a fenced rectangular arena along the near side of which rose a squat wooden tribune allowing an elevated view. At either end stood a flagpole whose banners were already raised and fluttering in the light breeze: here a Union Jack, and there a white standard fringed in red, the colours of North End. Once we had gained entry at the gate Berry and I took our time to stroll from one end of the ground to the other. We discovered a tidily mown field at the boundaries of which rudimentary steps had been laid for spectators at various points according to the natural contours of the field. A team of fellows were readying the pitch, a pair hammering down the corner posts, each decorated with a pristine white flag like four freshly laundered handkerchiefs. The air was crisp and the grass shimmered in the sunshine. It struck me as being a splendid place for a football match.

When I was introduced to the hosts' club secretary, a Mr William Sudell, before the kick-off, he told me that they had been playing fixtures there for ten years. The gentleman was also responsible for managing the team and had little time for me. He suggested I speak with the representatives of the press in order to confirm the names of the players and the match details.

Berry and I established ourselves across from the main enclosure on the halfway line. It was here that we had time and space enough before the crowds arrived in earnest to partake of the tasty refreshments kindly provided for the pair of us by Edward's mother. By a quarter past three there was not a foot of space to be had and hundreds of spectators jostled noisily one behind the next for a better view of the field of play.

Presently the umpires appeared and the referee took his seat directly opposite our vantage point. Then came the players, running through a gap in the crowd and out on to the grass, chests puffed out, three or four in each team holding footballs which they threw out ahead of them. They settled into impromptu groups, kicking the balls between them as the cheers rang out, principally for the home team, I have to say. The blood red stripes of the Preston shirts seemed to blaze in the fragile sunlight. Hyde's players, in their blue halves, gathered in one of the goalmouths and I caught sight of Jos Hall having a final, rousing word to his teammates. Meanwhile the North End players were drilling: racing in lines from one side of the pitch to the other, stopping to stretch out their leg muscles, forming squares of four and hitting hard, low passes between them. A couple of forwards were testing the goalkeeper with shots from close distance, both high and low, left and right.

Whether this display was a regular activity for the players or designed as a ploy to intimidate their opponents we could not say. Talking to some of the Preston supporters standing close to us, we were made to understand that today's team was no reserve side. Even though they were facing F.A. Cup novices – what one fellow called "small fry" – North End were at full strength. The undercurrent was that the club officials were still peeved at Hyde's refusal to rearrange the match to a more suitable date and as such they were determined to teach us a lesson.

The preliminaries over, the referee blew his whistle and the Cup tie began. Everybody around the ground was expecting Preston to win and most probably a wide margin of victory was anticipated, but no-one could have foreseen the slaughter to come. The game remained goalless for five minutes but it was clear that the hosts' clever Scottish players were going to take charge. Charlie Bunyan was kept very busy and acrobatically kept many a shot from his goal. At Greenhays we had seen Hyde try to play a more thoughtful, passing style of football, using the extreme width of the pitch and clever wing-play rather than flooding the central area with scurrying bodies and brute force. At Deepdale, even after just ten minutes, we realised we were watching Preston adopting similar tactics but putting them into practice with infinitely more speed and skill. Each player controlled the ball effortlessly, teammates ran into areas of the field where the Hydonians were absent and passes between them were struck hard and accurately, leaving our players chasing shadows. A mix of Scottish voices and Lancastrian accents punctuated the movement while the away team's players were soon blowing too hard to speak.

Time after time the Hyde defenders, drawn to the man on the ball, would be nowhere to be seen as, by means of a sly feint and dribble or a rapid series of short, cunningly angled passes, the ball suddenly appeared at the feet of two or even three forwards left unprotected and with the goal at their mercy. For all of the huffing and puffing of the Hydonians, for all of the spirited effort, for all of the agility and bravery of the overworked Bunyan, the goals kept coming. Without wishing to be unkind, the impression I had was that of watching a flat race of a couple of furlongs between a galloping thoroughbred and a lumbering carthorse. Of course the local crowd were in raptures, applauding and cheering the red and white stripes as yet another shot was driven between Bunyan's posts.

There came a point in the match, or rather in the visitors' mental approach to the match, when the light dimmed, when the breathless voices were less strident, when the belief began to ebb away. I believe it was as early as the fourth goal for Preston, Dewhurst's second, scored from close range after twenty-five minutes. If not that precise moment, then certainly five minutes later when the winger Drummond headed in an aerial pass from the right. It was already five goals to nil and the match had an hour still to go.

I had heard of great swings of fortune in sporting contests. Certainly they can occur in cricket with its generous allowance of time for the tide to turn and Berry had spoken to me of dramatic changes of momentum even within the shorter span of a football match. The pivot of the half-time interval, the opportunity to make some tactical adjustments or simply to stoke up a fire in the belly – these elements have, so I understand, served to cause upsets and wiped the smile off the faces of players who had enjoyed a comfortable lead after the first forty-five minutes. In addition, the gradient of the pitch, the wind direction, the setting sun in the eyes of the defenders – one or all of these geophysical factors could conceivably alter the course of a match.

After thirty minutes of play at Deepdale, however, everyone in the crowd knew that there would be no reprieve for Hyde F.C., no snatching of victory from the jaws of defeat. For a start Preston were already kicking uphill – I have to say the slope of the pitch was barely noticeable – and they would enjoy downhill advantage after the break. The afternoon's weather was unremarkable: there was barely a gust of wind and little sign of a blinding sun. Instead we had merely the fading glow as it sank shyly behind a bank of cloud on the western horizon, taking our hopes with it. At five-nil the players from Hyde already knew the game was up. By the time the referee signalled for half-time the score had reached twelve goals to nil. There would be no recovery today. No miracle. No humbling of the giant.

At a point during the first half poor Harry Bowers fell on his arm and was obliged to leave the field for treatment. He returned a little later but Hyde were forced to start the second half without him. With the score beyond us and the result a formality, the Preston captain graciously allowed the visitors to use a replacement.

In the second half, with or without Bowers, we witnessed no change in the course of the match. At certain moments it was like watching a conjuror playing tricks on a bamboozled child, the victim unable to tell where the penny might next appear, which card would turn up from the pack, under which cup the marble was to be found. The goals rained down, relentless as a waterfall. The North End goalkeeper had nothing at all to do; there would be no reason to wash his clothes once the game was over. Hopkinson and Pressdee, Robinson and Wood all spent the game largely back in their own half of the pitch without the football and as such offered no threat. Needless to say the urgency of the Hydonians to chase the match diminished with each goal conceded, but in spite of the torture, as *The Football News and Athletic Journal* reported, "the game was very pleasantly contested". The final score was twenty-six-nil, a record margin of victory at this level of the sport. The Scottish international Jimmy Ross scored seven times.

At the final whistle, in a display of some ironic good humour, several of the Hyde players came together to lift up their exhausted goalkeeper Bunyan and carry him off the field as a hero. In many ways the tribute was appropriate for he was oftentimes left exposed, making save after save to keep the score down. With a lesser goalkeeper to beat, Preston could have scored thirty-six. Of our weary team, Gregory, Hurst and Joe Hall also weathered the defeat with some credit, as the newspapers reported the following week. I read one journalist's description of Hyde's players as "a strong-looking lot and they have the makings of a good team".

Such consolation seemed far away as the large, excited crowd slowly dispersed and Berry and I trudged away from Deepdale back into town towards the railway station. The pair of us were somewhat dumbstruck, our emotions veering from sadness to sympathy, from amazement to grim amusement. In the blur of activity, in the pitiless onslaught I had forgotten about my ankle but now on this sorry return march the pain began to flare up once more. Almost on cue, as we saw the lights of the station entrance in the distance, a light rain started to fall.

After the match the players and staff of Hyde F.C. had been invited as guests of North End to stay in Preston for a meal. So it was that with no players for company this time, Berry and I boarded the train to Victoria with groups of fellow supporters, most as demoralised as we were. All of us having witnessed something quite spectacular and unprecedented, it was noticeable that nobody was talking of shame or even of embarrassment. Our players had tried hard but they had met a superior opponent on top of their form. Any resentment was directed at the football fates who had contrived the cruellest of draws for a team like ours trying to find its feet.

The evening had set in dark and cold by the time we reached Hyde. The rain had stopped but a wind had picked up and was gusting into our faces as we plodded up Market Street. By the time my friend and I were at the crest we had left our travelling companions behind and we pressed on wordlessly towards the high chimneys of Slack Mills. I had never known the unfailingly optimistic Edward so distraught but he rekindled the flame as we finally separated at the corner of Osborne Road.

"It'll never be as bad as this again," he said with a faint smile. "And there's always next year, Walter."

"There's always the next match, Edward."

"That's very true. Next Saturday, in fact. Against Manchester, at home. Will you be there?"

"Do you need to ask?"

We shared a tired chuckle and shook hands before going our own ways.

It had been a long, long day and still I had another slow mile to walk. I saw very few people out on Hyde Lane that evening. There were no stars, a curl of the moon shone feebly on my path as the heavy clouds were ripped apart in moments by the winds. Wearily I trod, hands in pockets, the ache of hunger in my stomach, my coat collar turned up against the chill. The fretful air felt like a harbinger of a winter I was unprepared for. Once I passed the Big Tree at least the dwellings of the village looked a little more welcoming. Lights glowed behind closed curtains, noise emanated from beyond the unlocked doors of alehouses. The tall silhouette of the chapel spire was all but lost in the blackness above it. *How do?* grunted a fellow stepping out of the Boy and Barrel, most likely on his way home to his wife. Another squall of fat raindrops blew in as I was passing the Cheshire Cheese and in spite of my throbbing ankle I quickened my step towards my door. The cottage looked dark and uninviting.

As I reached the threshold, however, I notice that inside the parlour window, between the part-drawn curtains, a little candle was flickering in a jar left on the window sill. I let myself in and shook off the wetness from my coat. The place was warmer than I expected. In the scullery I discovered a fire had been lit: guarded by the wire gate, the coals were glowing orange, timid fingers of flame awoken by the draught I had created. On the table, set in a lantern, a second candle had been burning for a short while prior to my arrival, filling the room with a delicate light. Sharing the table, in between a polished knife and fork, was a china plate upon which sat a pie, its lid of browned pastry crust still warm to the touch, giving off the sweet aroma of meat and potatoes. Next to it, to the right, stood a bottle of beer. On the left was a glass jar of pickled red cabbage.

I looked around for an angel but the room was empty save for shadows. No other soul was present to witness the width of my smile. I believe I was trembling with gratitude. If Mrs Harrop had been standing in front of me, for this kindness could be from the heart of no other person, I would have embraced her without a second thought and kissed her effusively on both cheeks. After such a demoralising day of defeat, suddenly I felt as though at least someone in Hyde had won something.

# Book the Fifth
# Beyond Preston

# Chapter 1

Almost a year and a half has passed since Preston North End progressed into the second round of the 1887-88 F.A. Cup at the expense of Hyde Football Club. On their way to the Kennington Oval they overcame Bolton Wanderers, Halliwell, Aston Villa, The Wednesday and Crewe Alexandra. So confident were they on the day of the final that William Sudell, the team's manager whom I briefly met at Deepdale, apparently asked for his players to be photographed with the trophy before the kick-off while their shirts were still clean. The referee refused the request, insisting quite correctly that the team must win the Cup first. In the event Preston lost to West Bromwich Albion by two goals to one, but it will not be the last we hear of them.

Far from an omen of collapse, Hyde's defeat by the absurd margin of twenty-six goals was quickly put aside in both the mentality of the players and the attitude of the committee. It was the middle of October, they reasoned, and the season had only just begun; there would be ample opportunity to restore confidence and self-belief. I remember talking at the time to men like Bowers and Pressdee, Tom Gregory and the Hall brothers. In some ways it was a fragile moment for there was no denying that every player was chastened by the result and the mark it had made on the national scale. In some quarters Hyde's footballers were ridiculed, it was true: at the match itself I had heard taunts from several Preston supporters, raucous and disparaging – remarks that to my mind overstepped the line between jollity and cruelty. Most fair-minded commentators, however, preferred to praise

North End and were sympathetic to our team's stumble at their first hurdle. The players could accept sympathy for only so long, however, and a determination to take the rest of the season's fixtures by the scruff of the neck was soon to take hold.

I can vividly recall the intensity of the team's efforts in their very first game after Preston: a hard-fought victory by three goals to two against a Manchester Select. Harry Bowers stood watching it with us for most of the second half with his arm in a sling. Jimmy Wood scored twice and Jos Hall claimed the other. The players and their relieved supporters felt they had laid the ghost of Deepdale and it had taken just seven days to do so.

The following week Jimmy Pressdee was our scorer but the feisty game away in Denton, just a couple of miles down the Manchester Road, was narrowly lost. The taste of that defeat was bitter but short-lived. Never have I been prouder of our town's representatives than for what they achieved after that. From the beginning of November to the end of March the following year – that is to say, from the middle of autumn to the springtime – they played twenty-three matches and were unbeaten in every one of them.

It was a marvellous series of games, as remarkable in its own way as the F.A. Cup defeat. The supporters surged back to Ewen Fields in their hundreds (indeed in their thousands for certain matches) and visits to grounds in Lancashire towns such as Gorton, Darwen and Oldham were rewarded with success. There were nineteen victories and four ties. The team scored seventy-three goals and conceded only fifteen. In the short history of our club it was surely our golden period. Of all the joyous occasions on the fields, the ones that brought me the greatest delight were the one-nil win against Hurst (the stick-legged winger, "quick-as-a-whippet" Arthur Hopkinson scored the important goal), an unexpected four-nil victory in a New Year's match against a Derby County Select and an unusual fixture on St Patrick's Day when a team from Ireland, Belfast Athletic, were invited to play us: we beat them by three goals to one.

For most of the locals in the crowd I am certain that the pick of the season was the four-nil revenge victory over the neighbours from Denton. This result caused such pleasure and pride amongst certain supporters that they were moved to write poetry about it, the best of which was later printed in the *North Cheshire Herald*. I make no apologies for including my favourite verse:

> *Now they are put to rout,*
> *And as they face about,*
> *Twenty-six none they shout,*
> *Poor Dentonians.*
> *Do not your fingers flirt,*
> *For with your Sunday shirt*
> *Hyde has wiped out the dirt*
> *Rubbed in by Prestonians.*

At the end of April, Hyde F.C. played their final match of an unforgettable season on their home pitch against Newton Heath L.Y.R. Founded ten years earlier as a team for the engineers and stokers, the carriage repairers and plate-layers of the local railway depot, this was an ambitious club which was about to be a founding member of the Combination, a league of the strongest local teams. In view of Hyde's momentous unbeaten run earlier in the season, the *North Cheshire Herald*'s correspondent dubbed the match an unofficial championship of Manchester. It finished with honours even in a one-one tie, and I have more to write about our opponents later.

I duly completed our club's records and happily admit to reading and re-reading through the details of the season for weeks after the last ball had been kicked. Apart from the numbers, the inevitable flux of characters was a feature of the pages. Nothing in this world lasts forever and the elements of a football team are just as ephemeral as the changing earth around us. Our heroic goalkeeper Charlie Bunyan left the club in March to sign for Sheffield United; his final game was the last of our long invincible run. The effervescent Jimmy Pressdee made a lasting impression on me but due to a series of knee injuries he played barely a handful of matches for the club. He left Hyde even earlier than Bunyan: days before Christmas he packed his bags for a grocer's job and another try as a footballer in the city of Liverpool. Shortly after Preston our forward line was improved by the addition of a pair of goal-scoring brothers from Chesterfield, Jack and Jim Bladen. Meanwhile the stalwarts of Joe Hall and Tom Gregory remained at the heart of our defence for the entire season and they have continued to play most consistently during the current one.

For both Jimmy Wood and Harry Bowers the Newton Heath fixture was to be their last in the blue halved shirt. I was especially sorry to see Harry depart; he had become a most important member of the team and indeed a friend, but an offer to play at a higher level for Derby County was one he could not refuse. It was sometime later, when I was in conversation with Frank Hibbert about the gardens at Brookbank, that I learned that the hydrangea cuttings that Bowers had transplanted for me were in fact healthy new plants which he had paid for from his own pocket. They are now twice the size, stand in large clay pots at either side of the coal shed in my backyard, and in the summertime are awash with petals of contrasting depths of blue just as he promised they would be.

As the 1887-88 season ended so did my first-hand involvement with the club's affairs. A new committee was elected and although Joseph Maloney remained a member of it he relinquished his secretarial duties to a colleague at the Newtonbank Printworks, Mr Robert Howland. I was introduced to the gentleman, who struck me as a progressive. His fair hair was as curly as the moustache he had cultivated with a degree of artistic flair. He wore a modern suit of pale grey and looked to be no more than thirty years of age. He was passionate about the football club – the least one would expect – and I was led to believe that along with Mr John Turner, the newly elected chairman, he was ready to explore the possibility of bringing in some Scottish talent, following the successful recipe of some of the more prestigious clubs.

"A young organization like ours cannot afford to stand still, Mr Ramsbottom," he said.

Ignoring his mistake, I allowed him to continue.

"Forward motion, sir, is essential. It's like ridin' a bicycle. If you've sat on one you'll know exactly what I mean. You have to keep pedallin', keep rollin' forwards or else you'll fall off and end up in the gutter."

Howland was also keen to cultivate a more productive connection with the local press. For that reason, and I dare say with the blessing of Maloney, he relieved me of my duties as a match recorder. Without saying the word outright, he explained that my role had become redundant. Instead I seem to remember him describing me as superfluous. I was surprised at first, faintly wounded for a little while, but I understood his rationale. For my part I had helped the club in a small, amateur way for almost two seasons and felt quietly proud of my contribution.

Meanwhile the club's accounts were in a healthy state, such had been the interest in the team's fortunes. Revenue from match attendance had never been so high and the new treasurer hinted at plans to improve the Ewen Fields ground. Money would be found to drain and refresh the pitch and the area around it was to be permanently enclosed. The wooden boards on the four sides of the playing area would be replaced with staging of better quality and the prospect of a pavilion being built, including changing rooms, was also mooted.

It was in this atmosphere of optimistic, and yet for me somewhat wistful change that the curtain was drawn on the season.

From a national perspective the 1888-89 football season was a most significant one. The strongest professional clubs in the country had for some time wanted to play in more than F.A. Cup ties and randomly arranged fixtures of limited competitive value. Early in 1888, to take advantage of the growing interest in the sport, a group of the game's most ambitious administrators, including William McGregor of Aston Villa and William Sudell of Preston North End, proposed the foundation of a national league in which teams would play each other twice during the season for points, leading to the awarding of a championship for the overall winners.

In September the first round of matches kicked off between the twelve clubs invited to form the Football League, as the competition was named. A point of interest for me was that in my short time as a football enthusiast I had seen four of the twelve members play in matches against Hyde F.C.: Blackburn Rovers, Bolton Wanderers, Derby County and, of course, Preston North End. As I write and with much of the season passed, the team from Deepdale, incidentally now playing in plain white shirts, look certain to win the inaugural championship title. No team has beaten them so far. In addition they have already reached the semi-finals of the F.A. Cup where they will face West Bromwich Albion, no doubt determined to avenge last year's final defeat. Perhaps it is indeed superfluous for me to add that Hyde F.C. did not apply to enter the F.A. Cup competition this season.

It appears that local groupings and leagues are forming to create championships at every level of the game and Berry has heard rumours that for the 1889-90 season Hyde will apply to join what is expected to become the Lancashire League. It is an ambitious target to compete on equal terms with clubs such as Bury, Blackpool and Southport (for these are amongst the names mentioned) but one totally in keeping with our club's view of itself.

As for Hyde's current season, the pattern so far is one of more wins than losses. The committee decided to maintain links with Belfast Athletic, somewhat extravagantly to my mind, although I do believe that the Irish subsidised travel to the game played over the sea in September. A return match took place in Hyde on Christmas Day. We won both matches comfortably. The majority of our opponents are in our closer geographical orbit, of course, and are becoming familiar to us, but the momentum of a long unbeaten run has proved elusive this time around. Nevertheless, Berry and I continue to attend every match on Ewen Fields, some in the company of young Danny Harrop, and all in the company of a fervent, noisy and ever hopeful throng of several hundred like-minded others.

# Chapter 2

When his father was taken from him, a victim of chronic bronchitis and heart failure, Daniel Harrop kept his tears to himself. Perhaps his poor mother helped to dry them but the boy made a point of hiding his grief from me. Almost two years later I was to witness him weeping for the first time. The tears were not shed for his invalid parent, long since dead and buried, however. They ran down his cheeks almost unannounced, struck as he was by the consequences of the awful disaster that visited our community in January of 1889, just two months ago.

The tragedy happened on the morning of the nineteenth, a Friday. The first Benjamin Lloyd and I heard about it was at dinnertime when several mothers appeared at the school gates with news of an explosion at the Hyde Coal Pit on Manchester Road. One woman was adamant that I be told first and should be allowed to use my professional judgement in how and when the horrific news should be passed on to the scholars. I had to be circumspect: I knew that very few of the villagers were employed in the mine but it was most likely that some of the children had relatives living in Hyde who were colliers. As it was I could only introduce the disturbing idea of an accident in the vaguest of ways as the details I was given were sketchily provided from second- and third-hand accounts.

From the top of Knott Lane the smudge of a grey cloud of dust could be seen, hanging above that side of the town, stubbornly refusing to disperse. I joined a crowd of silent watchers, each man and woman brought to a shiver by the sight of the grim, unmoving shadow it cast.

It was not until the evening that a grisly death toll emerged. On the following day newspapers reported that the explosion had occurred in the Two Foot Seam at a depth of over three hundred yards. The use of candles to illuminate the tunnels was accepted practice as the pit was well ventilated and signs of coal gas were rare. However, a collapse in a section of the roof released trapped gas and the naked flames were the cause of the conflagration. Of the forty-three men and boys working in the level at the time, twenty-three were reported as dead – in the main, it appeared, as a result of suffocation rather than from burns or falling debris.

It was when Danny saw me studying the following day's newspaper, digesting the shocking details, that he became agitated and pushed me for information. He sat down by the fire and I passed him the paper but I knew he would not have the patience to scour every paragraph.

"Does it say who were killed?"

"There are no names, Danny. Not yet. I think they are guessing at about twenty-three poor souls who perished. They have to be identified. It all takes time."

"So 'ow do we find out who died?"

"You could go down to the colliery. I dare say they'll have posted an announcement somewhere. Or wait 'til Monday's newspaper."

The boy sat quietly, the paper folded between his fingers, the flames in the hearth casting their dancing light on his ashen face. Presently he spoke again:

"I were thinkin' o' Toffee."

I had quite forgotten that his friend from the football team worked at the pit.

"There's no reason to believe Toffee was in that seam, Danny," I said with as much conviction as I could muster. "He was more likely in some other tunnel. If he were even underground at all at the time. It says the explosion went off at just gone nine o'clock. We don't even know what time his shift started, do we?"

It was at that moment that the boy began to sob. I hated to see him so anguished, shuddering in pain that way. I prayed to God that it would turn out to be for no reason. I crouched beside him, put an arm around his shoulders and did my best to comfort him.

"Your friend will be alive," I repeated, my voice no more than a whisper. "He will. He really will."

Eventually the trembling stopped. He took a deep breath, wiped his eyes with his knuckles and looked up at me. A catch in his voice made his words all the more piercing:

"You'd better be right, Mr Rowbotham. I'll never forgive you if you're wrong."

It was a day later when I cast my eyes down a long, harrowing list of names and addresses of those who had lost their lives in the explosion. Mr Dowson had procured the record from someone he knew – possibly somebody in the employ of our Member of Parliament Mr Sidebotham who, in partnership with his brother, owned the colliery.

Now it was I who was trembling. There were a full twenty-three names on the roll, from a fourteen-year-old jigger to a sixty-five-year-old miner. A woman from Cheapside had lost both her husband and a fifteen-year-old son. I read the names of six youths under the age of twenty. Mercifully Toffee Mellor's name was not amongst them.

Football played its part in helping to heal the distraught community. I was touched by the generous gesture of Preston North End, our club's tormentors fifteen months earlier, who agreed to play a special fixture on Ewen Fields to raise money for the pit disaster fund. Berry and I were part of a huge throng and for much of the time our view of the play was impeded. *The North Cheshire Herald* reported the crowd to be eight thousand strong. Mr Sidebotham, in his role as colliery owner or M.P. or perhaps both, performed a ceremonial kick-off and shared a meal with all of the players at the Norfolk Arms afterwards. This time Preston were deliberately not at full strength and a second thrashing would in any case have been wholly inappropriate. It was a much less fraught afternoon for the Hyde players, especially Joe Hall and Tom Gregory (the only remaining pair who had suffered so much at Deepdale) and the visitors narrowly won by two goals to one.

A second most worthy football occasion has taken place even more recently. This one, late last month and only six miles from where I now sit writing about it, was a benefit match at which I was not present. Also arranged as part of the relief fund to support the bereaved families, a game was played in the artificial glow of floodlights at Belle Vue between two football teams that have become the strongest on the eastern side of Manchester. My friends the Berry brothers, Edward and Clarence, were amongst the large gathering of spectators. Indeed it was reported that ten thousand supporters paid to watch the green and yellow shirts of Newton Heath L.Y.R. beat the black and whites of Ardwick A.F.C. by three goals to two.

# Chapter 3

As I perch here at my table by the parlour window, the weak sunlight of a spring morning falling on my final pages, I shall recount to you, dear reader, no more tales of football or footballers, but instead relate a bright summer of nuptials. For indeed in the month of July 1888 a matrimonial breeze seemed to sweep through the dusty lanes of Gee Cross.

Firstly, on a chilly morning, the first Saturday of that month, Mr Quigley the shoe mender married his distant cousin Mona O'Brien. A relative distant enough to prompt no objections, she was the shop girl he had taken on as an employee under duress at the time that Martha Harrop lost her job. The pair of them being Irish, the service took place at the Catholic church in Haughton Vale, where most of the bride's family lived. Nevertheless, neighbours in Gee Cross were generous with little presents for the popular couple and in their best wishes for their future. The normally reticent Mona needed no persuasion in showing off her wedding gifts, including the shoes that her husband had lovingly made for the occasion: their leather was the colour of dairy cream and as soft as a milkmaid's cheek.

Secondly, one week later, took place a more flamboyant affair, a wedding about which I dare say almost every person in the village had an opinion. Witnessed by a large congregation squeezed on to the pews at Hyde Chapel, Miss Louisa Thornley became Mrs Robert Howarth, married and blessed by the Reverend Henry Dowson. Missing from the official guest list but finding myself on the roster of chapel serving duties, I was in attendance as the couple were pronounced man and wife. Needless to say, Louisa presented a radiant picture as the happiest of brides. For once her mother, though dressed in the most ostentatious fashion, was obliged to vacate the centre of the stage for the younger generation.

Following the ceremony Maria caught my eye and was generous in her cordiality towards me, thanking me effusively for collecting up the hymnals and supervising the ushers. My threat, if there ever was such a thing, had long been nullified. Her husband Jesse, a man who once removed from his workplace seemed always on the verge of being surprised, stood at her shoulder in a tight-fitting suit, shifty-eyed, uncomfortable in religious surroundings. He was fidgety, twisting his own wedding ring around his third finger as if he was unscrewing a tap nut with a broken thread. I wondered if the imminent prospect of having to address an expectant audience at the wedding breakfast was weighing on the poor fellow's mind. Apparently over seventy guests had been invited to the Grapes Inn. I barely knew the man but it was obvious to me that he would be happier alone or working with a single apprentice at most, with sweat on his brow and soot on his bare arms, hammering out strips of glowing metal on his precious anvil.

Although it is not in my character to play tricks, Charles Knott at first believed I was jesting when I asked him, calmly and respectfully, if he would be prepared to be my best man. For the third wedding, on the final Saturday of last July, was indeed to be my own.

"Walter Rowbotham!" he cried, pulling me into a deep embrace. "You are a man of mystery. A man of secrets!" He grabbed my hand and shook it as hard as he might swing a cricket bat. "Congratulations, old man!"

A broad smile beamed from his face, then I saw that inquisitive look, a hint of confusion in his pale blue eyes.

"So you're gettin' wed, Walter, but tell me, I need to know. Who's your bride?"

"It's Martha Harrop," I announced with a smile of pride. "You'll recognise her, I'm sure of it. A Gee Cross lady, a widow. She's been looking after my domestics these past twelve months and has been an angel. Well, now we've decided we want to be looking after each other. Really, Charlie, she's the most generous, warm-hearted woman I've ever known."

It was no exaggeration. I believed it then and I believe it still.

"I don't need a best man to convince me I'm doing the right thing," I went on, "but I do need one to help make the wedding day perfect."

"Best man?" he was pondering. "I've been man o' t' match in a game o' cricket a time or two but I've never been a best man."

"But you'll do it?"

"Course I will, Walter! It'd be an 'onour."

Excitedly I informed him of the date we had settled upon and the location: Hyde Chapel, it went almost without saying.

"And of course, Blanche Berry is invited too."

"Blanche? I dunna expect she'll be comin', Walter. All that's over."

"Really? That's a shame."

"Aye, in some ways it is. We broke it off a month or two back. She's a nice enough lass but there were summat missin', you know. That spark we 'ad, it just seemed to blow itself out. Then there were 'er mother: daft as a bat. An' I've 'eard it said that lasses allers turn into their mothers in th'end. You know what she 'ad me do, Walter? Blanche's mother, that is. She 'ad me traipse upstairs after 'er in her big 'ouse to look at a bloody great shiny sausage machine. Expected me to stand an' admire it. Can you believe it? A sausage machine, as good as new, never been used, sittin' on a cabinet on t' landin' like we're in some religious shrine."

I said nothing, offering only a smile of disbelief which disguised my amusement.

"An' summat else you should know," he went on. "I've left t' bank. Couldn't be doin' with it. T' fella that owns that 'ouse where I stay, he reckons he can get me a job at t' Town Hall. Failin' that, I might be off, Walter. Be leavin' Hyde for a bit. There's plenty o' work in Manchester."

Here my expression changed to surprise.

"You've read about t' ship canal, no doubt?"

"I know there's been grumbles for years about the dock charges they have to pay in Liverpool."

"Aye, well, Manchester will 'ave its own port soon enough."

"I did read somewhere they're about to start work on it."

"They already 'ave, Walter, at t' western end. Imagine t' jobs there'll be in a couple o' years over in Salford. Great new docks, wharfs an' warehouses as far as you can see. An' not just labourin' jobs neither; clerical jobs an' all. There'll be summat there for an argumentative pen-pusher like me, I'm sure there will."

"I dare say you're right."

"You know what I'm like," he continued. "A restless soul an' no mistake. You see 'ow England is nowadays. You dunna 'ave to stay in one place no more, not if you dunna want to. Look at your footballers – a season or two with a club then they move on, get 'emselves a better contract somewhere else."

I knew he was right. I had known him since he was seven years old. He'd always been a thoughtful young lad. He was wise and honest and wore his heart on his sleeve. He was the best man I knew.

I will never forget our wedding day. It was a day I never imagined would happen, so set I had been in my steady, bachelor ways.

We had no more than thirty guests. Martha's family was even smaller than my own. My sister Esther replied to our invitation with a short letter in which her happiness was seasoned with surprise. She had firmly believed that I would never wish to marry, never be willing to share my life with a companion, and especially not in what she called "my advancing years". She was delighted to be proved wrong, she wrote, and was eager to meet the lady who had turned her convictions upside down. She and her husband duly brought their sons down from Saddleworth; it was the first time I had seen the boys, both already strapping young men, wearing neckties. I knew they would much rather be on the farm in their muddy boots than sitting quietly in the Chapel.

I invited Edward Berry, of course. He was accompanied by his fiancée Sarah, whom I was honoured to meet for the first time. He was most generous with a wedding gift which he offered, he said, on behalf of his mother and the rest of the family: a set of white cotton bedlinen and towels of the highest quality.

A bouquet of fresh summer blooms arrived unexpectedly, dispatched from a florist's shop in Bakewell, Derbyshire, courtesy of Harry Bowers.

Mr Quigley, whose fondness for Martha had never left him, provided my bride with a pair of shoes of a similar design to those he had made for his Mona. They were just as exquisite: hand cut from the finest leather she had ever laid a finger on, the colour of butterscotch.

Arthur Roscow, Martha's mentor at Apethorn Mill, a tall, thin man, slightly stooping, was proud to give her away at the altar. He and his wife, never gifted a daughter of their own, insisted on paying for her wedding dress.

Joseph Maloney and his wife were also invited, unofficially representing the football club, I suppose. He kindly paid a photographer he knew to take half a dozen images as we left the Chapel. He also handed me an envelope of money collected from former and current members of the committee which was their contribution to our modest honeymoon. Martha and I spent three nights in Buxton; our days in the sweet mountain air were blessed with sunshine. On arrival at our hotel, and to our complete astonishment, the manager showed us up to his very best room, in fact a suite of rooms, at the request of (and paid for by) Mr Frank Hibbert on behalf of Hyde F.C.

I had sent an invitation to Fitzalan Street and was most pleased that the Reverend Frederick Ashton was available to officiate. The Reverend Dowson and his wife were, of course, also in attendance. These days the old sea swimmer talks of little besides the new public baths in Hyde. He has supported the project with a passion, and they will open to all in two months' time. During the service Benjamin Lloyd took to his harp to play a moving version of *Crimond*, the melody of a favourite hymn of mine, *The Lord is My Shepherd.*

Of the photographs, we have a framed one of myself and Martha at the chapel gates: I grin like the Cheshire Cat while my wife is more self-conscious. It stands on the mantelshelf where a smeared wine glass once stood. My favourite photograph is a different one, however: the one in which Danny has joined us, standing at the front between the pair of us, offering his best chipped-tooth smile to the camera, as smart a young fellow as you could wish to see. I took him to the barber's shop with me the week before the wedding and had his hair dramatically tidied up for him for once in his life.

He has very recently, and still most hesitantly, started calling me Walter, which I am glad about. "Mr Rowbotham" has long been too stilted and although he was more than willing to use the word, I was not so comfortable with the term "father".

I will be sixty next year. I am conscious that a reorganization of the school system is imminent, and on a national scale. It has crossed my mind that the day for me to finally retire from teaching is probably on the horizon. Schoolteaching is an occupation that favours the younger man, I do believe, and increasingly the younger woman too. Let us leave it to the Benjamin Lloyds and the Blanche Berrys, those closer in age to their charges, those with energy and vitality and new ideas. As for my secondary role as an inspector, I can envisage myself continuing with it some while longer. It is less onerous, suits a man of experience and so far I have found satisfaction in imparting to others a little of the wisdom I have gained from near forty years in the classroom.

Meanwhile at Apethorn Mill my wife still works in the accounts department under the eye of Mr Roscow. As far as I am concerned she can work as much or as little as she likes, but she is a good deal younger than me and that is not a conversation we have yet approached.

Hyde beat Hurst last Saturday. It was a comfortable three-nil win. It seems that for the moment we have nudged ahead of Ashton-under-Lyne at least in terms of the fortunes of our football clubs. It was a result that cheered the soul. The afternoon was bitterly cold and the frosty air was gnawing at my knees as the sun dropped. On days like that Berry will run and fetch me a hot tea from the man in the tent. Of course, when the game is over I warm up again on the brisk march up Back Lane. Oftentimes I will stop in at Osborne Road and pay my respects to Mary but last week I declined to do so. I was eager to get home.

I hope I will never lose that eagerness. Each time I return, as I walk past the early evening chatter coming from the Boy and Barrel, then on down Gerrard's Street beyond the Cheshire Cheese, I look out for the glow at the window of our cottage. Danny will be in the parlour with a book or a puzzle. He will be ready with a volley of questions for me about every aspect of the match. *Did we win? Who scored the goals? Was Jack Bladen as good as he was last time?* Meanwhile Martha will be in the scullery, stoking the fire, setting the kettle on the stand, and when I step through the door she might smile and pull a loose strand of hair away from her sweet face, help me off with my boots and plant a welcome-home kiss on my brow.

*Walter Moses Rowbotham*
*March 1889*

# APPENDIX

## FA Cup First Round

October 15, 1887

Deepdale, Preston

Kick-off: 3.30 pm

Attendance: estimated 2,000

Referee: Mr R G Barlow (Manchester)

| PRESTON NORTH END | 26 - 0 | HYDE F.C. |
|---|---|---|
| | (Half-time: 12 - 0) | |
| Red and white stripes | | Sky and royal blue halves |

| | | |
|---|---|---|
| Addison | Goalkeeper | Bunyan |
| Howarth | Right back | Gregory |
| N Ross | Left back | J H Hall |
| Goodall | Right half | Hurst |
| Russell | Centre half | Bowers |
| Graham | Left half | Wilson |
| Gordon | Outside right | J Hall |
| J Ross | Inside right | Pressdee |
| Thomson | Centre forward | Robinson |
| Dewhurst | Inside left | Wood |
| Drummond | Outside left | Hopkinson |

**Goal scorers:**

> J Ross 7, Gordon 5, Thomson, 5, Dewhurst 3,
> Drummond 2, Graham, N Ross, Russell, Goodall

Hyde Football Club joined the Lancashire League for its inaugural 1889-90 season, the only member located in Cheshire. In spite of lavish spending, sustained success eluded them and each season saw them struggling to balance their ambition with financial security. They joined and withdrew from various local leagues before finding a consistent level at the turn of the century. At this point began the club's most successful spell: they were a leading team in the Manchester League, indeed its champions in 1901-02.

Following the chastening FA Cup exit at Preston, Hyde FC did not re-enter the competition until 1906. In that year on land close to the club's old pitch, a new ground was opened. It retained the name Ewen Fields and has been used ever since. Some years later the Great War precipitated the club's demise.

A new club, Hyde United, was founded in 1919. Red shirts were adopted in 1927. The high point of this club's fortunes came in the two seasons 2012-13 and 2013-14 as members of the Football Conference Premier League, just one tier below the Football League.

Charlie Bunyan, the young goalkeeper who had the misfortune to concede 26 goals at Preston, had a long and successful career in football. He played for several English clubs until the turn of the century, was a referee in South Africa and later a coach both in Canada and in Belgium, where he played a significant role in the development of the game.

From its founding in 1878 until the Second World War, Hurst FC was the foremost club in Ashton-under-Lyne. They were Hyde's main local rivals for many years and were renamed Ashton United in 1946.

Having defeated Hyde in the first round of the 1887-

88 FA Cup, Preston North End went on to reach the final where they lost 2-1 to West Bromwich Albion. That they were becoming the best team in England was not in doubt the following season. As founding members of the Football League they became its first champions by completing the season unbeaten. Their record: played 22, won 18, drew 4, lost 0, goals for 74, goals against 15, points 40.

They went on to earn the nickname "The Invincibles" by winning the FA Cup in the same season, beating Wolverhampton Wanderers 3-0 in the final.

They retained the Football League championship in the 1888-89 season and were runners-up in the following three years.

The founding members of the Football League played their first round of matches in September 1888. The twelve members were made up of six Lancashire clubs and six from the English Midlands:

| | |
|---|---|
| Accrington | Aston Villa |
| Blackburn Rovers | Derby County |
| Bolton Wanderers | Notts County |
| Burnley | Stoke |
| Everton | West Bromwich Albion |
| Preston North End | Wolverhampton Wanderers |

The two Manchester clubs that contested the benefit match in February 1889 to raise funds for the bereaved families of the Hyde Colliery Disaster have famous histories.

Newton Heath Lancashire and Yorkshire Railway FC were

formed in 1878. They joined the expanded Football League First Division in 1892 and ten years later became known as Manchester United.

Meanwhile Ardwick AFC, founded in 1887 from a team from St Mark's Church, Gorton, were admitted to the Football League Second Division, also in 1892. Two years later they changed their name to Manchester City.

The Reverend Henry Enfield Dowson (1837-1925) left a far-reaching legacy on public life in Hyde. He was a Unitarian minister, an educationalist, a Liberal and a humanitarian. He served as pastor at Hyde Chapel for fifty-eight years. He was involved in the management of several local schools and in his later years he was often referred to as "the Bishop of Gee Cross" and "the Grand Old Man of Hyde". Two roads in the town bear his name: Dowson Road, a main thoroughfare built in the mid-1920s, and Enfield Street, on which stood Gee Cross County Primary School. This building, which opened in 1890, replaced the school featured in the novel; a century later it was turned into a residential care home as a larger, modern village school was built on land very close to where the novel's imagined cricket match was played out. The new premises were named, to nobody's surprise, Dowson Primary School.

Dowson was also the President of Hyde Cricket Club and the President of Hyde Seal Swimming Club. The latter organisation was established a few years after the opening of the public baths in 1889 and produced a water polo team that dominated the sport. Hyde Seal were English champions nine times between 1903 and 1924 and world champions in 1904,

1905 and 1906. George Wilkinson of Hyde Seal captained the Great Britain water polo team that won the Olympic gold medal both in London in 1908 and in Stockholm in 1912.

Adjacent to the baths on Union Street, Hyde Free Library was opened in 1899. Sadly the baths were demolished in the 1980s and the library building was closed in 2014.

By the 1880s the cotton industry in Hyde was already some way past its peak of production. Apethorn Mill, later known as both Linnet Mill and Gee Cross Mill, closed as a cotton factory in 1934. The buildings continued to have some manufacturing use until they were demolished in 1987.

Clothing manufacturers James North & Co purchased Slack Mills in 1959 and remained in business for almost forty years. The area is now a housing development.

Some of the place names referenced in the novel have disappeared over the years. The Boy and Barrel public house, barely a hundred yards down Gerrard's Street from the Grapes Inn (now the Grapes Hotel), was demolished in 1909. Gerrard's Street became known as Stockport Road towards the end of the 19th century. The Royal Hotel, where the first meeting to establish a football club in Hyde was held, changed its name to the White Lion in the early 1900s and remains as such today. The pub on the corner of John Shepley Street, known as the Moulders Arms for more than century, has suffered two changes of name in recent years.

Chapel Street, across Knott Lane from the Hyde Chapel gates, is now Enfield Street as mentioned above. Fairbrother Street was the old name of Grange Road North. Lumn Street became the northern end of Lumn Road, and Back Lane renamed as its southern end. Stockport Road continued through the village of Gee Cross as far as where the James North clock now stands, replacing the name Hyde Lane.

# AUTHOR'S NOTES

I thought I had written enough about Hyde. *Blessèd are the Meek* was a labour of love in some ways, as I felt a very personal pull to the story of the Chartist James Shore, a mill worker from the middle of the 19th century, who I believed could be a distant relation of mine. The discovery that we were not directly related mattered not in the end as I was already emotionally attached to him. That novel also introduced a bookish, self-effacing schoolteacher whose friendship allowed James to tell his story. Walter Rowbotham was my fictitious narrator and as such stayed in the margins.

The book's reception, especially in Hyde, was gratifying and I enjoyed the opportunity to talk about it in local forums. Two years later, and with a contemporary novel set in France in between, I decided I wanted to revisit my hometown, and once more with a late nineteenth-century background. I realised that an event in 1887 that put Hyde in the sporting record books took place only six years after Rowbotham signed off his story of James Shore.

Three elements fell into place. Firstly, Hyde Football Club's record FA Cup defeat at the hands of Preston North End gave me the chance to write about the young town's ambition to make its mark. Secondly, I was finally able to justify indulging my own love of football in the pages of a novel. Thirdly, I could rediscover Mr Rowbotham and this time place him as a fully rounded character at the heart of the piece.

As with *Blessèd are the Meek*, the majority of the characters in the story were real people with whom I have had to take creative liberties. In the main, names associated with Hyde are real and those in Gee Cross (the Dowson family aside) are fictional. Similarly, apart from the football matches which are all factually reported, I have imagined scenes and dialogue to dramatize the tale. Like Walter's mother's Noah's Ark cross-stitch around a Bible verse, I have taken the historical record of Hyde FC's first three seasons and embroidered a novel around them.

Thus, *Twenty-six Nil* is not simply a football book, and certainly not a book about one historic football match. Instead the infamous Cup tie gives a context to a story about community, civic pride, friendship and the development of a man who begins to look beyond himself and is allowed to blossom. I suppose the main theme of the novel is that of ambition and its double edge: on the one hand the risk of trying to run before you have learned to walk, and yet on the other the conviction that without it nothing worthwhile will ever be achieved.

My principal source of information was Mike Pavasovic, unofficial historian of Hyde United FC, to whom I offer unlimited thanks. He was generous with his help and suggestions, and his brilliantly researched *Charlie Barber's Boys – A History of Hyde FC 1885-1917* became a reference work for me of biblical significance. I also wish to thank Preston North End Football Club, Hyde United Football Club, Victoria McCann at the Lancashire Archives, Pat Winterbottom, secretary at Hyde Chapel, and Mark Ridgway of the *Hydonian Chronicles* Facebook group.

The following books were invaluable: *Looking Back at Hyde* edited by Alice Lock (a collection of illustrated essays which includes *1885 : Hyde 'Town Hall'* by F R Stott and Alice Lock's *Henry Enfield Dowson 1837-1925)*, Ian Haynes' *Hyde*

*Cotton Mills* and *The Football League: The First Hundred Years* by Bryon Butler. I was, and remain, a regular visitor to the website *hydonian.blogspot.com* where David Barlow's contributions were particularly useful. Finally, many thanks are once again due to Warren Shore whose help and advice never fails to hit the mark and to Honeybee Books for their expertise and support.

My interest in the football club is genuine, life-long and was at its most intense in the late 1960s and early 1970s when I was a schoolboy. Our fiercest local rivals were, and are still, Stalybridge Celtic. I can still name a regular starting eleven from those days (Cheshire League/Northern Premier League) without missing a beat. My paternal grandfather played for the club in the 1920s and my maternal grandmother's house on John Shepley Street was two minutes from the ground.

In these days of the domination of wealthy super-clubs, I salute the directors, players, staff and supporters of not only Hyde United but of all the smaller clubs around the country who help to keep football's grass roots well nourished.

*Brent Shore*
*July 2021*

# ABOUT THE AUTHOR

Brent Shore grew up in Hyde, a small town on the eastern edges of Manchester.

He studied Modern Languages at the University of Nottingham, where he also trained as a teacher. Following a varied career which took him via North Yorkshire and Bermuda finally to Dorset, he now channels much of his energy into writing fiction, both contemporary and historical.

He has published six novels:

*Shillingstone Station*

*Bailing Out*

*An English Impressionist*

*Blessèd are the Meek*

*Inappropriate Behaviour*

*Twenty-six Nil*

Visit: www.brentshore.co.uk

Contact: stories@brentshore.co.uk

The Plug Riots of the 1840s: violent, significant steps on working people's long road towards justice and equality.

Based on historical truth, **Blessèd are the Meek** reflects on the life of a man who lived through these times: James Shore, a machine mender in the cotton mills of Hyde, seven miles to the east of Manchester. Politicised by poverty and injustice, he became a Chartist, a rioter and a convict but his story amounts to far more than that of a lengthy prison sentence. A son, a husband and a father, he was a man who sacrificed his freedom for the prize of equality, who glimpsed its light in the distance, but who was born too early to bask in its glow.

MURDER!
SUSPENSE!
STEAM TRAINS!

*"A great story line, with suspense and atmosphere right to the end."*

*"What a ride! I could not put it down until I had finished it."*

MYSTERY AND MORAL DILEMMA
IN 21st CENTURY WESSEX

*"Excellent writing and characterisation"*

*"A very entertaining read; it gave me a great deal of food for thought."*

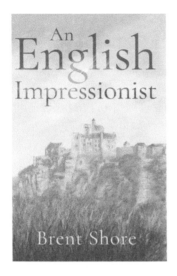

TO BE, OR TO SEEM TO BE?

*"Penny is a wonderful character creation, a fascinating sociopath!"*

*"WOW! – what a brilliant read!"*

HOW FAR CAN TRUST BE STRETCHED BEFORE IT SNAPS?

*"A challenging subject, skilfully explored."*

*"I was hooked from page one; another excellent read."*

All titles available at the Shop at
www.brentshore.co.uk

BV - #0020 - 051121 - C0 - 203/127/16 - PB - 9781913675226 - Matt Lamination